FERAL

FERAL

Glenis Wilson

The Book Guild Ltd

First published in Great Britain in 2022 by
The Book Guild Ltd
Unit E2 Airfield Business Park,
Harrison Road, Market Harborough,
Leicestershire. LE16 7UL
Tel: 0116 2792299
www.bookguild.co.uk
Email: info@bookguild.co.uk
Twitter: @bookguild

Copyright © 2022 Glenis Wilson

The right of Glenis Wilson to be identified as the author of this
work has been asserted by them in accordance with the
Copyright, Design and Patents Act 1988.

All rights reserved. No part of this publication may be
reproduced, transmitted, or stored in a retrieval system, in any form or by any means,
without permission in writing from the publisher, nor be otherwise circulated in
any form of binding or cover other than that in which it is published and without
a similar condition being imposed on the subsequent purchaser.

This work is entirely fictitious and bears no resemblance to any persons living or dead.

Typeset in 11pt Minion Pro

Printed and bound in the UK by TJ Books LTD, Padstow, Cornwall

ISBN 978 1915122 377

British Library Cataloguing in Publication Data.
A catalogue record for this book is available from the British Library.

Dedicated to the readers and residents of Radcliffe-on-Trent who, like me, respect and appreciate this very special wild place.

PROLOGUE
2020

Panthera pardus. The words on the sign outside the big cats' enclosure spelled out far more than the Latin name of the animal. They created a picture in the mind of white fangs; deadly claws; powerful, rippling muscles racing at phenomenal speed under a black pelt. But above all they created a gut-clutching fear at the merciless savagery meted out by nature's perfect killing machine – the black panther.

ONE
2020

The Cessna Skyhawk droned smoothly over the English Channel in the gathering dusk of the January evening and flew on above the Home Counties, holding fast to its flight path; destination: the Scottish borders. Meticulously, as ordered, the pilot maintained complete radio silence. Continuing on, with Birmingham sprawled out way below, its mess of interconnected roads looking like disembowelled intestines, the plane approached the East Midlands. Up ahead was the dark mass of Sherwood Forest. Visibility to the west was worsening rapidly. A gale-force wind swept the heavy, rain-laden clouds across the country in a wide swathe of grey curtain, and buffeted the light aircraft.

Anan Isooba yawned widely, rubbing a rough palm over his face, feeling the scratch of two days' growth of stubble. A good job Mara wasn't around to give him hell about it. She had very definite ideas about the standards and performance she wanted – and expected! – from her man. At the thought of her beautiful smiling face – and she smiled a lot – he felt a stir in his loins. Now it was his time to smile. They'd be making sweet music when he got back home. *When*. He'd only been away from her a couple of days and already he was missing her like crazy.

He reached for the stick, eased it forward and, losing height, dropped down and flew low over the Trent Valley. The wind was less of a problem now, and he followed the course of the river as it snaked north. He was tired; so goddamned tired. It was over thirty hours since he'd slept. Preferring to supervise the entire operation, he'd watched the zookeepers load the tranquilised animal into the wooden crate and onto the plane. The Cessna had been modified by removing two rear seats, and the crate, measuring five feet long by three feet high and three feet wide, rested on metal rollers, secured by leather straps. Apart from its animal cargo, the crate contained a deep false bottom. That was full of an altogether different cargo.

Isooba glanced at the control panel. In a few minutes the Cessna would be over the heavily wooded belt and looking towards Yorkshire. The Scottish borders weren't far away. When he landed his job would be done. Others were waiting to take over, and they would deal with the unloading while he ate and bedded down.

He unclipped his seat belt and stepped back into the body of the plane. There was time for a quick check on the crate, to make sure it hadn't come adrift amid all of the turbulence. Despite the buffeting wind, it didn't appear to have slipped much; the weight of the big cat held it down well enough. He turned to return to the cockpit – and then he froze. In the small, enclosed space the screeching squall was so loud it vibrated painfully in his ears.

One huge black paw, resting against the slats of the wooden crate, twitched violently, claws flexing in the air. Fear caught at Isooba's guts. The tranquiliser was wearing off and the panther, Kala, was coming round. It was always a possibility but it had never happened to him before. On three of the four previous occasions, the animals had remained unconscious all the way to the zoo in Cumbria. One young and heavily pregnant lioness had never regained consciousness. It was a tricky business, tranquilising animals in transit. Too much and the animal wouldn't make it. Too little and they would come round during the flight. Following the lioness's death, the order to reduce the dose must have come from the zoo's owner, Mr Smith, the boss. No one argued with him; not if they had any sense. Certainly not Isooba, who was rigorously obeying his orders to maintain strict radio silence *at all times*. Orders were set in stone, and he was following them to the letter. But that meant he was totally isolated. He had always felt completely safe before. Not this time. A shiver of fear ran down the full length of his spine. Without contact, he was on his own. And just how strong the crate was to enable it to contain an irate, struggling big cat, he didn't know.

He stumbled back to the cockpit as rain lashed at the windscreen and thunder rolled out over the land. Seconds later, forked lightning slashed across the sky, lighting up the interior of the plane. The trapped animal hissed in fright. Isooba glanced back and saw the black paw claw its way round the wooden slat. Watching in fixated horror, he saw the wood splinter and give way. The big cat screeched in pain as her claw caught in the wood and, as she struggled to free herself, tore away from the paw. Blood pooled onto the floor of the plane. Inside the crate, Kala became a dervish, thrashing and banging against the sides. How long? How long before ten stone of enraged panther smashed the crate to matchsticks? Long enough to land? If Isooba could land and get away from the plane, maybe climb a tree, before Kala escaped… It was his one slim hope. Very slim – panthers could climb trees. But he had to try.

Below, the patchworked countryside spread out: fields, woods – not a built-up area; it was just possible that he could bring down the plane intact. But a crash landing would almost certainly result in a fireball. He thrust away the ghastly thought of being engulfed in searing flames. Sweat stood out on his forehead and dripped down onto his shirt; his hands were slippery on the controls. He reduced altitude rapidly, and the plane responded, diving towards the ground. Making an emergency landing was extremely difficult even with a good runway, but ditching, possibly into a field *and* avoiding the trees, was a nightmare.

He cast a glance behind him. Bits of the crate were snapping off but as yet the cat was still imprisoned. Did he have long enough to seek a flat piece of ground? Drawing his gaze back, he cried out in panic. The plane had been flying low, avoiding the gale-force wind and following the river, but now, suddenly, it was flying far too low over a small village. And the village, which had begun down at the river level, had followed the swiftly rising ground. Houses, clinging precariously to the side of a steep hill, wound their way up almost to the summit; the terrain had altered drastically. Facing him was an old, disused brick quarry. The red-clay cliffs rose sheer and abruptly right in front, their tops ringed with trees – an impossible place to attempt a landing.

Isooba gasped in fear. Two choices, then: crash into the cliffs and burst into flames, or fly on and be ripped to shreds when the panther got out. Either way, he was dead meat. His pilot's instinct took over. He fought with the controls to bring the plane's nose high enough in time. The Cessna responded, its single engine roaring in protest as, with barely moments to spare, Isooba managed to clear the rim of the quarry and the encircling trees. It was testament to his prowess, but even as he felt a surge of relief, the manoeuvre left him shooting wildly over a wide expanse of wooded wasteland, and he wrenched the stick forward. His relief died. There was no flat, open ground in sight. Even as he scanned the area, he heard, above the scream of the engine and the thunder, a splintering crack. Looking over his shoulder, he saw that Kala was getting out. One part of the crate hung at an angle, creating a gap through which she had managed to force one front leg and shoulder. Isooba had only a few seconds at best before she demolished the crate entirely. One chance left: land, anywhere!

Seizing the controls, he throttled back, lowered the undercarriage and prayed. As the plane dropped, Isooba aimed for what must surely be scrubland on the other side of the wood directly in front of him. But the plane was already disastrously low. An eighty-foot ash tree near the middle of the wood proved its nemesis. Snagging the topmost branches, the plane juddered, flipped sideways, turned a half-somersault and came down. Right on cue, a deafening clap of thunder rolled on and on. When it stopped, there was only the sound of the gale and the rain. The plane, caught up and buried deep in the trees, had miraculously escaped impact with the ground.

Inside what remained of the crate, Kala lay stunned and motionless, an open head wound steadily dripping blood. Isooba struggled feebly to free himself, but it was useless. Both his legs were crushed and trapped from the shins down. Strangely, he felt no pain. But with no response at all from his legs he gave up the struggle, knowing he wasn't going anywhere. With bitter, fearful resignation, he accepted that there was no hope of escape. A picture came into his mind of grim-faced Mr Smith, the boss man, and he knew that even if, against all odds, he somehow survived this crash, he was still a dead man. He closed his eyes, and now a picture of Mara, his beloved wife, swam before him. She was smiling. He kept his eyes closed and waited for the fire to start.

TWO
2020

He was choking. No breath. Sheer terror swamped him, took over. Struggling, coughing hard to clear his mouth and throat, his airways contracting with the effort of sucking in life-giving air. Sour, scalding bile seared the back of his throat. Only partly conscious, he flung out an arm and his knuckles hit the solid oak headboard. The sharp pain brought full consciousness flooding back and Kent Evans threw himself forwards, gagging desperately. Leaning over, retching helplessly, unable to stop himself, he whimpered like a scared puppy as he vomited all over the duvet.

Kent! For God's sake... No compassion. He could still hear her voice yelling inside his head. Her only concern: clean up the mess, wash the stinking bedcovers and the spattered oak floorboards, make sure everything was wiped clean. No wiping clean of his tormented subconscious; no allowance made for his inability to control the nightmare that had prompted his vomiting.

He'd thought that maybe he was over it; that the hellish root cause had finally abated. So strange that he'd never vomited, not once, during his time out in Afghanistan. Some of them had, but he'd never awakened throwing up, not even with the bloody, daily horror he'd witnessed – and 'bloody' was definitely the right word. The metallic smell seemed part of the air they all breathed. The spartan living conditions, and the blinding white heat that sucked dry every bit of energy not only from the body, but from the mind too, were demoralising enough. But the relentless, nerve-stretching waiting, watching and hard graft in that dusty, arid countryside, the polar opposite to England, wore down the very soul. He'd awoken to the shouts of other soldiers who, fast asleep, were reliving the hell of the day just gone; their muffled sobs; and their prayers. He'd turned over, buried his face and pretended, like they all did, that they'd get through this term of active service unscathed and would soon be back in the cold drizzle and greenness of England, where the loving arms of their own women were waiting. Then they woke to daylight and reality, to the clatter, smoke and stink of another day in Afghanistan's inferno. But he'd never thrown up. That delight saved itself for when he was back in England.

Kent! Stop it! As if you *could* stop in the middle of being sick. *Other men go out there. They don't come back and barf all over their beds like children.* She said that – yelled it – every time. If only she wouldn't; at those words, his stomach always heaved again and nearly always managed to relieve itself of any residual contents that had escaped being thrown up the first time. Then Chloe would really lose it, smacking him, flat-handed, round his head and face. *Stop it, stop it! Just look at yourself. What an excuse for a man. You're not a man, you're... you're... pathetic.* She'd really spit out the words, or similar ones, full of venom, conveying her total disgust and revulsion. And his precious, much-anticipated days or hours of remaining leave would be spent trying to appease her, to cross the no man's land between them, all the while aware that time was running short. Returning from a war zone to a war zone wasn't a situation he could stomach. He needed a loving home to return to like a diver needed air.

The last time, on the very last night of his leave, as they were getting ready for bed, she'd suddenly relented. 'Kent, you're going back in the morning.' She'd traced a fingertip down his right ear and along the line of his jaw. 'Don't let's part as enemies. I mean,' she'd laughed, 'you're surrounded by them out there.'

He'd stared at her, shaking his head. He couldn't believe she'd actually laughed as she said those words. But taking a very deep, steadying breath, he'd convinced himself that she had no idea what he and all the other poor devils had to face in Helmand Province. How could she? It wasn't her fault. And so, for comfort, he'd reached for her, carried her to the bed and spent the greater part of the night making passionate love to her. He'd kissed every inch of her silky, perfumed, beautiful body; buried his face in her sweet-smelling hair; committed it all to memory. It would have to last him the long months until he returned home again – assuming, of course, that he survived.

THREE
2020

The Wild Ark private zoo occupied a vast acreage on the Cumbrian–Scottish border. Most of the week it remained closed, but on Fridays and at weekends it was open to the general public – at a price. Those three days ensured that the zoo was a legitimate, self-sustaining and taxpaying business. Mr Smith, the owner, ensured that his accountant/vet, George Gregson, confirmed this. The books were always up to date and presented immaculately for whatever inspection HMRC might deem necessary. The end-of-year tax return was all done on computer now and Gregson was a forward-thinking man; he'd been preparing for this change for three years or more. Everything was done exactly to the government's stipulations. Gregson couldn't afford the slightest slip-up. While the zoo was seen to run on correct and approved lines, there was no need for any investigation. The fact that the zoo was merely the legitimate front for the real business was something the government knew nothing about. And considering the excellent salary he received, Gregson would keep it that way.

And the zoo did do very well. The numbers of visitors had increased year on year for the past four years. One of the reasons for this was Kielder Forest, just north of the zoo; people could easily drive up to take in both attractions if they wished. But the main reason was the sheer range of the Wild Ark's exhibits. To ensure it didn't diminish, an ongoing supply of new animals was essential. On this Sunday evening, Smith was waiting for the telephone call from Brittany to his burner phone that would confirm that his latest acquisition had left France and was on its way. Immaculately dressed, as always, in suit and tie (until nine o'clock found him attired in dressing gown and slippers), he paced the floor of his private office. There was the normal office, part of the reception buildings near the zoo's entrance, and then there was the private one within the house itself; 'house' being a loose description of what was virtually a mansion. This was Smith's personal residence. Situated down a winding, tree-lined drive on the zoo's far northern boundary, it was well away from any inquisitive visitors.

A raging gust of wind flung rain against the triple glazing of the west window behind Smith's desk; a massive, nine-drawered mahogany piece complete with gleaming brass cup handles. Smith ceased pacing and went over to peer out at the wild night before pouring himself a large Scotch from the decanter sitting on the desk's red-leather top. Isooba's flight would be far from smooth. Smith downed the Scotch in one gulp and poured another – but then the disposable phone rang. Before he could answer, there was an artillery rattle of hail against the glass. His hand hovered over the mobile, letting the noise abate before he answered. 'Yes?'

'Cargo loaded and lifted.' There was a click and the phone went dead.

The corners of Smith's mouth relaxed and curled slightly. He tossed the phone into the wastepaper basket under the desk to join two others. When the number of phones in the bin reached three, he paid a visit to the aquarium and reptile house. Captain Hook, the largest of the zoo's crocodiles, tidied up anything that needed disposing of, and he wasn't fussy what he ate.

FOUR
2020

You needed ice-cold nerves and shit-hot reactions, and Phillip Lemmingham had both. His nerves were made not simply of steel; more titanium.

The plane, a British Airways, was directly in front, and flying straight towards him at two hundred miles per hour. From his seat in the control room he could see it clearly through the wide glass panels... well, almost clearly. At fifty metres tall, the East Midlands Airport control tower was a marvellous feat of engineering. Phillip was proud to work there as an air traffic controller. Having started at twenty-nine, he had now completed almost twenty-seven years' service.

He took a tissue from his pocket, placed it against his left eye socket and the side of his nose, and pressed. Grateful for the release, salty fluid trickled from his eye and down his cheek. He blinked rapidly. Better. A swift glance sideways at Mickey, the rookie on duty beside him, confirmed that he hadn't noticed, and Phillip, letting the tissue drop swiftly into the palm of his hand, blew his nose hard.

Without taking his eyes from the view in front of him, Mickey said, 'Not coming down with it too, are you?'

'No, hopefully, not.' They were struggling; manpower down at least twenty per cent due to the latest virus sweeping the country.

'And your retirement do down the pub tonight. Need you there to receive whatever it is they've bought you. I mean, twenty-seven years…'

'And of course you've no idea what that is, have you, Sonny Jim?'

'Can't say, Mr Lemmingham, can't say.' Mickey was about to laugh, but instead found himself sneezing twice, violently.

By four o'clock Mickey had been sent home, his eyes and nose streaming. Phillip, his last shift almost finished, was confident he'd cope brilliantly as he always had. But just before six, his left eye was playing him up again. It was quite a simple thing – a blocked tear duct – and straightforward to put right: a small operation to insert a thin instrument to clear the duct. But Phillip knew that if he owned up to the minor malfunction, the optician would discover what he already knew: that his eyesight was deteriorating. Once that was known, his job would be gone. OK, after this last shift he was retiring, but what he hadn't come clean about was that he'd known about his vision problems for at least six months now. He was obliged to take an eye test every year, but knew that well before the next test his life would change and it wouldn't matter anyway.

And, indeed, the not-unexpected phone call he'd received a few days ago regarding his mother had certainly changed his situation. But up to now, he'd needed his salary, desperately. He felt as if he was standing on a tightrope and doing a juggling act all at the same time. His ninety-three-year-old father was in a nursing home, which meant sky-high care costs. Phillip's salary was very generous and he'd budgeted to be able to take care of the finances even if he couldn't physically care for his father. But about the time he'd become aware of his sight problems, the doctor at his local practice had taken him aside and broken the news that his mother also needed to go into care. The doctor's prognosis was that at best she had only a few months to live. Phillip was damned if he was going to let her down when he had already done the right thing by his father. And after all, he convinced himself, when he could no longer do the job safely, he'd come clean and hand in his resignation. It was just a balancing act.

The illegal, disastrously low-flying Cessna, already below radar, didn't register on his screen. It flew on. Phillip knew it was simply a question of holding his nerve. No way would he sully his reputation by putting passengers' safety at risk. Right now it was just a necessary balancing act, before the company required his next eyesight check and he needed to pay his parents' care costs. He could do it.

Two further airplanes landed safely. Phillip took another tissue and pressed it gently against his left eye. As the time moved round to seven o'clock, knocking-off time, he felt a Cheshire cat grin spread over his face. Unless a rogue plane had slipped past under the radar – and he laughed at the very idea – he'd completed a full twenty-seven years with an unblemished record. He bounced a clenched fist on his knee in triumph. Now he could book that optician's appointment, he could play golf (he loved golf), and, at fifty-six, he could do anything else he fancied. He'd earned it. He hadn't let anybody down – not passengers, not crew, not family. And an appointment had already been made at the village church for next week. He wouldn't need to ask for time off work now to attend his mother's funeral – she'd died four days ago. However, retirement wasn't the end. He was still very much needed. He was pushing his father's wheelchair to the church.

FIVE
1986

Kent had always wanted to be a soldier. Even at three or four years of age he had lived and breathed – and dreamed about – the thought of being in the army when he grew up.

Many a time his mother bewailed the fact that she had bought him an Action Man as a Christmas present. 'It's my fault, Bryn,' she said to her husband. 'That's what started it all off.'

'Give over, woman. Kid's just playing soldiers. Doesn't mean he'll enlist when he's through wi' school.'

Bryn looked across at the kitchen window. Swirling white flakes hit the glass as the wind roared around the farmhouse. It had been a long, hard winter, with lots of losses of newborn lambs. But if they'd still been at the Welsh farm, it would have been even harder. Not for the first time, he realised that he was glad his father had bequeathed the family farm to his eldest brother, carrying on the family tradition. OK, Bryn had had to make the tough choice of where to move to; where to take his family. But it had worked out all right in the end. They were over the border in England, the Midlands, and the weather wasn't so grim, not by a long chalk. Kinder winters and early springs were more the norm. That equated to fewer lost lambs, and Bryn's annual income reflected this.

Ruth shook her head. 'Oh, he will. My Kent's got a mind of his own. Once the idea's in his head, you won't sway him.'

'Not just *your* Kent. He's my son an' all.'

'You know more about the damned sheep than people.'

'Maybe. But you know what?' Bryn added. 'Kent's got a feel for them too.' He nodded over to the corner next to the Rayburn.

The little boy was sitting cross-legged inside a large cardboard box well padded with straw. On his knee was a tiny Black Welsh Mountain lamb. Cooing encouragement, he held a bottle of warm milk and touched the teat to the lamb's mouth. A few drops bathed its lips and, responding to the taste, the little creature cottoned on and began to suck. Kent raised the other end of the bottle and, contented, the lamb sank to its knees on its two forelegs. Its rear end stood proud, its short tail wagging vigorously as it suckled greedily.

'See what I mean?'

'OK, Bryn. Yes, he'll make a good farmer.' Ruth rose from the table and, going over, rubbed her hand across her younger son's dark curly hair.

The child looked up, his face alight. 'This one's not going to die, is he, Mum?'

'No, son. He'll pull through just fine.' She glanced along the table towards Kent's brother, Jack, three years older. He was totally engrossed, as usual, in a Meccano set. Unaccountably, a faint, cold shadow passed over her. At some point in the future, she sensed there was going to be trouble.

SIX
2020

A deep feeling of disgust and disappointment swamped Kent. He didn't need Chloe's nagging voice in his head to feel shame at the state of his bed – a single one now. Despite it being barely 5am, he gathered up the soiled bedding and sluiced it off in the kitchen sink downstairs. Then he loaded the washing machine and left it to do its work while he scrubbed the oak floorboards in the bedroom. Despite the cold outside, he flung open the casement window, letting in an icy blast of winter wind. Unusually, last night he'd had a pint of beer after his meal, and, on top of curry, the stink in the bedroom was sour and overpowering.

Tearing off his pyjamas, which had miraculously escaped the tide of vomit, he tossed them into the linen basket in the bathroom and stepped under a scalding shower. After ten minutes he rubbed himself dry with a rough towel. Feeling considerably better, he walked naked down the landing and into the bedroom to fetch clean clothes. The wind through the open window had cleared the worst of the smell, but it struck his bare skin with a merciless arctic blast that had him gasping at its intensity. He grabbed some thick woolly gear and shut the door on its hostility. It was certainly scouring his bedroom and removing the unpleasant odour. He just wished that he could as easily scour his subconscious and remove the memory that had prompted his body's involuntary response.

Clad now in three warm layers and leaning against the Rayburn, rubbing a stockinged toe against Jess the sheepdog's ear as she lay in a snug basket at his feet, he chewed on a piece of honeyed toast. Then he washed it down with strong, hot tea – the first of the two breakfasts he always had – and prepared to face the battering going on outside. It wasn't snowing yet, but the weather was making every effort towards it, and his livelihood was out there on the hillside. His precious flock, all five hundred Black Welsh Mountain sheep, were enduring it, and he was needed out there with them.

Clicking his fingers to Jess, he opened the door.

SEVEN
2020

Darkness. Darkness surrounded her. The smell of man filled her nostrils. And blood. Tentatively, Kala sniffed at her left paw and growled low in her throat as the movement sent pain flashing across her head. But it wasn't just her own blood; there was the blood of man too.

Wrinkling her muzzle, she sniffed, determining the direction and strength of the scent. For long moments she lay without moving, just using her sense of smell. But she detected no increase in the man's scent. Her ears flicked as she listened. All around, she could hear the howl of the wind, the pounding of rain on the earth. But there was no other sound; no sign of danger approaching.

She was well used to the smell of man. Often she associated it with the coming of food; hunks of raw meat or fowl. She wasn't hungry right now; there had been an extra feed before the man with the rifle had raised it in front of her. The last thing she remembered was a sharp sting as the dart had driven into her neck. But while she wasn't hungry, she was in pain. All over her body it flared and receded from numerous abrasions and bruises. It was worst in her head and left forepaw, but a gash on her flank also throbbed fiercely and oozed blood. She twisted her head, ignoring the extra jag of pain, and licked feebly at the wound, her rough pink tongue scraping the black fur again and again, instinctively cleansing away the trickle of blood. As her left paw stabbed sharply where the claw had been pulled out, she raised her muzzle and growled angrily, deep in her throat.

Kala struggled to get up but it was too much effort. The effects of the drug were still running through her system and the battering she'd received had left her weak and vulnerable. She sank back, closed her eyes and let the darkness sweep her back into oblivion.

EIGHT
2010

'What did you say?' Bryn Evans clenched his fists and slowly pushed himself up from his chair at the farmhouse kitchen table. His knuckles whitened as his grip tightened.

His elder son, Jack, lifted his mug of tea and took his time drinking it. His Adam's apple rose and fell.

Bryn shook his head. 'And you've driven up from Southampton to tell me that? I don't believe you could have been such an idiot, our Jack. What the hell would your mother think, eh?'

'Dad, Mum's been dead these last few years. She's at rest now, not suffering. Nothing *can* hurt her any more.'

'Ruthie and me, we looked after you and our Kent; brought you up decently, knowing wrong from right, and this is how you repay us?' Bryn sat down heavily, clutching the scrubbed oak tabletop.

'I didn't plan it, did I? I mean, it's not something you'd plan. It's just life.' Jack shrugged. 'I planned going to college and qualifying as a mechanic. That's the sort of thing you plan.'

'Yes, even though your mother and me didn't want you to, and you knew that well enough. But we gave you your head; let you do what you wanted.'

'Oh, yes,' Jack sneered, 'to "get it out of my system". That was what Mum said, wasn't it? Just like she said it to our Kent when he was desperate to join the army. And look at him. Signed away nine years of his life.'

'Don't you criticise your brother. If nothing else, he's a brave lad, away fighting for his country. Trying to help make the world a bit safer.'

'But you were against him going, weren't you? Wanted him here at the farm, not miles and miles away.'

Bryn dropped his head into his hands and nodded. 'Kent had such a feel for this way of life. Yes, I did think he'd grow out of his obsession with the army.'

'Well, he didn't.' Jack curled his lip. 'The days when you could dictate to kids what they were going to do have gone. Why don't you accept it, eh?' He crashed his fist down onto the table, making their mugs of tea bounce and slop over. 'Get over it.'

Bryn lifted his head and looked at his son. ''S no good blustering, Jack. You used to do that when you were a kid – an' in the wrong, same as you are now. You're in a bloody awful mess, an' you know it. You've got a wife, but are you satisfied? Oh, no. You had to bed another woman and get her pregnant. So, what y' going to do about it, eh?'

Silence filled the kitchen; a silence that stretched as Jack finished his drink.

Bryn sighed heavily. 'No, I didn't think you'd have an answer. Because, by crikey, there isn't one, is there?'

'Well, there you're wrong, Dad. Dead wrong. I know exactly what I'm going to do.'

The two men eyed each other across the table.

'Go on then, tell me.'

'I'm leaving Liz. I'm going to divorce her. She can keep the flat. I don't want it. Then I'm going to marry Juliette. Her dad's already offered me a job in his engineering company.'

Bryn dropped his gaze and studied his fingernails minutely. He was silent for a few moments. 'In that case, if you've made your mind up, made a choice, there's no point in me saying any more, is there?'

'No.'

'When are you leaving?'

Jack glanced at the wall clock. 'In the morning – too late now.'

Bryn stared at his son, sadness and distress battling with anger. 'Don't bother coming to find me to say goodbye, then. I'll be up on the hills with the flock.' He rose to his feet. 'I'm for bed.' At the kitchen door he hesitated. 'I hope it all works out for you, son. Goodbye.'

NINE
2013

It had been a long journey, most of it a blur, from Afghanistan. Now Kent was on the last leg home. Every turn of the train wheels seemed to chant, *Going back, going back*, vying with the words that went round and round inside his head; the words his commanding officer had said to him earlier that morning. Being called into the adjutant's office had rung warning bells before he'd even gone through the door. And it was the worst of all news.

'I'm afraid I have some bad news, Sergeant Evans. I'm sorry to have to tell you, your father has died.' The shock effectively obliterated the rest of what the CO was saying, but Kent had come back to reality in time to hear the words '…of course, compassionate leave is granted, with immediate effect.'

At sixty-seven, Bryn Evans had looked a good decade younger. He could still work a sixteen-hour day when it was required, and it often was, in the late winter when the lambing season began. Being a shepherd wasn't simply a job; it was a way of life. Bryn's health had seemed perfect. There had been no indication that there was anything in the slightest bit wrong. That made the news all the more shocking. He had, apparently, suffered an aortic aneurism; it had been quick death. Kent's first coherent thought was, *Thank goodness Mum passed on first; at least she won't have to suffer the shock and distress of this.* It would have been very hard for her to cope. She and Bryn had been a really close, loving couple. His second thought was, *What the hell will happen to the farm and the animals?* With a massive effort, he brought his attention back to the man in front of him.

'I'm very sorry for your loss, Sergeant Evans.' And indeed, there was sympathy in the CO's eyes.

'Thank you, sir.' Kent stood passively, letting the finality of it all sink in.

'I understand there is a farm and livestock involved?'

'Yes, sir. But I have an elder brother who will inherit.'

'Ah, I see… no doubt he will take up the reins admirably.'

'Sir.'

'I note from your file, Sergeant Evans, that you are within two months of completion of your signing-on period. And this was for nine years.'

'Yes, sir.'

'Very good, then. I'll see you on your return.' The CO stood up, concluding their conversation.

Considerably shell-shocked, Kent saluted and walked out of the office, dazed and shaken. He'd then been flown to Brize Norton and was now aboard the diesel train fast approaching Nottingham Station. On time for once, the train slowed, groaned and shuddered to a stop. Kent waited for the green light to appear, pressed the button and alighted onto the platform. Still dressed in fatigues and with kitbag, he was aware of the somewhat embarrassing yet at the same time ego-boosting respectful looks and nods from some of the other passengers. They spoke without words of the esteem in which the general public held serving soldiers, and their admiration for their courage. Checking the destinations board, he made his way to Platform 6. He supposed he could have bought a cup of tea – there were a few minutes between connections – but all he could think about now was watching for the arrival of the Grantham train; the tiny last lap. Only two stops down the line now to his station: Redcliffe-on-Trent.

The train pulled in and Kent stepped aboard and slumped back in a corner seat. Beyond the window, the countryside slid past as he let the skimpy facts given to him run through his mind. He hadn't let Chloe or Jack know exactly when he'd be arriving – he didn't even know himself. He'd told them it would be somewhere around teatime on the 5th June, and that would have to do. But first he needed time alone, back on home territory; time to sort out his thoughts and absorb the familiar, comforting normality of known surroundings. The loss of his father had shaken up something inside him. The foundations of his life had suffered tremors, almost like a tiny earthquake. This further shock emphasised just how much, without being aware of it, he had missed England and home. He was suddenly aware of a vulnerability that he'd not known before.

The farm was way above the village and the tiny railway station. He supposed he could try to ring a taxi but with just one operating, success would be unlikely. A good walk, followed by a strong climb to reach the farmhouse, would be a soothing balm, calming and steadying his fractured feelings and emotions. It was what he needed: clean, cool air; the verdant greenery of the countryside he'd missed so much just lately, and increasingly in the past year of serving abroad. Above all, he wanted to listen to the silence of the hills, to the total absence of gunfire; the direct opposite of where he'd just been. Even though he was coming home to bury his father, this was where he wanted to be. His married quarters in Derbyshire had no pull whatsoever, and there would be no point. Chloe had already temporarily decamped to the farm following Bryn's death. She would be there now, waiting for him.

TEN
2020

Isooba felt as if he was floating in black water. The darkness was all around him, sucking him down, but, conversely, he also sensed himself beginning to rise above that almost suffocating darkness. Somewhere high above, thunder rolled. The noise reverberated inside his head, punctuated by heavy, driving rain battering against hard surfaces. The raindrops penetrated the wrecked fuselage and dripped steadily onto his forehead before running down the contours of his face.

Slowly, very slowly, Isooba became aware of the blackness beginning to lighten to grey, and the rising sensation intensified. The raindrops trickling down his face triggered a primal awareness of overriding thirst that involuntarily parted his dry lips. As the life-giving water found its way between them, he swallowed convulsively and full consciousness returned. His eyes flew open; his heart pounded madly. The rain continued to drum down and he lay with his face angled to catch it. For a long time, he remained unmoving, gratefully letting his mouth fill with raindrops and swallowing them. A very small blessing, but it was enough. Man could live without a lot of things, but not water.

Gradually, his eyes adjusted to the dim light. Moonlight filtered down through the trees as, blown and ripped by the wind, thunderclouds moved wildly across the sky. Restored a little by the rainwater, he tried to move his legs. Nothing. The only relief was that he wasn't yet feeling any great pain. He would at some point, he knew that, but for now he could cope. He put a shaky hand to the back of his head; touched the sticky, congealing blood and the swelling beneath. Obviously he'd sustained a bash which had knocked him unconscious but maybe there wasn't too much damage done. He wasn't seeing double; didn't feel sick. The miracle was that the plane had come down in exactly this spot, supported by the massive tree. Not only had he survived the crash but, because there had been no impact with the ground, the plane had been saved from going up in flames.

And then the full horror of his situation returned, flooding his mind as he remembered the disintegrating crate and the big cat. Fear caught his guts and twisted them, his heart once again beating in overdrive. Stiff with fright, he lay and listened. Had Kala perished in the crash? Or maybe the crate had broken up completely and she'd escaped. He prayed that she had; that she hadn't suffered any dire injury and had raced away to freedom. It was a long shot, but then again, he had survived – so far. He could still smell the rank animal odour, but the plane always reeked of cat.

As he lay, ears straining, amidst the howling wind and rain he became aware of another sound: a gentle, rhythmic scraping, repeated very slowly over and over again. It couldn't be the twisted metal of the aircraft cooling; it was far too soft a noise for that, and he estimated that the metal would have cooled whilst he'd been unconscious. Without a clock he had no idea what time it was, but judging by the cold stiffness of his muscles, it must be several hours at least since he'd ditched. The soft rasping continued. Somehow he found it soothing; hypnotic in a way. The *rasp, rasp, rasp* was comforting and reassuring, almost like a ticking clock. His head began nodding gently to the rhythm. Gradually, his eyelids closed and sleep took him unawares.

ELEVEN
2020

It was nearly ten o'clock. The storm battering the animal houses at the Wild Ark had reached its peak some while ago and was now beginning to move away east; the thunder grumbling in the distance before losing itself out over the North Sea. The animals – who, despite being under cover, had sought ever deeper shelter within their dens and beds – welcomed the respite as lightning ceased to fork across the sky, illuminating the night with jagged white flashes. A relaxed air settled over everything.

Except for Mr Smith, who was growing increasingly uptight about the fate of his aeroplane. The modified Cessna was flying illegally. If it had crashed it would be a disaster that could wipe him out. The plane would be found, together with Isooba, the panther… and the secret cargo. Everything would come out. His fingertips drummed the leather-topped desk in agitation. While registering on one level that Isooba was a good worker, a real yes-man who never queried anything and was committed to carrying out Smith's orders to the letter, he couldn't understand the total silence since the Cessna had taken off from Brittany. And it had certainly taken off; the phone call from the zoo in France had confirmed that. If Isooba had been forced to land, if he was still alive, he could have left the plane and called Smith's burner to confirm his location. But there'd been no call.

It would be a real loss to the Wild Ark if anything had happened to the replacement black panther. Her quarters were all ready and waiting. She would undoubtedly create a rise in the numbers of visitors. Not immediately – that wasn't how Smith operated. He was a man possessed of great patience; he needed to be. Kala would be shielded from the general public's view for a few months until the cubs she was carrying were born and fully weaned. Just how many she would produce would remain a mystery until Gregson had done a scan. Whilst Kala herself was being imported illegally, once her cubs had arrived and been passed off as being born to the resident panther, Nanna, they would not be subject to the same restrictions. A safeguard he'd operated previously with Nanna could also work. She too had been pregnant when she had arrived, and her two cubs had sent visitor numbers soaring that year. But the Wild Ark's original panther – lawfully imported and registered – had been too old to bear cubs and, once her offspring were old enough to face the visitors, Nanna had effectively been swapped in her place. However, Nanna herself was getting older now and had suffered grave setbacks in her latest pregnancy. The result: two stillborn cubs and a sterile mother. The opportunity to buy Kala, who was expecting cubs very soon, had been too good to turn down. He'd got in quick before anyone else had a chance. She was valuable.

But where the bloody hell were Isooba, the plane and the panther – not to mention the all-important second cargo? The storm, seemingly unexpected, had caused problems with air transport across the Midlands and north of the country. A crash landing now seemed not only possible, but very likely, and that meant an explosion and, inevitably, fire. A shiver ran the full length of Smith's spine just thinking about the consequences of a crash. Every hour that passed increased the likelihood that an unforeseen disaster had overtaken the plane. Surely, if Isooba had managed to find somewhere safe to land, he could have left the plane and made a call to say where he was? Anger rose in Smith, and he poured another whisky from the decanter. As well as the possible loss of the big cat, there could be a huge loss from the hidden cargo. Isooba knew nothing about that. As far as he was concerned, his job was simply to make sure that he delivered the panther from the French zoo to the Wild Ark. Compartmentalising jobs ensured that there was no continuous chain to follow should the worst happen. But supposing it already had? However, if the plane had come down over the Channel, it would be the saving of the situation. Still a massive loss, but with no trail leading back to Smith or the zoo. Even as the thought occurred to him, together with a corresponding rise in hope, it was counteracted by a second theory. Isooba wouldn't have been coping with the storm that far south. So, if he *had* crashed somewhere in England…

Smith tilted the tumbler and knocked back the spirit in one swallow. If, as he now strongly suspected, the plane had come down in the storm, all hell was about to break free. How apt, then, was the meaning of the panther's name? Kala: black destiny.

TWELVE
2013

The train juddered to a standstill, parallel with the platform at Redcliffe-on-Trent Station. Kent climbed out and made his way to the flight of steps at the far left corner. Ascending the curving concrete stairs, he reached the bridge spanning the railway line. At the middle of the bridge he stopped, leaned his forearms against the coping stones, waited for the whistle and watched the train snake away beneath him, heading off for Grantham. He waited until the last carriage disappeared around the bend in the track before beginning the nearly three-mile walk uphill to Hilltop Farmhouse. What had once seemed a poor substitute for the farmhouse in Wales had quickly become home to the young Kent, his brother Jack, and their mum and dad. The road from the station initially ran downhill out of necessity until it joined with the main road through the village. To the right it was lined with shops leading directly to the village centre. Following it further brought the walker to the River Trent. To the left it wound itself up through a series of bends, and the houses and cottages climbed as the road dictated.

Kent came to the T-junction. A young woman and a small boy of about three were on their way to the shops.

'Look, Mummy.' The little boy pointed excitedly at Kent. 'A soldier.'

His mother smiled indulgently. 'Yes, Sam, he's a soldier, isn't he?'

Sam, a big grin on his face, nodded vigorously. '*Yeees!*'

Aware of the effect of his fatigues, Kent grinned back and raised a hand in salute. It was about thirty years since he had been at that impressionable age but he could still remember the thrill of unwrapping Action Man on Christmas morning, and he knew exactly how Sam must be feeling right now.

Sam's eyes widened. He tugged at his mother's hand. 'He s'luted. Wow!'

His mother laughed. 'Thanks.' She smiled at Kent and led the most reluctant child, looking back over his shoulder every couple of steps, towards the village.

Whether she had meant thanks for the salute or for his military service wasn't clear, but it didn't matter. The encounter had brightened Kent's day despite the sadness in his heart, and he was so glad to be back on home soil. And it was quite possible that the chance encounter would live on in Sam's memory, bringing him happiness in the future. For a moment, Kent found himself wondering what it would be like to be a father. For sure, life would never be the same again; his own wishes would come a very poor second to the child's needs. And what would Chloe think? Would she like to be a mother? Maybe he'd ask her.

He turned left and walked on. Half an hour later, he had left the lower village behind and was climbing steadily. The houses thinned out as the hill rose, allowing glimpses of the countryside all around; its fields and wooded areas. And there was the gateway to the farm track that stretched away to the right, leading on upwards. Reaching the five-barred gate, Kent paused and looked back at the village far below. The railway track ran away in the distance towards Grantham; the train now long gone. He was here, on home ground. It was all so familiar and so precious. Taking a deep breath of satisfaction, he turned to face the last climb. At the end of the track was the farmhouse. Chloe would be there. He suddenly realised how much he'd missed her. Hefting his kitbag, he strode on. He was coming home.

The smaller of the two barns was empty, he noticed as he entered the farmyard. The big Gator quad bike was missing. No doubt old Jeremiah had taken it up onto the hillside and was running an eye over the flock, looking out for any stranded sheep. Despite his age – eighty on his last birthday – he had worked for Kent's father since they had arrived here and, although he'd officially retired last year, Kent was sure he would have offered his services given these sad circumstances. No sign of Jess anywhere either; nor her welcoming bark. She'd be out there with Jeremiah – try and stop her. Kent smiled. She was a clever sheepdog, very much part of the team. Then the smile died as he remembered that his father wasn't part of it any more. Bryn had spent a good deal of time training Jess but, as he'd said, in the end she had really trained him. Her instinct was inborn and couldn't be taught. Kent swallowed hard and gripped the strap of his kitbag. He hadn't just come home for a visit; he had a job to do. There was a funeral to be organised.

Letting himself in the kitchen door, he dumped the kitbag on the big wooden table and pushed open the living-room door. There was no one around. He was about to call Chloe's name when he heard a creak of floorboards above him. The farmhouse was old – over two hundred years old – and an oak door closed off the staircase. If she was upstairs she wouldn't hear him. Kent opened the staircase door. He'd surprise her; come up behind her, put his arms around her waist and kiss the back of her neck. She liked him to do that.

Walking up the twisty stairs, avoiding the fourth from the top – it really could do with another screw putting in to stop it creaking – he made his way down the landing. Approaching the master bedroom door, he heard her. She was giggling. Kent halted. The door wasn't fully closed. There was a gap of about six inches and he could see a sliver of the room beyond. Chloe giggled again, louder. His heart began to bang uncomfortably in his chest. The white duvet was slewed sideways, and part of it lay on the oak-boarded floor, partially covering something else. Kent stepped closer. Now he could see what it was. Thick material, heavily ridged and dark brown in colour: a pair of men's corduroy trousers. There was a leather belt threaded through some of the loops at the waist, and he recognised the buckle. He knew who the trousers belonged to.

A movement caught his eye and, lifting his gaze, he saw a man's naked leg and buttock. If he'd needed further confirmation as to who the man was, he needed it no longer. In the centre of the bare buttock was a tattoo. Even as the impact of recognition hit him, he saw a hand reach around, cup the buttock and squeeze hard. It was a woman's left hand with a ring on the third finger – a ruby surrounded with diamonds. He recognised that, too. It was the engagement ring he'd given Chloe.

THIRTEEN
2020

Phillip Lemmingham awoke at his usual time: 6.30am. Snug under several blankets and an eiderdown – he abhorred duvets – he lay comfortable and at ease, watching the red digital numbers on his bedside clock flick on to 6.40. The clock sprang into life, shrilling a wake-up call. Raising a hand, he flattened the alarm button on the top.

And then realisation of his new situation hit home. Retired! He was now officially retired. There would be no more infuriating, crawling commute, no more putting in the daily hours, no more control tower. He was free. And he was going to celebrate by going out onto the golf course. Yes, it was January, cold and bleak, but he'd never been a fair-weather golfer.

He thought with sadness about the sudden death of one of his golfing buddies, Bryn Evans. They'd enjoyed many rounds on Redcliffe Golf Course. What a damn shame Bryn had died at such an early age. Only the last time they'd played, Phillip had said that once he had retired they'd be able to play more often during quiet periods in the farming calendar. Now it would never happen. Of course, Bryn hadn't been his only partner. As a long-standing member of the club he knew most of the other members and had played with and against many of them. But his main golfing buddy had been Bryn. Like many older people Phillip disliked change, but now that Bryn had died, he realised with a sigh, that period of his life had gone and wouldn't be coming back. That left him looking for another golfing partner; one with whom he could strike up a compatible friendship so they could both enjoy their game.

Then he remembered that when Bryn's son, Kent, had come home on leave, both of them had sometimes come to the club for a game. Phillip could still recall Bryn's words from years ago. At the time, he'd acknowledged to himself that he'd experienced a twinge of jealousy as he hadn't any children of his own. But he was pleased for the farmer's sake that he had family around him.

'Our Kent's been badgering me to let him play. Promised the lad after the lambing was done, I'd get him started up at the clubhouse. As a treat, y' know – works damn hard, he does, for a young 'un. Only juniors, mind, but if he shows aptitude, I'll maybe arrange a few lessons for him…'

And Kent had proved that he could work hard not only on the farm, but also on improving his swing. He'd given it a hundred per cent effort and had become a popular young member of the club.

Phillip mulled it over. He'd heard a rumour that Kent was now back at home. But Phillip himself hadn't played as much since his parents' health problems had taken up so much of his time and energy. However, it might be an idea to call at Hilltop Farm and check out the possibility of having a round now and again with the lad. It wouldn't be the same, of course – not like with Bryn – but they might hit it off. Be nice if they could. It would be the next best thing, especially given Phillip's new freedom. Whenever Kent found the time to play, he'd certainly be able to accommodate the lad now he'd retired.

Phillip threw back the covers, slipped on his woolly tartan dressing gown and his slippers, and padded cheerfully downstairs to make the first lovely mug of tea of the day. After breakfast, he'd head over to the club and ask the pro if anybody needed a partner this morning. Despite the weather, golfers, like farmers, were a hardy breed. As the kettle burbled to a boil, Phillip joined in the happy sound and found himself whistling 'Straight Down the Middle'.

FOURTEEN
2020

Hilltop was an apt name for the two-hundred-year-old farmhouse. Far above Redcliffe-on-Trent, it was built of bricks from the red-clay quarry at the extreme top edge of the village that began over two miles below in the basin of the River Trent. Running alongside at one point was the former golf course, which had been made obsolete when the new eighteen-hole course was laid out almost parallel to it. The original course had been sold to the council over seventy years ago. At the time, there had been plans to turn it into a bypass, but, like similar ideas and plans elsewhere in the country, they had died a quiet death, most likely for financial reasons, and had not been mourned by the local residents.

Now, however, with mounting concerns about climate change, and because the land had never been disturbed by development, it had been elevated to the status of wildlife reserve. It was generally managed by the parish council, in that in the springtime a motor mower was used to negotiate the steep hill and cut the grass forming a plateau part way up. For the rest of the old golf course, nature revelled in her wildness and her victory over the planners, and the villagers revelled with her. It was used by local dog walkers – hardy souls who, when the negotiable rising ground gave out, weren't put off by the further fifty steps of steep climb. Paths mown by the council, usually in May, stretched along the boundary opening into the forty-yard-wide area at the top adjacent to the new golf course. There was a bench at the highest point for walkers to sit and admire the view. Those who made it to the top of the steps could stand to get their breath back and take in the fabulous view to the north towards Rufford Abbey and Sherwood Forest. Then, turning to face the south and the wildlife reserve, they were met with a wild sweep of rough grassland covered with dense vegetation, gorse bushes, brambles, and hawthorn bushes – twelve feet high, angling for full tree status – reaching upwards to the wide inverted bowl of sky. Tiny coverts of trees covered the reserve, with narrow, hidden paths opening and disappearing from sight that spoke of foxes and badgers passing through swathes of tall fern and waving, snowy-topped cow parsley that grew to shoulder height in the spring. A great deal of the reserve was inaccessible as blackberry brambles rioted in all directions, encircling the lower trunks of the hawthorns and spreading over wide areas of vegetation to heights of eight or nine feet. It was a marvellous secluded and safe habitat for all manner of wildlife. At the furthest part of the reserve stood the wood that, undisturbed for seventy years, gave shelter and housing to creatures including foxes, badgers, squirrels, rabbits, stoats, weasels and, more recently, muntjac deer.

And stretching away on one side was Hilltop Farm, encircling and sweeping on upwards for a further hundred or more acres; the grass hillside where the five-hundred-strong flock of Welsh Mountain sheep owned by Kent Evans roamed. Hardy, black-fleeced beasts with tightly curling horns, they suited their terrain perfectly. In the grim January weather, the animals, both wild and farm stock, had the hillside all to themselves.

In the farmhouse kitchen, Kent left the washing machine whirling round, cleaning and freshening his clothes, and opened the kitchen door, breathing in the icy blast. At his heels, Jess danced back and forth in eager anticipation of the freedom of the hills, but waiting for him to step out first. He was her adored master. He gave the orders and she was only too willing to carry them out. It was her reason for living. Descended from generations of sheepdogs, all her hardwired instincts ensured that she had been born to work sheep. A dry, comfortable bed and a bowl of food at the end of a long and strenuous day were reward enough; that and the caressing praise of her master's voice and hand. Kent called her to heel as he walked across the yard to the smaller of the two barns, lightly frozen puddles cracking beneath his boots. A dog whistle, its sound too high-pitched for human ears to catch, was in the pocket of his jacket. High on the hills where the wind snatched away his voice, it would be needed. But working instinctively in difficult situations, Jess often pre-empted his whistle. She was a brilliant sheepdog.

The barn housed not only the John Deere Gator quad bike, but also the hopper filled with sheep pellets and the stock of empty bags. The trailer was already attached to the quad, but the feed bags needed filling. Kent grabbed the first bag, secured it beneath the hopper and let the pellets run down. It was a job he'd been doing, or assisting with, since he was a kid on the farm in Wales. He'd felt the loss keenly when his grandfather had died and, because the farm then passed to his Uncle Alan, they'd had to leave his childhood home. However, it hadn't taken long before he and his family had put down new roots and established themselves in the English Midlands. Securing the neck of the bag, he loaded it into the trailer. By the time he'd filled and loaded the fifth bag, he'd removed his jacket and was warm and sweating despite the frost outside. Jess was circling, knowing the routine and accepting it, but for her the work didn't begin until they drove off up the hill.

Fully loaded now, Kent shrugged back into his jacket. Jess leapt up onto the trailer, and Kent swung aboard the quad and powered up the engine. He eased the quad and trailer out through the yard. Jess, tongue lolling despite the cold morning, gave one small yip of excitement and then braced herself as the trailer tilted, meeting the rising ground. Kent smiled. She was an extremely good sheepdog. His father had trained her and she'd worked alongside the older dog, Buddy, emulating him and picking up good habits. But Kent had to admit that she was getting on a bit now; she'd be nine this year. He ought to be thinking of getting a pup to bring on beside her. Nothing taught a pup so well as following the example of an older dog, especially a skilled and instinctive one. He might fall lucky if he went to the Skipton sheepdog auction; it was one of the best in the country for Border collies. With only himself and Lennie working the farm and the sheep now, he knew he was very much reliant on Jess's help. OK, Lennie Brown was his official farmworker and, at nineteen years of age, six feet six inches tall, and strong as a tank, he ate up the heavy work with relish. He certainly had the brawn, and could turn a sheep over with a deft flick. But he wasn't great on initiative and needed to be instructed.

Kent had noticed Jess quartering the yard before they set off, trying to pick up Lennie's scent, but she was out of luck. It was his day off today. The appeal for Jess was that Lennie always kept a supply of dog treats about his person, and he doted on her. She was always in line to receive something tasty. She whimpered softly near Kent's ear as they approached the scattered sheep. Feeling her muzzle resting on his shoulder, he smiled, took a hand from the wheel and scratched her gently below her ear.

'Sorry, Lennie's not here today, Jess.' It was doubtful that she understood, but then again, she was sharp as a tack and maybe she did. Kent slowed the quad right down and gave a hand signal. 'Come-bye.'

The bitch needed no second urging. She leapt from the trailer and was gone, racing away towards the sheep in a black-and-white blur.

FIFTEEN
2020

The storm raged mercilessly across the Midlands. It showed no sign of easing. All forms of human and animal life had gone to ground.

Slowly, Kala stirred, stretching out her forepaws, becoming aware of her surroundings. The effects of the drug were wearing off. But as consciousness returned, so did solid waves of pain. The gash in her shoulder had stopped bleeding, but the movement reopened the wound and immediately the blood flow resumed. She wrinkled her muzzle and snarled impotently.

The wind – gale force, with savage gusts of up to eighty miles per hour – sent a raking side sweep against the top branches of the old ash tree that was supporting the severely damaged plane. One of the lower, whippier branches that had provided a precarious hold to the left-hand vertical wing was blown sideways. Unable to withstand the force, the branch bent and scraped its way down and under the lower edge of the wing before coming loose and springing violently upwards. Deprived of its flimsy grip, the badly damaged wing slammed against the trunk of an adjacent tree. The entire plane shuddered and lurched downwards. The higher branches of the ash, free from restraint, whipped back upwards. For a few seconds the shattered wing remained attached to the body of the Cessna, but a further blast of wind took hold of it and shook it like a flag. The wing snapped clean away from the fuselage, crashing to the ground, and the plane slid down further after it. Far above, the dense canopy of the wood sprang back and reassembled itself, bending and swaying with the dictates of the storm and blocking out the wild sky.

Kala, ears clamped flat to the sides of her head, eyes wide with fear, pupils dilated to their maximum, braced herself as she felt the plane tilt and start to slip. With claws fully extended, she gripped what remained of the wooden floor of the crate and resisted the pull.

The full weight of the plane was resting on the right wing tip that was just skimming the ground, but without the weight-bearing branches high above supporting it, the plane continued to inch downwards. Each massive gust of wind shaking the trees sent it slipping further and further down. The wing tip met the ground, pressing harder and harder into the soft earth until it reached the resistant clay beneath. But the weight of the fuselage was far too great for the flimsy wing to support, and very slowly it started to bend before crumpling under the overwhelming force. For a minute or two it held, whilst above the storm continued to lash the wood, screaming through the trees, snapping twigs and smaller branches, and throwing them around like darts. Until the inevitable happened and the right wing, unable to take the pressure any longer, ripped apart with a scream of metal before falling. The rest of the mangled plane followed it, plummeting to the ground with a mighty crash that dislodged and took off the access door. The crate disintegrated, releasing the false bottom and its cargo and tossing the big cat out.

Kala, racked with pain and terrified, snarled and flattened herself against the floor which had come to rest at an oblique angle, her claws flexing wildly, seeking a firm hold but finding none. One paw landed on top of a soft, slippery surface, causing her to lurch forward. As she fought to anchor herself, her claw penetrated the slippery surface and her paw sank into something soft. A puff of fine whitish powder rose up. Kala sneezed.

SIXTEEN
2020

The African sun was burning everything beneath; a white-yellow furnace in the sky. Isooba rocked gently in his cane chair and felt a trickle of sweat run down his face. Mara emerged from the house and came out onto the stoep, her movements languid in the afternoon heat and a wide smile on her lovely face. He lay back in the chair and drank in the sight of her. She was a delight to the eye. She carried a small bowl with a spoon in it, and he watched her approach, watched the sway of her hips in her thin cotton shift, savouring every inch of her. What a woman – his woman. Coming close, her perfume filling his nostrils as she leaned over him, she dipped the spoon into the bowl and took out a scoop of vanilla ice cream. She tilted the spoon between his lips and slid the ice cream into his mouth; something she had done a hundred times before, knowing his weakness. The ice cream tasted delightfully sweet.

And then, suddenly, his chair tilted. Everything tilted. In a flash, Mara was gone, and Isooba jerked awake. He was no longer at home in Africa. The sun wasn't shining – the moon was up. It wasn't sweat trickling down his face, but rain, and the cold wetness filling his mouth was no longer sweet; it was tasteless. His ears were filled with the sounds of wind and rain, and he was still tilting. The familiar pilot's seat and tight belt held him firm, yet the whole seat – the plane itself – continued to tilt and slide, accompanied by a horrible metallic scraping noise. Inside his head, drums joined the cacophony of sound; it felt like the biggest hangover he'd ever had. He wasn't in Africa, nowhere near. Mara wasn't here either. He'd been dreaming – this was reality, the terrifying reality.

The plane jerked again, sliding down a few more inches, and, trapped in his seat, Isooba knew he was totally helpless to prevent whatever horror was about to happen. The plane inched towards the ground, each screaming gust of wind shaking the trees and causing it to slip further. Isooba knew the weight of the fuselage would continue to force it downwards; knew that if, as he suspected, the wing was the only support that was keeping the plane above ground level, there could be just one end to this situation. And it came. The wing was crumpling – the angle of the fuselage told its own tale. And even as he desperately clutched the restraining belt with both hands, he heard the scream of tortured metal as the wing finally gave way, pitching the wrecked plane the last few feet onto the sodden earth where it lay at a crazy angle.

Then, above the lashing rain and wind, he heard another noise; one he definitely did not want to hear: Kala snarling, just a few feet away, somewhere behind his seat. Involuntarily, he turned his head as far as he was able – which wasn't far. In the fitful moonlight, he could make out the gaping hole in the side of the Cessna where the door had been. Moving his neck sent shock waves along his spine; the pain sudden, hot, razor sharp. Holding back a cry, he clenched his jaws and focused all his attention on the open doorway. If the panther had freed herself from the crate, that would be her only escape route. He was still confined, but fifty per cent of the immediate danger came from the cat. But could he be sure that the sound he'd heard was her snarling? Might it have been the wind soughing through the gaps in the fuselage of the stricken plane? Then, as if in confirmation that he hadn't imagined it, he heard Kala sneeze very loudly – right behind him now, it seemed – and saw what looked like a fine white mist float upwards. Obviously, she had survived the crash. But was she still inside the crate, or was she free? Kala sneezed once more and leapt over the wreckage of the smashed floor, through the gaping doorway and out of the plane. Within a split second she had disappeared into the dark wood.

The relief was a tsunami that flooded Isooba, washed over him, and left him beached, weak and trembling. With shaking hands, he let go of the seat belt. Cupping his palms, he held them below the trickle of rain that ran down his face and dripped off his chin. With eyes closed, he lay there for a long time until his palms began to overflow. Then he lowered his face and slurped the cold water between dry lips, letting it cool his burning throat, sluicing it over his face. How many times he performed the action he didn't know; after a while it became routine, automatic. He stopped thinking about what he was doing and just did it, until his parched mouth and throat were sufficiently slaked. Then he let his hands part and fall limply at his sides. An overwhelming exhaustion gripped him and he was powerless to resist as his heavy eyelids closed and he fell asleep.

SEVENTEEN
2020

'It's a grave situation.' George Gregson, the Wild Ark's vet, smoothed a little finger across his ginger moustache, twisting his lip; a mannerism initiated in his twenties when he'd first grown a moustache. Now, at fifty-six, it was an ingrained habit he didn't even notice himself doing; one that increased in direct proportion to his stress levels. 'The only chance, I'd say, is if the Cessna came down in the Channel before it reached England. Of course, big cats can swim but not really for any great distance, so it's reasonable to assume that she'd have drowned.'

'Hmm,' Smith grunted. 'I'd already considered that possibility.'

'And how likely is it?'

Smith shook his head. 'I don't know. That's why I'm bringing Rawson into it. As a local pilot he can advise on flight conditions. He should be here in a couple of minutes. Just thought I'd speak to you first. What I anticipate he'll say is that Isooba wouldn't have met the bad weather until he'd actually crossed the Channel, but we'll see.'

'As I say, a grave situation – in more ways than one.' Gregson gave a dry snort of laughter, totally devoid of humour. 'However, it would certainly save *our* skins if he'd ditched in the sea. Not his own, of course.'

'He's paid to take risks.'

'True enough.'

'But say the plane did manage to cross the Channel – if it ditched somewhere in England, what then?'

Gregson adjusted his moustache. 'Two scenarios: if the panther was killed in the crash we've only got the problem of Isooba, but if the cat survived – and indeed actually escaped – then we've got a very dangerous situation as regards the general public as well. And that could get very nasty.'

'You're forgetting something,' Smith interjected.

'Which is…?'

'We're also facing the potential loss of two million pounds' worth of cocaine.'

'Ah, yes, of course.' Gregson groaned. 'I was concentrating on the escaped panther scenario. I had forgotten.'

The stretching silence was broken by a tentative tap on the office door. Smith gave the merest inclination of his head and Gregson went and opened it.

'Come in, Rawson,' Smith said.

'You wanted me?'

'Yes. We want your expert knowledge applied to the situation we've got right now.'

'OK.'

'The Cessna hasn't returned.' Smith drummed his fingers on the red leather of the desktop.

Rawson grimaced, lips pressed together in a thin, hard line. 'It was the usual southwesterly blow. Last night was a really rough one – gale force nine. Isooba would have had his hands full. Most likely he's had a forced landing lower down the country somewhere.'

'That's what I want you to work out. He was coming in from the Channel late afternoon. At what stage would he have encountered the storm? Could it even have caused him problems *over* the Channel?'

Rawson flicked a quick glance at the two men. 'You're asking me if he ditched in the sea?'

'Is it a possibility?'

'Without knowing his air speed and altitude, I can't give you a definite answer – an approximate one, possibly. But one thing I feel sure of is he hasn't got his feet wet. I'd bet on that. Like I say, the storm was blowing from the west, sweeping northwards through the country, and it wouldn't have troubled him earlier – like when he was coming over the Channel. He'd have been feeling it around Somerset, or even Wiltshire; the wind would have been funnelling up the Bristol Channel. By the time he reached Leicestershire, yes, he'd certainly have had to drop altitude.'

'So, we can rule out an English Channel ditch?'

'Oh, yes, I'm pretty sure about that.'

'Could he have been brought down in, say, Leicestershire then?' Gregson put in.

'Hmm, could have been… or even a bit higher; say, Nottinghamshire. They were experiencing gusts of up to seventy miles per hour, together with several electrical storms that converged. Or he could have decided to land, sit out the rest of the bad weather and carry on later. Sensible thing to do.'

'Something you would have done, in the same circumstances?'

'I definitely would, yes. Safest thing.'

'OK, Rawson.' Smith jerked his head towards the office door. 'Don't forget, I'll be needing you later this morning.'

'Yes, sir.' Rawson left, closing the door behind him.

Smith pressed a button on the side of the desk and, two or three minutes later, his housekeeper brought in a tray of coffee, cream, a glass bowl full of brown sugar cubes, and a set of silver tongs. She placed it on the low table between the two matching settees and disappeared, closing the door after her.

Smith sighed heavily. 'Not looking good, George.'

'No. But we have to give him time to get back – if he *is* getting back. From what Rawson said, we must assume that Isooba was forced to land further down the country and see out the storm.'

'Could be the reason he hasn't phoned. Until the weather improved and he could estimate flying time, he wouldn't have been able to give me a time.'

'That's true.'

'He was well over the flying limit time-wise. I know he always supervises the loading – doesn't trust anybody.' Smith gave an ironic guffaw. 'So, assuming that's what's happened, he probably got his head down for a few hours, sharpened himself up for the flight back. Might even still be asleep, lazy bastard. Didn't get much sleep myself last night.'

'Sounds reasonable. And that theory would shelve the issue of the white stuff too. Well, for now, anyway. Let's hope so, shall we? Until we know any different.'

'Think we're going to have to. Anyway, let's have some coffee – I just realised, starting this early, I haven't had any breakfast yet.' Smith grabbed the handle of the coffee pot and poured himself a near-overflowing cup before switching the handle around towards Gregson. 'Mrs Milton does make damn good coffee.' He shrugged. 'Well, she is half Italian, y' know.'

Petrina Milton left the office, closing the door behind her and letting the obligatory subservient smile leave her face. It was too bad: her one day off a week cancelled at such short notice. It had never happened before. Monday was sacrosanct; her precious day for herself. But she'd not questioned it when Mr Smith had told her that this Monday she'd be working. Well aware that her whole livelihood depended on her job, she'd acquiesced. And it wasn't just her job – her home, the tiny flat built onto the side of the main office at the zoo, belonged to Smith as well. They'd called it a 'tied cottage', and it was rent free. She'd thought it marvellous to begin with: a paid job and a free home. The hours were long, but the pay was very good.

However, she'd soon come to realise that absolute obedience to Smith's rules and wishes – and there were a lot of them, not least of which was discretion and absolute silence regarding anything she might see or hear – was what kept her in relative comfort. Any other housekeeping job would, no doubt, have meant deducting rent from her wages, be it for a single room in the employer's house – not what she wanted at all – or a self-contained flat. This would have left her with little remaining for savings. And she needed the money. Each week she squirrelled away whatever she could spare in the building society in Penrith. Her one extravagance – and really it was more of a necessity – was her little Fiat. The zoo was isolated and the bus service pretty infrequent, so she used the car every Monday when she drove into town, firstly for her personal shopping, before going on to enjoy afternoon tea in the company of her best friend (her only friend) Lisa, at the best tea shop in Penrith. They chatted and people-watched, swapped news about their grown-up children and grandchildren. It was a real treat to choose a cake from their delicious range, none of which Petrina had to make herself. That fact alone added to her pleasure. And come two o'clock that afternoon, Lisa would be there, saving her a chair at their usual table in the alcove by the window. Only Petrina wouldn't be able to join her. She grimaced. She'd have to let her know; let her down. She hated having to do it. Going into the kitchen – the one place Mr Smith hardly ever deigned to set foot in – she picked up her mobile from the worktop and called Lisa's number.

Predictably, Lisa was fairly bristling with indignation on her behalf. 'But it's Monday. We always meet on Mondays.'

'I'm so sorry, but I've been asked to work.'

'That man expects the earth from you. It's so unfair.'

'I'm really sorry.'

'Did he say why he wants you to work today?'

'No, but he says I can have a day off later in the week. He'll let me know when.'

'Hmm… when it suits him.'

'Shall we say next Monday, then?' Petrina bit her lip. 'You know, to be absolutely sure?'

'Yes, better do that because I don't know when else I might be able to get away from the farm. We've got a very big order for later this week; one of the hotels in Penrith. Seems they've got a wedding party booked and the bride-to-be is mad on chocolate ice cream.'

The mood lightened, and the two women laughed and ended the call.

EIGHTEEN
2013

'I'm not discussing anything with you, not after you've stabbed me in the back. Not before Dad's funeral. What I've got to say to you and Chloe…' Kent swallowed hard, battling to keep his anger under control. 'It'll keep until after we've buried him.'

'Leave her out of this,' Jack sneered. 'But somebody's got to *discuss* something or there won't even be a funeral.'

Kent stared at his brother. 'You mean you haven't arranged anything with the undertakers, or Dad's solicitors?'

'Nope.'

'But I was in Afghanistan, for heaven's sake. I came home as soon as I could. I'd no idea nothing had been done.'

'Dad and I parted on bad terms last time I visited.'

'It's your right to take charge; you're the eldest.'

'No, what you mean is, you want me to do all the work, so you don't have the bother.'

'*The bother?* For God's sake, it's his funeral we're talking about.'

'So, go ahead – *bother*.'

'Don't you want a say in the arrangements, then? Not even whether it's a cremation or a burial? What hymns are sung, the flowers for the wreath – nothing?'

'Look, little brother, you're the one who signed up for nine years in the army, then swanned off abroad.'

Kent shook his head slowly and backed away. He couldn't believe the coldness in Jack's voice, in his eyes. He'd come home the previous evening expecting some semblance of family unity. What a bloody laugh. Sick to his stomach on finding his wife and his brother betraying him in bed, Kent had snatched up a change of clothing, including his suit, and driven his father's Land Rover down to the village. There he'd booked himself in at Redcliffe's only B&B for a couple of nights at least, possibly longer. He knew there'd be talk – a soldier back from a war zone and not staying with his wife – but he couldn't have stayed at the farm. How the hell it would all shake down was unknown.

The one certainty was that there would be a funeral. The way Kent felt about Jack right now, there might easily be two. This morning, he'd driven up to the farm to find out the facts of his father's funeral – it had to take priority, even above his marriage; it wasn't something that could be put off – only to find that nothing had been done. On the train home he'd assumed that Jack, being next in line, would shoulder the responsibility, maybe ask Kent about his preferences, but at least contact the undertaker regarding the collection of their father's body from the mortuary at the Queen's Hospital in Nottingham. Davidson's was a village firm of long standing and an excellent reputation, and as part of their premises they had a dignified chapel of rest. They had handled Kent's mother's funeral; she had been respectfully removed from the farmhouse and taken to the chapel of rest until her funeral had been organised.

Standing in the farmhouse kitchen, feeling Jack's coldness coming at him in waves, Kent was shocked to the core – again.

As for Chloe, last night after some wild, hysterical screaming, she'd locked herself in the bedroom and refused to see or talk to him. He clenched his hands hard and felt his nails bite into his palms, welcoming the pain. 'OK,' he said slowly. 'I'm going down to Davidson's right now. And when I'm done there, I'm going to see the solicitors. If Dad made a will, they should have a copy. See what he wanted done about his funeral.'

'That's right, our Kent. You can start to do a bit of work around here. It's about time.'

The funeral took place four days later, by which time they were all observing an unspoken truce, mostly by avoiding each other, and Kent had left the B&B – its proprietors no wiser as to why he'd needed their services – and returned to the farmhouse.

Davidson's had admitted that they weren't overly busy. 'Normally,' Tim Davidson had said, 'you'd be waiting anything up to two weeks.' But it was, after all, June, not January. Kent supposed that, like farming, undertakers' work was influenced by the seasons.

They'd had a visit from the local vicar. He'd driven up to the farm in an antique Morris Minor, cassock flapping round his ankles as he alighted. For the sake of propriety, Kent, Jack and Chloe – again mostly without speaking more than was necessary – had managed to congregate in the living room and show a united front. And because it was in front of a comparative stranger – none of them were churchgoers – they combined forces in answering his sometimes probing questions regarding Bryn's life, interests and ambitions.

'Ah, yes, Bryn was a true son of the soil.' The vicar sat nodding, smiling, comforting. 'I have known him for thirty years.' That was a total lie because, to Kent's knowledge, his dad had never set foot inside the parish church apart from for his wife's funeral. But some things you didn't challenge, and today was one of those occasions as they tried to give him the answers that would enable him to use them in his eulogy.

Part way through his visit, Chloe disappeared into the kitchen and returned with a beautifully laid-out tray: Kent's mum's best china cups and saucers, and individual matching plates with slices of freshly cut ginger cake. There had always been a ginger cake on the go. It was – *had been*, Kent corrected himself – his dad's favourite. But this one was fresh; the delicious smell filled the room. At the sight and scent of it, he felt emotion welling up inside. It seemed so ironic that Chloe was carrying the tray. They were all mourning the loss of his dad and yet Kent was also mourning the loss of his wife, who, at least for now, was standing right in front of him.

He swallowed down the overwhelming feelings of grief. 'Sorry, Vicar,' he managed to say. 'It's just… ginger cake was Dad's favourite.'

'I see.' The vicar nodded, smiling affably. 'Do you know, I'm going to use that in my eulogy. The little personal touch – just what the congregation likes.'

Kent managed to smile back before dropping his gaze to the floor and praying for this farce to end.

Obviously, like the undertakers, the vicar wasn't swamped with work either, and when he suggested eleven o'clock four days hence, for the first time they answered as one voice: 'Yes.'

It was a bad mistake. After two weeks of brilliant sunny weather, on the morning of the funeral it was siling down. The undertakers scurried about with umbrellas, trying to keep everybody from getting soaked. But somehow it seemed appropriate as, seated in the church with the rain pouring in rivulets down the beautiful stained-glass windows, Kent thought of the many, many mornings when his dad had shrugged himself into waterproofs and stoically set off up the hill through the driving rain to tend his flock. He bent his head and unashamedly let the tears roll down his face in communion with the rain.

NINETEEN
2020

Phillip finished his breakfast. He'd done himself proud. Not the full monty, not quite, but it had him smacking his lips as he mopped up the last of his fried egg's yolk, then speared the remaining piece of succulent short back bacon and ate it with relish. Normally, when he was working in the control tower, breakfast had been cereal, maybe followed by a piece of toast. But today was different. It wouldn't come round again: the first morning of his well-earned retirement. It had to be marked; a little celebration leading to the rest of his new life.

He poured himself another cup of coffee. There was no hurry. Outside the rain was still bucketing down. The force of the storm had woken him once or twice during the night, and his thoughts had gone out to anyone abroad in the wild weather. It had calmed a lot by daybreak but the garden path was more a stream than slabs, and the lawn running alongside it was waterlogged. Certainly not a day for gardening, but, hey, he'd already decided it had to be golf. Now he had the time, he was going to spend a great deal of it practising his golf. No doubt about it, he'd let golf slide in the past few years, and he needed to reconnect with his golfing buddies. Without Bryn he'd have to make even more effort to catch up with the others, but by now it was possible that one or two of them had also passed on. He definitely needed to make some new friends.

Finishing his coffee, Phillip washed up the few dishes and the frying pan, flung the eiderdown back into position on top of his bed, and disappeared into the cupboard under the stairs where he stored his shoes and coats. He didn't need to think which coat he'd wear: it had to be his extremely expensive, but wonderfully waterproof, Gore-Tex. Dipping a hand into the capacious pocket, he pulled out his golfer's rain gloves. They made such a difference to his grip when the weather was bad. Taking up a soft clothes brush, Phillip opened the kitchen door and gently brushed off a sizeable, sticky cobweb from the raincoat's shoulders. Just showed how long it had been since he'd last worn it. The rain was still pouring down, bouncing off the pavers outside the back door. He hesitated. Maybe he should make sure the course was playable before he set off. But as soon as the thought occurred to him, he dismissed it. He'd arrive, find all the other golfers – men and women – out on the fairway, and look a complete fool for querying it.

All the same, he had to drive his Vauxhall at a steady speed, the wipers working hard to clear his screen even at forty miles per hour. Coming off the main A52 outside Bingham, he cut across country through Cropwell before taking a right turn that left him cruising gently up Dewberry Lane. The club was about a mile in front. It was fairly isolated. The lane culminated in the circular car park adjoining the golf course. Phillip found a free spot easily. Too easily – ominously, there were very few vehicles. The captain's Volvo was in its usual reserved space, and Phillip recognised the pro's car and that belonging to Bill, the office manager who'd been there for years, but apart from that the car park was empty. He screwed up his lips ruefully. It looked like he'd been wrong to assume it would be business as usual. Pulling on the handbrake and locking the car, he squelched over to the main doors and went in. There was no one about, so he went to the office door and knocked.

Bill opened it and beamed a welcome when he saw who it was. 'Hello, Phillip. Been a while. How you doin'?'

'Would you believe, I've just retired – my first day of freedom and…'

'…and you get this.' Bill waved a hand towards the wet window. It was almost impossible to see out. Rain ran down it like a curtain.

'Daft question, then, I suppose: any chance of a game?'

Bill laughed and shook his head sympathetically. 'Sorry. All this water's already adversely affected the greens. They'll need time to recover. Plus, I'm afraid the bunkers are flooded. We're keeping our fingers crossed that the faces won't collapse.'

'That's a blow.' Phillip sighed. 'Any suggestions?'

'Well, if you don't mind driving, I know two or three courses that seem to have escaped. Sleaford, for one, and I've just been speaking to John, the pro at Skegness. It looks like they missed the worst of the storm so they're still up and running.'

'Definite, is it?'

'Oh, yes. It's business as usual at North Shore Golf Hotel. The course is a little up the coast towards Winthorpe. You've played there before, have you?'

'Certainly have, and really enjoyed it. Stayed overnight, too – lovely room, cracking good food.'

'There you are, then. As you say, you've retired. Nothing to rush for now, is there? I mean, you've only got yourself to please. Why not make it a mini golfing holiday, eh? I mean, you can't do any gardening in this, so it's just you and the telly otherwise. A no-brainer, I'd call it.'

'And I'd say you're dead right.' Phillip laughed.

He squelched back over the car park to his vehicle. With disappointment running through him, he sat behind the wheel for a few minutes, watching the rain trickling down the windscreen. It was Sod's Law that Redcliffe Golf Course was closed. He'd been really looking forward to a game and Redcliffe was his local course. But it was no good bellyaching about it. *Go home first*, he decided – he'd left his mobile charging there, knowing that there was no one he needed to contact, no golfing partner to liaise with. Well, there hadn't been. Now there might be. He reached forward and switched on the engine.

The A52 was clear of any flooding and it was only when he turned off at the Bingham crossroads and drove down the lanes near Belvoir Castle that he had to take care and slow down, driving practically in the centre of the road to avoid mountainous sprays on either side. Reaching Harby, he drove through the small village before pulling up on the gravel drive in front of his bungalow. Going in the back door, he glanced at the kitchen wall clock – barely 8.30. Placing a palm over the plastic casing of the phone charger, he found it barely warm. The pulse had finished running up the right-hand side of the phone's screen: it was fully charged. He disconnected it and went into the spare bedroom he used as an office-cum-storeroom.

His address book was in the top drawer of the desk. It was some time since he'd played with Smith. Maybe the man wouldn't welcome a call out of the blue. Very likely he'd be busy. But then he shrugged. He'd never know if he didn't try – and they *had* played some excellent rounds at North Shore. It had been Bryn who'd introduced them when he and Phillip had spent a weekend at the hotel attached to the golf course. North Shore was sited right next to the sea, its car park barely yards from the sandy beach. It was a beautiful venue that attracted not only golfers but other visitors as well. One or two famous golfers had enjoyed rounds there: Lee Westwood for one; Harry Radcliffe, champion jump jockey, for another. Phillip and Bryn's visit had, of necessity, been during the summer months; Bryn was always far too occupied with the lambing early in the year. But subsequently when Bryn had been unable to extricate himself from farming commitments, Phillip had gone over to North Shore without him and partnered Smith. Still, he hesitated. By now, other partners would have come along, and he certainly didn't want to be a hanger-on. The worst scenario was that Smith would turn him down. A valid excuse would be business commitments – a saving of face for them both. And indeed, that excuse could very well be bona fide. He wouldn't know for certain, of course, because Smith was a very successful businessman, running what appeared to be an extremely lucrative leisure complex and zoo in the Cumbria area. When they'd first met, Phillip had checked him out on the internet and it had made impressive reading. Undoubtedly, Smith was a multimillionaire, and the first time they'd met for a round Phillip had struggled to shake off an uncomfortable feeling of inferiority. However, from the first green they'd hit it off and, fully focused on the game, Phillip had forgotten the difference in their social status. With golf it wasn't down to money; it was all down to the game. However, that had been several years ago and maybe Smith was no longer in that line of business. But Phillip would never know if he didn't make the call.

He shrugged – why not? Opening the address book, he turned to 'S' and punched in the number on his mobile.

'You're right. It is damn good coffee.' Gregson drained the last drops from his cup with satisfaction before setting it back down on the tray. He lifted his gaze and followed Smith's pacing of the office carpet, his coffee being imbibed in quick, snatched sips. 'No good getting stressed. Isooba will ring when he can.'

'It's nearly 9am. He's had time, for God's sake.'

Outside, rain was thrashing down. The tops of the tall poplars lining the drive to the house were still being shaken from side to side in the strong wind.

'I think we both know he's not going to be back any time soon,' Gregson said, pointing to the window. 'So, hadn't you better let Collection know?'

Smith's shoulders dropped and he followed Gregson's example and returned his empty cup to the tray. 'Yes. Yes, I'd better. Don't want them turning up when we have no bones to throw at them. That would never do; they might turn nasty – they need to know just who is in charge of this operation. Without us they have no business. And Mrs Milton's around today.' He went over to the desk, pulled open a drawer and took out a new phone. Dialling from memory, he said, 'X here. Cancel for today.'

Gregson watched him throw the phone into the wastepaper basket before kicking it backwards, further under the desk. 'You need to calm down.'

'Like you're a walking advert for calm yourself?' Smith snarled.

Gregson shook his head. 'I wish. But now I shall go and watch the seals in their pool. Works wonders.'

The phone on the desk rang. The two men exchanged looks.

Smith lifted the receiver. 'Yes? Who?' He listened for a few moments. 'Oh, yes. It was at least a couple of years ago, I'd say.' Then he nodded. 'Yes, yes, I remember; the weather was abysmal that day too.' He gave a short, dry chuckle. 'Didn't stop us, though.'

Gregson raised an enquiring eyebrow.

'We had a terrific round. And a terrific meal after.'

Gregson's eyebrow lowered and he met Smith's eye. A smile creased the vet's face.

'Yes. D'you know, Phillip, it's probably just what I need right now. What about Stockton-on-the-Forest? No? Too far to drive, hmm, I see. OK, well, yes, North Shore would be fine; lovely greens. I'll get Rawson to flip me over in the chopper.'

Gregson, seated in his chair, was still smiling and nodding gently.

'See you at the pro's shop, one o'clock, then?' Smith replaced the receiver and addressed Gregson. 'Don't look so smug. You have seals; I have golf.'

'Horses for courses.' Gregson rose, went to the office door and opened it. 'Enjoy.'

'Oh, I intend to, George, I intend to.'

TWENTY
2013

Rain had been pouring down before the funeral service, and it was still raining when the mourners left the shelter of the church porch. Kent stood just inside along with Chloe and Jack, all three with emotions firmly clamped down, putting on a show of unity and shaking hands with each person as they left the church and went out to face the rain. They thanked everyone for coming to pay their respects to Bryn. Kent, for one, meant it sincerely. It was a truly foul day. His father, he knew, would have appreciated their fortitude. Bryn had spent his life outdoors and it had given him a tough resilience to anything the weather could throw at him, but he would have known that many of the mourners were not outdoor workers, and most were elderly. Kent hurried to instruct them to make their way straight to The Royal Oak in the middle of the village, where refreshments were waiting. He assured them that, after Bryn's interment, he and the other two would join them at the pub. Walking right up Vicarage Lane to the cemetery was not on in this weather. There was a polite murmur of dissent, but he also detected a feeling of relief.

So it was only the immediate family who found themselves protected by large, solicitously positioned umbrellas and then seated in a single undertaker's car. At a suitably deferential pace the car glided round the corner from the church and through the village before turning sharp right into Vicarage Lane. At the recommended ten miles per hour, the big Daimler made its way up the long, narrow driveway flanked on either side by dripping yew trees, their foliage turned almost black by the deluge. At the graveside, artificial grass covered a mound of unearthed red clay that lay above a layer of topsoil, before unrolling down to meet the drenched natural grass. The striking red clay was a geological feature from which the village had got its name. From the north and south, steep cliffs of red clay held the village above the River Trent in a natural elongated bowl. It mattered not a jot that Kent's tears sprang afresh as his father's coffin was slowly and reverently lowered into the gaping hole. Even the vicar had raindrops rolling down his cheeks. And then they were ushered back into the waiting car and driven to the pub to fulfil the rest of a united family's duties.

Nearly two hours later, the ordeal over, they were back at the farm, dry if not comfortable; just the three of them. But, away from the view of the mourners, they were no longer a united family.

In the living room, Kent went over to the sideboard and set out three tumblers. Removing the glass stopper from the decanter of whisky, he poured a generous tot of Glenlivet into each. Passing one each to Chloe and Jack, he took the last one for himself. 'The village and Dad's friends have done their bit by turning up to his funeral in this siling rain. Now I propose that we raise our glasses and drink to Dad – a final send-off, just from the family.'

Chloe and Jack raised their glasses and gave silent nods.

'So, to our dear father, Bryn Evans – who always did his best for us, no matter what the weather – may he be reunited with Mum and may he find peace and rest after his lifetime's hard work. To Dad.'

Three tumblers were raised, three toasts drunk. Then, almost as if scripted, from out in the yard there came a prolonged howl. It went on and on. Unexpected and mournful, it froze them all for a few seconds.

'I'll fetch Jess in,' Kent said suddenly. 'She's still working for him, and will be until she passes over.'

Bryn had always treated his animals kindly. Jess had never been simply the farm sheepdog. Her basket was close to the Rayburn in the kitchen; her water bowl always clean and topped up. Bryn had respected the hard work she did for no tangible reward, and had kept his side of their unwritten bargain.

Kent opened the door and called her name. From her guarding vantage point inside the small barn, Jess flew across the yard and into the kitchen, tail well down between her back legs. He bent to reassure and comfort her, fondling her furry ears.

'It's how it goes, girl. You've had your howl. He'd want you to perk up.'

She licked his hand. With the sixth sense that animals have, she seemed to recognise and accept that Kent was now her master.

'OK, now in your bed.'

Obediently, the bitch trotted over to the Rayburn and curled up in her basket. She had stopped howling, but two soulful, sad eyes watched Kent as he went to rejoin the others.

At that point, there was a knock at the front door and Jess dutifully gave one warning bark. Kent shushed her and went to open it. He knew who it would be. Any friends or villagers would have knocked on the back door.

'Oh, Mr Peters, do come in.'

The solicitor had been invited to the funeral, not only in his professional capacity but also as a long-standing acquaintance of Bryn's. However, he had thanked Kent but explained that, as he would be attending a family gathering at that time, he couldn't come. Now he stood on the doorstep, briefcase in hand, sombre look on his face. He'd known Bryn for nearly thirty years, having handled his purchase of Hilltop Farm.

Kent had been holding himself in, containing all his anger with Jack and Chloe – until his father's business affairs were settled, he had to. He saw it as just one more gesture of respect for his father. His own affairs had to come second today. He opened the door wider. 'Come inside. The weather is awful, isn't it?'

'I fear it is, Mr Evans. And it seems to make these sad occasions so much worse, somehow.'

To Kent the very use of the name 'Mr Evans' seemed poignantly to emphasise that his father was truly gone and he was now an adult in this house, rather than just a son.

Chloe moved away from Jack's side, went to the sideboard and poured the solicitor a whisky.

'I'm sure you will remember, Mr Peters,' Jack said smoothly, 'that although my brother's name is Mr Evans too, I hold seniority to that title now that my father has died.'

Kent was only too aware that the farm was traditionally passed on to the oldest in the family. It was why the farm in Wales had passed to his Uncle Alan and his father had brought them to live here.

'Your drink, Mr Peters.' Chloe handed the chunky glass to the solicitor.

'And I assure you, Jack, it is a fact of which I am well aware,' Peters said, accepting the glass of whisky. 'Thank you, Chloe. However, with your permission, may I suggest a toast to Bryn?'

Following quick glances at each other, they all nodded.

'Our firm has taken care of Mr Evans Senior's needs for almost thirty years,' Peters continued. 'He wasn't simply a client; he became more of a valued friend. We played golf together on occasions. He will be very sorely missed in the village. So, I give you a farewell toast to Bryn. May he be reunited with his dear wife, Ruth, in love and peace.' He raised his glass. 'To Bryn.'

The toast was echoed by everyone.

'It's very good of you to come,' Kent said. 'I know you were already committed earlier today.'

'Well, as I said in my letter, your father's wishes, as detailed in his will, need to be made clear. And I thought today would be the best opportunity to present them, whilst both Jack and you, Kent, are at the farm.' Peters took an appreciative sip of the excellent whisky.

Chloe smiled broadly at the solicitor. 'But I'm sure we can all make a good guess, can't we?' Then she turned to Jack. 'Can't we?'

He nodded. 'I'm sure.'

'Then I suggest we get on to the business.' Peters cleared his throat and drained his whisky.

There was a significant charged silence. Kent felt the skin at the back of his neck prickle with apprehension. He had experienced enough shocks in the past few days but he had the impression that another was about to happen.

'You lost your grandparents quite a few years ago,' Peters began. 'And, as you are aware, your Uncle Alan and Aunt Pam had no children. And, of course, both Alan and Pam have predeceased Bryn.'

'That's correct.' Jack answered for all of them.

'That means there are no other living relatives, except for you, Jack… and you, Kent.'

Their nods confirmed his observations.

'And therefore, because there are no bequests to anyone else, the will is quite straightforward.' Peters paused and stared at the brothers in front of him. 'Bryn gave his whole working life to keeping the farm going. And in recent years, with profits decreasing, it wasn't easy. He struggled. Most farmers are struggling. But Bryn's will reflects his work ethic and his hopes for the future of Hilltop Farm. And I know that he took a great deal of time to make his decision, because he discussed his wishes with us.' He hesitated.

'It would be easier for all of us if you just told us what my father's wishes are,' Jack said.

'Very well. Mr Evans Senior has bequeathed the entire estate, including Hilltop Farm, all stock and equipment, all monies in his investments and his savings and current accounts, plus ownership of the sheepdog, Jess – with the proviso that she stays on the farm – to… Kent Evans.'

Stunned silence filled the room.

TWENTY-ONE

2020

Pupils dilated to their maximum to catch any slivers of moonlight, Kala leapt away from the wrecked fuselage of the Cessna. Her black pelt was plastered flat by the torrential rain, and only her blazing green eyes were visible in the dark depths of the storm-tossed wood. Her driving instinct was to get away from the crate and the plane.

She snaked her way through the trees as she ran, her lithe body twisting and turning, but as no sounds of pursuit followed, her speed soon slackened. The burst of energy – fuelled by the need to escape – ebbed. The sudden physical action had provoked the pain from her wounds, and blood was again dripping down her muzzle and flank. The injury where the claw had been ripped off was a sharp reminder every time she put the paw to the ground. As the fear subsided, her awareness of these pains increased and she began to limp. But the wood felt like familiar territory. Distant memories of freedom in the jungle surfaced and calmed her. Running free, away from the confines of the crate, and before that, from the panther enclosure at the French zoo, had awakened her wild instincts.

At the zoo, as the late-afternoon light faded, the big cats had been locked in secure pens for the night. She had got used to that routine, and now, filled with pain, she felt a dragging exhaustion urging her to find a safe shelter in which to sleep. In the jungle she would have chosen a tree, climbed it, then lain across a thick supporting branch, legs dangling either side to keep her balanced. But this was not the jungle, and most of the trees here were simply not tall enough, their branches not strong enough to support a ten-stone big cat. And Kala was not only exhausted; she was also thirsty, so very thirsty. The sedative leaving her system had given her a desperate urge to drink. In this, she was amply accommodated. Every dip and gully held rainwater – in parts, the wood was almost a swamp. Tired beyond measure and racked with pain, Kala limped to a stop beside a depression in the earth that had filled with several inches of rainwater. Crouched low on her forepaws, she lapped and lapped until she was fully sated. Then, rising shakily, she stood stock-still and scented the air. All around her the wood was full of the noise of the storm, but her acute hearing was focused on picking up signs of danger or of other nocturnal animals. There were none. All the burrowing animals – rabbits, foxes, badgers – were staying safely out of reach, preferring hunger pangs to the raging wind and rain above ground.

A particularly vivid fork of lightning slashed the sky, and for a split second the wood was fully illuminated. It was followed almost immediately by a tremendous crash of thunder. Crouching low, Kala wrinkled her muzzle and snarled in fright and pain. Above her head, a startled wood pigeon clattered its way to safety higher and deeper into the hanging clusters of last season's dried seed heads in the branches of a massive ash tree. She caught the scent of the bird, registering it not as a danger, but as food. However, she wasn't hungry – her appetite had been totally suppressed by her circumstances. Yes, she had craved water, but food was not something she needed right now.

However, the lightning had shown up a solid mass to her right. Swinging her head from side to side, whiskers twitching, she padded slowly into the undergrowth, away from the path. The smell of dead wood guided her towards the possible shelter at ground level. There were no caves or holes, but at some point three large trees had met their nemesis, probably in a storm as severe as this. No doubt as the rain had loosened the soil around their roots, the strength of the wind had sent them crashing earthwards. With their branches interlocked as they fell, the impact had torn their roots up through the ground, forming a low tunnel beneath. Over time, the rich soil had become a good seeding area. Now, decades later, only the main trunks of the three interwoven trees remained on the ground, their branches mainly rotted away. But the years had seen the growth of other trees around them. Hawthorn and holly had put down roots and reached up to the light. Taking advantage of assisted upward growth, ubiquitous ivy had smothered the trunks, twisting, encircling, and producing a natural living cave that screened the tree trunks.

Kala pushed her way through the outer layer of brambles surrounding this natural hide to where the great trunks had overlapped each other as they fell, one on top of another. At the point where they had hit the ground, a narrow tunnel some eight or nine feet long had been formed, enlarged into a sett by badgers in the past but empty now, totally hidden from outside view and, because of the thickness of the trunks keeping out the rain, barely damp inside. Almost spent, Kala crawled on her belly and, ignoring the pains racking her body, pulled herself into this compact, dark den. Safe now from the battering storm and any possible pursuit, she lay down and within seconds had passed out.

TWENTY-TWO
2020

Some ten miles away to the east of Redcliffe-on-Trent, at 9am in the small village of Harby an alarm clock sprang into life. Betty Sidcupp, still half asleep, still half drunk, reached out a groping arm and smacked it into submission. Groaning gently, she pushed herself into a sitting position and dug an elbow into the mound of bedding beside her. 'Arthur, wake up. The news will be on in a few minutes.' Their clock was always ten minutes fast.

There was merely a subterranean grunt from the recumbent form beside her.

Betty eased herself out of bed and stood up. With a mouth as dry as chalk dust and a splitting headache to boot, she tottered into the kitchen and stuck the kettle on. 'Tea… and more tea,' she mumbled to herself, and raised the blind. The scene outside was not an energising sight. The sky was filled with dark clouds being hustled along in ragged succession by a strong wind. The big sycamore in the lane was being buffeted roughly, its branches bending and sweeping almost to ground level. At least, for the moment, it wasn't actually raining. The kettle boiled and she made two mugs of tea.

It was not until she was safely back in the warm bed beside the still-snoring Arthur that she recalled the weather forecaster's warning the previous evening: a severe storm was expected to blow up from the south-west later on Sunday afternoon. Sipping the strong, reviving tea to ease her pounding head, Betty realised it was Sunday today. But the forecast was only one of the things that had occurred yesterday. Saturday had been her and Arthur's wedding anniversary – their thirtieth. At the small family party last night, both their children had been present. However, William and Michael were grown now, with partners and children of their own: Jacob, who was six years old, and little three-year-old Tommy. It had been a smashing party, what she could remember of it. Her mind was still in a fog – she'd drunk far too much. That was out of character. Normally, one glass of gin and tonic was her lot.

The clock radio came on with the nine o'clock news, followed by the weather for the next twenty-four hours. It reiterated what had been predicted the night before, though it seemed the storm had now been upgraded. Following the forecast, Classic FM played Schubert's *Trout Quintet*. Betty's head gave a particularly sharp stab of pain. Oh, yes, they'd certainly celebrated. It was a pity she couldn't remember the details. She closed her eyes to let the pain pass.

But a second or two later her eyelids flew open wide and she gasped at the sudden recollection. There'd been a lion in the garden! No, no, that couldn't be right, could it? She must have dreamt it, or possibly experienced an alcohol-induced hallucination. That was much more likely. Betty gripped the handle of her mug tightly. How likely was it? Her memory, still befuddled by many gin and tonics, was playing tricks. It must be. Turning to ask Arthur what he remembered, she found him still blissfully asleep, giving soft little grunts of contentment. No, he'd be no help at all. Well, he had matched her drinks with his own and was, like her, still under the influence. Neither of them was used to heavy drinking.

She put down the empty mug on the bedside table. It was probably a good job he was still asleep; he'd think she was completely mad. Ronald Binge's *The Watermill* was now playing. It was so soothing. Betty closed her eyes and slid further underneath the warm duvet. Right now it was just what she needed – soothing. In seconds she had joined Arthur in sleep.

It was nearly three hours later when they awoke. Arthur, seeing the mug of tea on his bedside table, reached for it and took a slurp. 'Oh, God,' he spluttered, 'it's bloody cold.'

Betty, rousing a second or two after, was too late to stop him. 'I made it at nine o'clock, that's why.'

'You know what, me duck, we both had a real skinful last night.'

'Hmm…' Betty attempted a nod and hastily gave up. *Never again*, she vowed silently, *never again*. 'Can you remember anything from last night?'

'Not a damn sight.' Arthur heaved himself out of bed, grabbed his towelling dressing gown and shuffled off as quickly as he could manage to the bathroom.

Knowing a lost cause when she saw one, Betty took herself off to the kitchen. Even if neither of them felt like it, what they needed was a lining on their stomachs. *A good brunch*, she decided, *with lots and lots of coffee – strong coffee.*

A little later, Arthur leaned back in his chair, patting his stomach gently, replete and with hangover well in retreat. 'What say we have a walk, eh? Get a bit of fresh air before this storm appears?'

Betty knew he hadn't switched on the television yet today. 'So you *do* remember last night, then.'

'Hmm?' He frowned.

'The storm, you said; the one that's supposed to be coming tonight.'

'Well, the forecast at teatime was bulling it up pretty well.'

'What else do you remember?'

'Our thirtieth, wasn't it? And, by crikey, we did celebrate. It was great to see the kids again – and the grandkids.' He chuckled. 'In their late twenties and I still call them "the kids".'

Suddenly, Betty was remembering herself. The haze in her brain was clearing, helped along by the coffee. 'Yes, it was lovely to see them all.' Her hands started to shake a little. 'But do you remember what else we saw? Or did I dream it – or maybe it was the drink?'

'Eh? What the heck you going on about?'

'Last night, Arthur. Late on, in the garden. Tell me it was just my imagination.'

'What was?'

'The lion, Arthur; the lion at the bottom of our garden.' She gripped his arm tightly. 'Did you see it?'

Arthur burst out laughing. 'Sounds to me as if you're still drunk as a newt. A lion, in our garden? More like next door's moggie.'

'So, you can't remember it?'

'Damn right, I can't. And I know I was three sheets to the wind – and if you were matching drinks with me, which you were, well… need I say more?'

'But you knew about the storm.'

Still laughing, he gently took hold of her shoulders and steered her across the room to the window. 'Look, lass, out there. Who needs a forecast, eh? You can see there's a storm brewing. And I suggest we take a short walk – down to the pub, maybe; have a hair of the dog – then come back home and go to bed.' He winked salaciously. 'Celebrate our thirtieth in the time-honoured way.'

Arthur had been right to suggest a quick visit to the village pub. And afterwards, when they'd got home… well, she'd showed him that even after thirty years, she was still in love with him. It had rounded off their anniversary weekend beautifully – it was one they'd never forget.

The gin and tonic at the pub had been nice, thought Betty, but you really couldn't beat a good cup of tea for hitting the spot. It was known to make everything better. Maybe that was why the English always mashed some tea in an emergency – any sort of emergency. Not that there was anything amiss right now; not at all. Arthur didn't need a drink; he was still fast asleep. Betty smiled, added some semi-skimmed to her mug and sat down next to the Aga, snug and warm, and watched the fat raindrops run down the kitchen windowpane.

The familiar tones of the *William Tell Overture* broke into the peace, making her jump and reach for her smartphone. It was her daughter-in-law, Larissa, her younger son Michael's wife.

'Hello, dear. Get back home safely? Little Tommy all right?' She listened and nodded. 'Good, yes, we're both absolutely fine too.' Then she frowned. 'What was that again?'

'Last night,' Larissa repeated, 'when Tommy had left his toy tiger on wheels out in the garden – you remember?'

'Well, Jacob came in first. I was pouring him some juice when Tommy ran back outside again. I left you to see to him.'

'That's right. He'd left his woolly tiger at the bottom of the garden, near the hedge; that wheeled toy we bought him last week when we visited the zoo. He went back outside to fetch it. He couldn't see me but I was watching him from the window, taking photos on my phone – you know, when they don't realise you're watching them, they are natural and funny. But then it wasn't so funny, Betty. He started shouting, "Lion, lion." Do you remember?'

Betty sat down suddenly. 'Yes, now you've prompted me, I do.'

'He came racing in, pulling his tiger toy and still shouting, "Lion."'

'"That's right, and we said, "No, Tommy, it's a tiger", didn't we?'

'Yes. And he got all agitated and screamed, "No, no – black lion."'

'Then I fetched the biscuit barrel and gave him a chocolate biscuit. It distracted him,' Betty said.

'And we thought no more about it.'

'But…?' Betty found her hands shaking.

'I looked at the photograph today and… oh, Betty, it was standing just inside the hedge, watching Tommy.'

'Oh, God. Not a lion; say it wasn't a *real* lion?'

'No, it wasn't.'

Betty felt her shoulders drop with relief. 'Thank God for that.'

'It wasn't a lion, it was a panther – a black panther. And it was in your garden.'

'No, no, it couldn't have been, Larissa. You must have snapped a neighbour's cat.'

'Sorry, there's no mistake. It was definitely a fully grown panther. I'll send you the photos.'

'But it wants reporting.' Betty's voice quavered. 'People should be warned…'

'Yes, and Michael has already forwarded a picture to one of the national newspapers. He says the news editor took all the details and assured him it will be in the paper tomorrow.'

'Oh, my word! I must wake Arthur and tell him. He was scoffing about it being just an ordinary cat…'

'I only wish it was. But I saw them when I lived in Kenya. Take care, both of you. But I have to say, panthers don't usually attack. They are secretive cats. Give me a ring later, when you've had a chance to see the pictures. Let me know what you think, OK? Bye for now.'

With exaggerated care, almost as though it might bite her, Betty put the phone down on the table and went to wake Arthur.

TWENTY-THREE
2013

The solicitor had gone. Jack had gone. The silence remained. Kent and Chloe stared at each other across the farmhouse kitchen.

It was Kent who broke the silence. 'Why?' It was the one question he'd wanted to ask her since he'd walked up the twisty old staircase to the bedroom door and seen Jack's belt and trousers lying on the floor – and his brother lying naked in the double bed with Chloe. It was a question he could not have asked before, not when his father's body was lying cold in the mortuary. Now, dignified by a church service and burial in a consecrated graveyard, Bryn was beyond any further help from his son. Now Kent needed to sort out his own life.

'Well...' Chloe shrugged her shoulders.

'Tell me, why did you do it? Why did you strip off and climb into bed with my brother?'

'Why do you think? To have sex, of course.'

Her blatant and deeply wounding answer hit Kent in his solar plexus like a kick from a horse. He gasped at the unbelievable pain it caused him. Clutching the edge of the kitchen table, he shook his head. 'You don't hold back, do you?'

'No. Tell it how it is. Saves a lot of messing about. Now, go on – ask me why I wanted sex with Jack.'

'Why did you?'

'You are so thick, aren't you, Kent? So bloody thick. You go away to play soldiers and leave me all by myself.' Chloe squared up to him, hands on hips, face screwed up with disgust and anger. 'What am I supposed to do? Sit knitting?'

'Other wives get left. They don't jump into bed with other men.'

'Oh, no? How do you know that, hmm?'

'They don't, I'm sure they don't, not if they love their husbands.'

'That's what you think.'

'Well, how do you know about these affairs? Do you have a weekly get-together and swap the dirt while all of us men are overseas?'

Chloe smiled chillingly. 'Wouldn't you like to know. Anyway, I've answered your "big question".' She indicated quote marks with her fingers. 'I'm not saying anything else. Right now, I'm going to bed. You can sleep where the hell you like, as long as it's not with me. If I were you, I'd try the dog basket. It obviously wasn't you your father was thinking about when he made the will – it was Jess. You're the only person mad enough to take on the farm. He knew that all right. Jack wouldn't have stayed here in a million years; he's got more sense. This place is a bucket with a bloody great hole in it, and it's been leaking money for years now. Farming has gone to the wall – and you know it.' She stamped out of the room and Kent heard the door to the stairs slam shut behind her.

The living room had been a place of stunned silence following the solicitor's words, so unexpected, so life-changing. Now the kitchen too was filled with an almost tangible atmosphere of shock. Kent sank into the armchair near the Rayburn that had been Bryn's usual seat. Chloe's words had sent him reeling. But almost immediately he rose again and lurched through to the living room, returning with a tumbler and the whisky. With an unsteady grip on the bottle, he sloshed in half a glassful. He raised the glass and gulped down a mouthful before slumping back into the chair. He followed the first swallow with several more, then refilled his glass. The fiery burn found its way down to his stomach and produced a warming glow, strengthening, steadying, easing the shock from his system.

He sat motionless, eyes shut, but this was one shock too many. Kent had held himself together rigidly during the time he'd been back here, knowing that someone had to be the pole around which the funeral revolved. He'd not allowed his deep grief and loss to escape. Undoubtedly, his military training had taken over and allowed him to attend to what had to be done. But now he felt a double loss: not only had he lost his father, but he knew without doubt that he'd also lost Chloe. Recalling the coldness in her eyes chilled him to the marrow – so far inside, the whisky could never reach. Salt tears oozed from beneath his closed eyelids and rolled down his cheeks, and Kent did nothing to stop them. There was no excuse that they could be raindrops. It wasn't raining here inside the quiet farm kitchen. But they continued to fall, trickling down his face, spilling over his chin, cleansing the hurt inside and leaving behind a hollow sadness. Although he'd never expected to, he had gained the farm, but his marriage was over, lost to him by her wounding words.

Taking his thoughts back to the moments before the solicitor had dropped the bombshell, he recalled that Chloe had been standing beside Jack. But then, after Peters had revealed Bryn's wishes, she had subtly moved away. She'd taken the solicitor's empty glass and refilled it, then come to stand at Kent's side. He hadn't given it any thought at the time – it had been such an immense shock to discover that Jack wasn't going to inherit the farm. It was an unwritten law in their family that, on the death of the farmer, the eldest male would automatically inherit. He'd been grappling with the implications of the solicitor's disclosure; trying to understand that Hilltop Farm really was his.

But now he had time to replay the scene in his mind, Chloe's movements assumed an unpleasant significance. She might very well declare that the farm was leaking money, but the house was still a very valuable building, and the acreage that went with it was worth a sizeable amount. So was she only interested in whichever brother inherited it all; whoever would be massively better off? Like Kent, she'd obviously expected Jack to inherit. It must have been a massive shock to her as well to be told that Bryn's wish was for Kent to take over. Kent shuddered. It was no good kidding himself. She was simply looking out for herself. He took a big pull at his whisky, choking as it burnt his throat. But it couldn't warm the chilling thought that Chloe was only interested in her own future, and whichever brother could best provide it. And since Kent had inherited, it begged the question: did *he* want *her*?

There was a nudge against his hand; cold and wet. He opened his eyes. Jess had left the warmth of her basket and was trying to cheer him; give him some comfort. She knew he was distressed and unhappy. He put out a hand and stroked her soft coat. She sighed deeply and laid her head on his knee. Her eyes were filled with unconditional love and loyalty.

'You know what, Jess?' he said. 'In the love stakes, dogs take a lot of beating. You can *always* depend on a dog.'

Kent stirred and groaned. He kept his eyes closed. The pain in his head was almost unbearable; too intense to allow daylight in. He ran a palm down his cheek; felt the stiff, almost gritty dried salt tracks and the unpleasantly sticky deposit that had trickled out of his mouth overnight. He must have been dribbling. Eyes still closed, he lifted his hand to his nose and caught the smell. Not simply saliva; this was last night's full-strength Glenlivet whisky. It smelled vile, which would explain why his head was giving him such a kicking.

'Are you ill?' Chloe was standing in the kitchen doorway.

Swiftly, his eyes opened. Wincing as he adjusted to the brightness, he looked across the kitchen at her. 'No.'

Her gaze took in the three-quarters-empty bottle on the floor beside him. 'I bet you've a king-sized headache.'

'Hmm…'

'Did you get to bed at all last night? Get any sleep?' She looked down to where his feet still rested on top of a cushion that was in turn supported by the edge of Jess's basket. 'I see you took my advice, then.'

'Eh?' Kent eased himself up in the armchair.

'I suggested you sleep in the dog basket.'

'So you did.' He made to stand up.

'Oh, for goodness' sake… stay there while I make you a strong coffee.'

Kent stared at her. 'Have you forgotten? I *always* have tea. Or does Jack take coffee first thing in the morning? Is that what you made for him?'

'I wouldn't know. He makes his own. I don't run round after him.'

'No?'

'*No!*' She slammed the kettle down onto the Rayburn. 'Look, we went through this last night. That's what married couples do: have arguments, rows. But the next day it's all over. Or it should be.' She stared hard at him, defying him to disagree. 'As far as I'm concerned, we argued, right? We cleared the air, and today's a new day.'

Chloe turned her back on him and made two mugs of tea. She handed one to him. Kent took it, shaking his head – very slowly, because it hurt so damn much, but he couldn't believe what she'd said.

'You're priceless, do you know that?'

'Of course I am.' Chloe sat down, watching him lazily, and began to drink her tea.

'I didn't mean…' He gave up. His head felt like it was about to explode. He couldn't cope with another row. The tea was scalding hot but he drank it straight away, welcoming the burning on the roof of his mouth – at least it offset the pain in his head. He drained the last drop and levered himself up, gripping the Rayburn rail for support. His head swam dizzily for several seconds and he fought down the accompanying feeling of nausea.

Jess sprang from her basket, knocking the cushion onto the red quarries.

'OK, girl, come on then. You need to go outside, don't you?'

Jess, eyes fixed on Kent's face, tail wagging furiously, took up position by the kitchen's stable door. A couple of seconds later, she was gone – a flash of black and white across the yard. Kent emptied out the stale water from her bowl and refilled it. Taking the plastic scoop from its hook on the pantry wall, he dipped into the big sack of dry dog food where it sat within a clean plastic kitchen waste bin, safe from being raided by Jess herself, if she ever got a chance, or any opportunistic mouse. It was a farm; there were always mice and rats around outside, and sometimes they got into the farmhouse itself. The dry kibble rattled into the stainless-steel food bowl and the sound brought Jess back, tongue lolling, eyes bright with anticipation of breakfast.

His duty to the dog done, Kent spun round to face Chloe. 'So where does your behaviour leave us?'

'Leave us?' she said innocently, sipping daintily at her hot tea.

'Oh, come on, Chloe, stop playing the innocent. Are we still trying to make a go of this "marriage" or what?'

'Don't be so dramatic. There's no "trying" about it. We're man and wife – we are married – and, of course, it's ongoing, as you put it.'

'And what if I don't want to, eh? What then?'

Chloe looked at him slyly from under her lashes. 'Oh, I think you do, Kent. In fact, I'm sure of it.'

'Really? And what makes you so sure?'

'The fact that I'm pregnant.'

TWENTY-FOUR

2020

Phillip, smiling, slid his mobile into his trouser pocket and rubbed the palms of his hands together. Sod the weather – he was going to enjoy the day. He'd forgotten what Smith played off – he was good, very good, he remembered that. The man had trounced him last time. But he'd always found it was better to play against a skilled opponent – being stretched enhanced the pleasure and, hopefully, improved his own game.

Smith had said to meet at one o'clock at the pro's shop at North Shore Golf Course. It would take Phillip at least an hour and three quarters to drive over. He looked up at the clock: it was only just after 9.15am. If he left in an hour and a half he'd have time for a coffee and maybe an indulgent toasted teacake when he arrived in Skegness. The Cosy Corner Café on Roman Bank did great coffee and superb cheesecake. He'd driven his mother and father over to North Shore for a short break once, and they had had coffee at the café. On spotting the cheesecake his mother had immediately opted to have a slice with her coffee. A very discerning lady, she'd been well impressed. It wasn't simply the refreshments on offer that set a person up: the whole atmosphere in the café – which was painted in a shade of palest turquoise that was immediately calming and soothing – was one of positive enjoyment. Around the walls were various affirmations – 'Enjoy the little things'; 'Happiness is an inside job' – and you came out feeling uplifted and ready to take on life's challenges. Calling in for coffee had become a sort of ritual whenever he was in the area.

Phillip grinned. He was acting like a big kid; all this freedom from work was going to his head. But when he thought back to the past couple of years and the tough times he'd come through – had had to be strong to come through – a small indulgence was surely in order. Besides, the sugar boost would set him up ready to tee off, and he needed all the help he could get. He wondered if Smith was still on form; if he had been keeping up his golf practice. He'd soon find out.

Right then his mobile rang. It was Smith letting him know that everything was all sorted – their tee-off time had been booked for 1.10pm. However, for now there was time to mash a mug of tea and have a read of the papers. Phillip flicked on the electric kettle and walked down the hall to where he could see the newspapers sticking out of the letterbox. Settling on the settee, he scanned the day's headlines: serious and informative from the broadsheet, and more sensational from the tabloid. Amongst the usual Brexit talk that everyone was totally sick of after three or four years was a report from much closer to home:

A panther prowls
Caught on Larissa Sidcupp's mobile phone camera, it seems that once again there is a panther on the prowl in the Leicestershire village of Harby.

Having just taken a mouthful of hot tea, Phillip found himself choking and spluttering – Harby, for goodness' sake! His own village? Dabbing his chin, he read the rest of the coverage, which included confirmation from Larissa Sidcupp that the animal was without doubt a panther – a black one. She added that she had later inspected the spot where it had stood and found a five-inch paw print. A further photograph showed the print.

Phillip got up and went over to the window. There was no sign of the big cat. He drew up his shoulders and shivered. Well, of course there wasn't – he'd not expected to actually see it – but all the same, it was a bit too close for comfort. He knew Betty Sidcupp; she and her husband Arthur lived further up at the top of Daisy Lane. Larissa was her younger son's wife, and had been born in South Africa. She wouldn't mistake a normal moggie for a wild animal. No – he looked carefully at the photograph again and, judging by the height of the hedge, could see that the cat was indeed massive. The authorities wouldn't catch it, of course. They hadn't been able to catch the previous one – years ago, it was now. That one had been nicknamed 'the Beast of Harby'. Its existence had never been in doubt – several people had seen it. Now, it seemed, there was another; wild, with all the finely honed instincts of self-preservation passed down through its genes. The big cat would easily outwit any pursuers. Phillip wondered why it had strayed so far into a populated area. Hunger, probably. There couldn't be much food around to keep an animal of that size going in the middle of January. He shivered again. It wasn't a comfortable feeling that he and his neighbours were sharing their gardens with a panther – and, more than likely, a hungry one.

At a quarter to eleven, golf bag and clubs stashed safely in the car, Phillip checked his wallet, patted a trouser pocket for his mobile and put the key in the front door. Then, stopping, he went back inside and picked up the tabloid before going back out and locking the door. Throwing the newspaper onto the passenger seat, he started up the car. It was possible Smith would be interested to see the report. At the least, it would be a talking point if they had to wait to tee off. After all, the man ran a zoo. Maybe there were black panthers on show there. Phillip chuckled softly as he drove away from Harby and down the lanes to join the A52. What a coincidence if one of Smith's panthers had escaped!

At 12.45, leaving The Cosy Corner Café after enjoying a restorative coffee and a deliciously buttery toasted teacake (he'd declined the tempting choice of jams), he drove north along Roman Bank for nearly a mile before swinging off right onto North Shore Road. Up ahead was the hotel: an impressive white-painted two-storey building complete with balcony, fronted by the sweeping golf course with its carefully tended grounds and greens dotted with trees and coppices. Phillip drove past and turned left into the huge gravel car park at the rear of the hotel. Locking the car, he straightened up and looked across the sparkling expanse of the North Sea merely yards away. The dull boom of the white-flecked waves breaking on the sand filled his ears and he could smell and taste the salt air. He breathed in deeply. Oh, yes, it had been a great idea of Bill's to point him in this direction. He was going to enjoy today.

He walked across the crunching gravel to the north gate leading to the private gardens. There was no sign of Smith's helicopter as yet. He sucked in a sharp breath when he saw the size of the lawns upon which it would have to land. The pilot must be extremely experienced. Even as he stood looking through the gateway, he heard the far-off whine and saw a dark smudge through the curtain of grey rain. The black-and-white helicopter became increasingly visible, and surprisingly quickly it was overhead, its rotors whirling madly. It flew right over, passing the gardens and heading out over the North Sea. Phillip saw it dip lower, make a wide circle and come back in from the east. There were no trees growing on that side of the gardens, and he watched as the pilot flew in until he reached the dead centre of the manicured lawns. Hovering for a few moments, the helicopter then began to descend very slowly. It had a black cross painted underneath. Phillip backed away into the car park as the wind whipped the trees and bushes at the edges of the gardens. The helicopter dropped lower, landing softly with barely a bump and with pinpoint accuracy in the dead centre of the lawn. When the motors were cut and the rotor blades slowed to a halt, Smith slid back the door and clambered down onto the grass. Phillip recognised him immediately, although he'd put on quite a bit of weight since they'd last met. He walked forward to greet Smith. They shook hands.

'Great to see you again, Phillip. Damn good idea of yours, I must say. I'm looking forward to whacking some balls, getting rid of my petty frustrations. What about you?' Smith pumped Phillip's hand.

'Oh, yes, indeed. Nice to see you again too. I'm looking forward to a stimulating round. Even though you'll beat me, I'm sure.'

Smith bellowed with laughter. 'Let's wait and see, shall we?'

Phillip could almost feel the waves of confidence emanating from the man.

They made their way to the pro's shop at the far side of the car park on the approach to the rear entrance of the hotel. 'Good day, gentlemen,' John Cornelius, the professional, greeted them as they paid their green fees and the extra cost of hiring a golf buggy. 'I'm afraid you'll find the dyke is full; overflowing, in fact.'

Both men nodded. They had played the course before and were aware of the long dyke.

'You're playing yellow markers, 494 yards. Par 5 over the ditch. It's a long carry for your tee shot, so I'd advise you to aim down the left side.'

'Thanks very much, John. We'll bear that in mind,' said Smith.

'Yes, thank you,' Phillip agreed.

Outside there was a line of about ten buggies drawn up, and they took the end one. Securing their golf bags to its rear, both men climbed aboard and Smith drove them straight up the short, steep slope to the back of the hotel and followed the narrow plum-slate-topped buggy path round to the right. The first tee reached, they alighted and removed the head covers from their drivers. Phillip teed off first. Considering John's advice, he widened his stance in order to try and hit the ball under the wind. It pitched out over the dyke, dropping into a good position on the edge of the first fairway.

Next to go, Smith swung even lower. A man of more portly build, saw him with a flat rounded swing as his usual one, and again the ball arced away and landed in the perfect position in the centre of the fairway. He turned to Phillip, a wide grin spread across his face. 'Not bad, eh?' he chortled.

And it wasn't. It took Phillip three more shots to get to the green, whereas Smith needed only one putt to obtain his par, which put him ahead of Phillip on the first hole. They stashed their clubs back behind the buggy and climbed aboard, marking the card before heading off to the second.

Smith was already three up by the time they reached the fifth. The fifth bordered the east side of the course and was exposed to the elements, and Smith's habitual flat swing didn't serve him well. The west wind was howling in, funnelled by a belt of trees over the ridge behind the green, and Smith's ball was sent sailing out over the sand towards the sea. Phillip, seizing his unexpected advantage, made full allowance for the wind's strength and put his ball down to the centre of the fairway, from where he was able to place his second shot onto the green and subsequently win the hole. Smith was now only two up.

They battled on against each other and against the grim weather, both grateful for the good grip their waterproof gloves provided as the rain continued to pour down. By the time they reached the ninth hole, playing back towards the hotel, both men were of a similar mind. Chilled, they agreed to have a swift hot coffee in the bar before tackling the remaining nine holes.

'Nobody's booked in for the next tee, apparently, so we've an extra ten minutes,' said Smith.

They seated themselves in leather bucket chairs in the warm bar, nursing steaming coffee and thawing out. At the crackle of newspaper in his pocket, Phillip put down his drink and pulled out the tabloid, smoothing it flat on the round table in front of them. 'OK. Since we've got time, thought you might like to see this morning's headline.'

Smith picked up the paper. 'Why, do you think it might interest me?'

'Well, you run a zoo, don't you?' Phillip ran a finger under the headline. 'Not one of yours, I take it?' He laughed.

Smith put on his glasses and read the words. His face whitened. 'Why should you think it's mine?'

'Do you actually *have* black panthers at your zoo, then?'

'Yes,' Smith said stiffly. 'But I assure you there's no way one of mine could get free and prowl around the countryside.' His colour returned suddenly, suffusing his face with dark red.

Phillip stared at him in amazement. 'Please, I wasn't intending to criticise your business. I simply thought you'd find it interesting. I was going to ask you whether, with all your experience, you thought it might survive in the wild here, especially in the winter?'

'Sorry, sorry – of course you weren't having a go at me. I understand, of course I do.' Smith spread his hands in a placating gesture. 'And as to your question, yes, I would say the cat has a very good chance of surviving. Panthers are amongst the most adaptable of the big cats. They can withstand widely varying temperatures. Lions can't, but panthers are exceedingly cunning and secretive. They're born survivors.'

'That's not a very happy thought.' Phillip groaned.

'And why's that?' Smith, good humour seemingly restored, slapped Phillip jocularly on the shoulder.

'Well, you see, I actually live on Daisy Lane in Harby.'

'Ah, now I understand.' Smith nodded, smiling. 'You are concerned for your safety.'

'Too true.'

'Don't be. Like I said, panthers are secretive beasts. It's hardly likely to creep up on you.'

'It certainly crept up on Mrs Sidcupp and her relatives.'

Smith dismissed the notion with a wave of his hand. 'It didn't attack them, though.'

'It might very well have done. I mean, little Tommy was out in the garden, apparently. He's only three. He wouldn't have stood a chance if the beast had gone for him.'

'But it *didn't*, did it? And why should it?'

'Hunger?' Phillip suggested.

'Hmm… that is a possibility, of course. However, panthers can cover upwards of thirty miles in one night, so the likelihood is, it will take itself off to a more suitable environment where there's plenty of food; a remote area, like a sheep farm. That would be ideal, what with spring lambs coming along and all that.'

'Let's hope you're right.' Phillip drained his coffee and put the newspaper back in his pocket. Smith had meant to reassure him, but it hadn't worked. Rather, the reverse. The big cat had been prowling for a reason: it was hungry. Phillip was sure it had had its sights on little Tommy, and he was just thankful that Larissa had been around. The alternative didn't bear thinking about.

Almost two hours later, they were approaching the seventeenth. Smith had been one up after the sixteenth, but on the seventeenth he three-putted and the game was now all square. Phillip had sensed his opponent's concentration wavering since they'd returned to the course. The reason for it could only be the article about the panther. After suddenly draining to chalk white, Smith's face had then taken on a very strong colour, and he had appeared somewhat flustered. OK, he had recovered quickly, even going to the extent of slapping Phillip on the shoulder, but it had still seemed a little odd. There was nothing else that could account for the dip in the man's confidence. But why the article should have so unsettled Smith, Phillip had no idea.

However, after the seventeenth he knew he was actually in a position to beat Smith; something he'd never done before. The thought boosted his own confidence. He'd got the measure of the wind now, was thoroughly enjoying the game, and was playing to the best of his ability. And then, to his delighted astonishment, at the eighteenth he made a fantastic birdie to win the game.

TWENTY-FIVE
2020

The long hours passed. Kala's body, aided by the copious amount of water she had drunk, was ridding itself of the last traces of the sedative. As the effects of the drug diminished, so too did the pain from her wounds; without movement to keep the raw edges open and bleeding, they had knitted up and were healing. The restorative sleep also took care of her exhaustion, refreshing and refilling her with vital energy. And she was soon to need it.

As dawn broke late and with little power, Kala stirred. She opened her eyes the merest slit, then lay motionless, allowing her pupils to enlarge and adjust. The inky blackness inside the narrow tunnel had lightened to charcoal – enough to allow her to see the entrance hole outlined some three yards away. All her senses – nose, eyes and ears – told her there was no danger, no pursuit. Still she lay motionless. Her pains had eased, except for one: a rolling wave of sensation, not too unpleasant, passing down the front of her body and over her belly. As the muscles, contracting and relaxing, rippled down, a deep contentment filled Kala and she began purring in rhythm. She'd experienced this sensation before

– once in the wilds of Kenya, and again during captivity in the zoo. She stretched herself out more comfortably, closed her eyes and dozed, conserving her energy for when it would be needed. All the time, the darkness around her slowly lightened as the dawn advanced. Now and then her ears twitched as a sleepy bird awoke and greeted the new day with a note or two, until, a couple of hours later, the wood was filled with their twittering.

The contractions were stronger now and Kala experienced pain and discomfort until she felt the need to push hard. As the first of her cubs passed down the birth canal and, after a lot of sustained effort, its head emerged, Kala gave a single squall of pain, quickly suppressed as the rest of its body slid out, pelt slick with fluid. Bending her head, she began licking and nosing the tiny creature. It lay motionless and silent. She continued cleansing and massaging it until, again, her contractions increased and she was forced to leave it and lie back as cub number two demanded to be born. This time the birth was over very quickly and the new baby began mewing straight away as she cleared its airways. Its head moved in Kala's direction and nosed into her belly. Purring loudly now, the big cat swiftly cleaned the cub and turned her attention back to the first one, still lying motionless. Despite the long, stimulating strokes of her rough tongue, the cub made no attempt to move or draw breath. But within a short time, Kala once again had to lie back as fresh pangs racked her body. The third cub's head was forced free, and she suppressed a cry as the rest of its slippery body quickly followed, taking away the pain with it. The last of her litter was born.

With the birth process all over, Kala dedicated herself to caring for her newborns with constant licking and a rumbling, reassuring purr. The last two cubs were both suckling, tiny pads, either side of their muzzles, pressing and stimulating their mother's teats, drawing the warm, life-giving milk into their stomachs. Their pelts now dry and their bellies rounded and full, they finally let Kala's teats slide from their mouths as they fell asleep. The first cub still lay lifeless and limp. The big cat, recognising the futility of her efforts to resuscitate it, and in the face of death, protected it in the only way she knew how: the way of the jungle.

For the rest of the day the family remained in the tunnel, safe and out of sight, but as dusk began to fall, Kala was once again assailed by a fierce thirst. She felt no hunger; had no need for food. But the craving for water was something she couldn't ignore. Reluctantly easing herself away from the two sleeping cubs, Kala belly-crawled down the tunnel. At the entrance she waited, ears twitching for any sounds of danger, nose questing the air. She could smell water: rain had collected in all the dips and hollows it could find and the wood was awash. The falling dusk had effectively silenced the birds and a hush had settled over the countryside. For long minutes Kala stayed where she was, but thirst was a driving force within her now. She desperately needed water. And it was an increasing need. The flow of milk from her teats dictated that she take in sufficient water. The lives of her two babies demanded that she leave the safety of their makeshift den and find water. But she was their only means of survival, and her protective instinct was very strong.

Slipping through the entrance, Kala paced silently to the nearest pool of water. She crouched, emerald eyes scanning the undergrowth all around, tail twitching, before she began to lap. Thirst slaked, she padded away into the trees and bushes and relieved herself. Then, lifting her head, she looked around the quiet wood, vigilant for sounds and smells of danger. With all her senses on high alert since the birth of her cubs, she would be a fearsome foe to anything that threatened them. But there were no signs of any predators. Retracing her steps, she again approached the water and drank deeply. Satisfied now, she returned to the tunnel entrance. The soundless call of her young was light as silk, strong as titanium, and it kept her bound to them. She dropped to her belly and in seconds disappeared inside the den.

TWENTY-SIX

2020

The storm had long since passed but it had started raining hard again. The drumming on the wrecked metal of the Cessna stirred Isooba from a light sleep. His eyes fluttered open. Disorientated, he lay still, assessing where he was and what the noise was. Attempting to straighten his legs, he found himself trembling with the realisation that he was still strapped into the pilot's seat with both legs trapped and unresponsive.

Then a picture came into his mind of the black panther, Kala, as she'd leapt out of the wreckage through the gaping hole in the side of the plane where the door had been. For a moment fear made him gag, hand going instinctively to his mouth. But gradually, taking several deep breaths to overcome the nausea, he gained control of himself. It was a diabolical situation in which to find himself but maybe it wasn't entirely hopeless. At least now he could forget the possibility of being mauled. He might still die, trapped here in the wreckage in the middle of the wood, but he wouldn't have to endure the agony of a wild animal's claws and fangs sinking into his flesh, blood pouring from his throat (that was where the cat struck first, tearing out the throat of its prey); even the unimaginable hell of being eaten alive! It was a truly ghastly thought.

He found himself starting to tremble again and, with a massive effort, forced the thought away. What he needed to do now was keep calm and think his way through this nightmare. This was the second day – by now he should have been very hungry, yet he wasn't hungry at all. Since there was no possibility of finding any food, he counted that as a positive – one less discomfort to endure. But he was thirsty. It seemed a long time since he'd had a drink. However, luck favoured him again, because the rain was dripping even more freely from what remained of the metal cockpit. It hit the top of his head and dripped down into his seat before finding its way out onto the ground below. As before, he placed both palms together, then widened the space between them to form a cup. Letting the rain fill it up, he drank greedily, satisfying his need before sloshing a handful up into his face. Gasping with the shock of the cold water, he wiped his face and removed some of the drops. Instantly, he felt more alert. If he leant back as far as he could, he could avoid the worst of the rain dripping incessantly on his head like the Chinese water torture. He could now understand that concept. It was extremely irritating. But no way was he going to let it drive him mad – all his senses were needed right now if he was to get out of here.

He mentally prioritised his other needs. His thirst was taken care of and he was not hungry. At that point he stopped almost before he'd got going. He might very well not be thirsty right now, but what if he were stuck here for several days? Food – OK, it was unpleasant to go hungry, but he could tough it out. However, no human could go more than three days without water – it was essential for life. So, what he needed to do was catch the rain whilst it was pouring down, because when it stopped, he'd really be up against it. Unless he collected a supply to last until someone found him – and surely to God, somebody, anybody (anybody except Mr Smith) would find him? It was odds on that they would – it would most probably be a dog walker. The English were known to be mad about their dogs and walking them, weren't they? They were said to go out in the midday sun and brave the wickedest weather to walk their beloved dogs. Yes, that would be it. If he could just sort himself out and hang on two or three days more, somebody's dog would come barrelling through the wood after a rabbit or a squirrel or something. He calmed down. Yes, he could almost hear it barking, urging its owner to come and see what it had found. And, of course, the owner would. They wouldn't go home without the dog. If it was friendly, Isooba could maybe catch hold of its collar and hang on to it so the owner would have to search for the animal. It seemed a very likely scenario.

In the meantime, collecting water was his first priority. But what could he catch it in? There was nothing he could use in front of him: the entire control panel above his lower legs was a buckled mess of metal, wires and smashed instrument cases. He turned to the left as far as he dared, knowing that the agonising pain in his spine would immediately shriek in protest. It had done the previous time. OK, it had eased quickly, but supposing he turned that little bit too far? It would be an utter nightmare if the pain didn't back off again. He wouldn't be able to stand that degree of agony. The very thought made his heart jump and flutter erratically, his palms sweat and his pulse race. Taking several deep breaths, he willed himself to keep calm. Mercifully, right now he had only a low level of pain; nothing he couldn't cope with. If he could just keep a grip on his fearful thoughts – because they brought on the panic and its allied symptoms – he would be all right. Not great, not fine, but simply all right. And for now that was enough.

With extreme care, Isooba edged himself very, very slowly to the left, ready to stop if needed. But nothing happened; no excruciatingly sharp knife strike assailed him. When he reached the limit of his mobility he was forced to stop. His left arm and hand were now clear of the pilot's seat. Moving his fingers gently from side to side, he tentatively touched and assessed what was immediately behind his seat. His questing fingertips found something cold, slippery and yielding. Concentrating hard, eyes screwed up tightly to aid his sense of touch, Isooba puzzled as to what it could be. Stretching his fingers as far as they would go in every direction, he ascertained that it was a fair size. Sliding one finger hesitantly along a dip at the top, which proved to be hard and finely ridged at the bottom between two grooves in the slippery surface, he scraped a fingernail along and it gave him the answer. It was a zip. A zip fastening on a bag. Realisation brought a tiny smile to his face. Mara had handed this to him as he'd left their home. There had been no need for him to use it on the journey over. He'd stowed it for safety behind the seat before taking off from Brittany. For several minutes he relaxed back in his seat, letting thoughts of Mara fill his head. A woman in a million, she took great delight in looking after him. This was one way, she said, that he could carry her love with him. On every trip that would take him away for a few days she packed a bag of surprises for him to unwrap, open and enjoy. 'Until you get home,' she would laugh. 'Then you won't need any home comforts; I'll be right here waiting for you.'

Slowly, Isooba's smile faded. She *would* be waiting for him, he knew that; he trusted her completely. But it cut both ways: she trusted him to stay faithful, to return to her. After every trip he had done so, and the homecoming was every bit as enjoyable as he'd known it would be. But would he return to her this time? The thought of never seeing her again caused him more pain than anything else ever could, and strengthened his determination to get through this. He'd survived the plane crash. OK, his legs were most likely buggered – they might never support him or allow him to walk again, and it was more than possible that he'd lose one or both of them – but he was still alive. And Mara was still there in

Africa, awaiting his return. Whatever shape he was in – and he knew he was almost certain to be disabled once he'd come through this – she'd love him just the same. He was convinced of that. They were two halves of an eggshell, one no good without the other. All he had to do was make sure he got back. He wasn't simply fighting for his survival; he was fighting for Mara as well. Gritting his teeth, Isooba let his fingers slide down from the top of the zip to the nearest corner of what he now knew was his overnight bag. It contained not only a change of clothing and his wallet with his papers, cards and passport; but also his sponge bag. And that was made of plastic. It would undoubtedly hold water.

It took a long time. His aching fingers teased and twitched at the corner of the bag, losing their grip, sliding off, struggling to find a grip again, but all the time moving the bag fractionally further and further to the left. But it didn't matter how long it took – as long as the rain kept falling, time was cheap to him now; he had plenty of it. There was, thank God, no longer any risk of the plane exploding and engulfing him in flames. No risk, either, of being savaged by the big cat. By now, Kala would be many miles away – probably still running. All Isooba had to do was hold his nerve and stay alive until somebody found him. And so he reached again and again for that slippery corner of his overnight bag; the only part of it he could reach with more than one fingertip. It was an awkward, unnatural angle to maintain, and he constantly had to ease his discomfort by drawing his arm forward and upwards before trying again. But ignoring the ache in his shoulder and the fierce protests from his fingers and wrist, he continued teasing and easing the bag ever further out from where it was resting behind his seat. What did the pain matter right now? The pay-off would be worth it if it gave him the means to stay alive for another two or three days. Slowly, very slowly, the tiny triangle in his grip expanded. Then came the moment he'd waited for as the bag itself suddenly slipped sideways and his whole hand curled around its edge. Panting with the effort, his shoulder muscles screaming for release, he gently manoeuvred the bag until he felt it come up and away from the dip behind his seat where it had been stashed. And then it slid right out.

Turning his head carefully to the left as far as possible, Isooba could just see the bag lying near the side of his seat. Elation roared through him. It hadn't slid too far; with a bit of luck, he could reach it. But first he withdrew his throbbing hand, arm and shoulder from behind the seat. If anything, the pain of release was even greater than holding the unnatural angle had been, and he ended up hugging his right arm around his left biceps. The sharpness brought sweat oozing from his forehead. Rocking back and forth might have eased the pain, but in his present situation it wasn't possible and instead, to hold back a bellow, he found himself reduced to biting his inner cheek, hard. But weirdly, along with his suffering, he was also inwardly shouting with triumph.

TWENTY-SEVEN
2013

'Pregnant?' Kent felt a strange mix of feelings surge up from his solar plexus, threatening to overwhelm him. Whatever he'd expected her to say, that hadn't been on the list.

Chloe turned to face him fully. She was smiling – a wide, contented smile.

'How can you be pregnant?'

'Oh, really, Kent,' she said coyly, and fluttered her eyelashes. 'And you a shepherd.'

'I've been away in Afghanistan, remember? So how do you explain that?'

The smile left her face. '"That" meaning our coming baby, presumably?'

Kent felt a stab of remorse. 'I'm sorry.'

'I should damn well think so.' Having gained the moral high ground, Chloe was being magnanimous. She crossed the kitchen and draped an arm around his neck. Leaning in close, she whispered in his ear. 'Have you forgotten the times you were home on leave?'

Even as the shock waves rippled through him, he was aware of a warning voice inside that said, *Are you* sure *it's yours?* He was ashamed to entertain the thought, but the memory of Chloe in bed with his brother overrode that shame. Yes, it was possible that the baby wasn't his. He'd been quite determined to end the marriage; had only held back from having a showdown with Chloe out of respect for his father and to allow the funeral to go off smoothly. Now he was on the back foot, reeling from the news. And if the baby *was* his, then of course there was no way he'd walk away. The child would be his responsibility. But if it wasn't... His mind juddered to a stop. If it was Jack's child, Jack would never do the decent thing. The pregnancy would blow apart his marriage and, undoubtedly, his job. Jack was on to a good thing down south. Following his divorce from his first wife he had, by marrying Juliette, earnt a meal ticket for life: she was the only daughter of a wealthy engineering company owner and would inherit the lot one day. That meant Jack was set for life – he knew it, and no way would he allow anything to threaten his lifestyle; certainly not the unwanted result of a dalliance with his brother's wife. And where would that leave Chloe? The stark facts of the situation faced Kent. No choice. That was the bottom line. The two words hammered themselves into his brain. He was trapped – whatever his own wishes, they were irrelevant.

'You do remember, don't you? I can see you do.' Chloe's arms tightened around his neck as she bent her head and nuzzled his neck.

'Of course I do. But that was then, when I thought we were a happily married couple.'

'As far as I'm concerned, we still are, Kent.'

'And what about Jack? What does he mean to you?'

'Jack? Oh, Jack was just providing a bit of comfort while you were away.'

'So, he's not the father, then?'

'Don't be silly; I was already pregnant.'

'And you told him that?'

'Well, yes. He knew he was quite safe. It couldn't make any difference.'

'You are bloody unbelievable.' Kent jerked upright, shook off her encircling arms and slammed his fist onto the kitchen table. 'You left me till last – your husband! I should have been told first.'

'I wanted to wait until after the funeral. I know how you felt about your father. There's only so much you can take.'

'Oh, yes.' Kent clenched his fists until his nails dug into flesh. 'I think you can say that.'

'That babby's the spit o' yer,' Jeremiah said, shaking his head. 'Eh, y' dad would ha' been so proud.'

Now that Bryn had died, the old man took an even greater interest in the future of Hilltop Farm. It had been his life for over thirty years. Bryn had employed him since his first day there and would have trusted Jeremiah with his life. As Jeremiah had said many times, it must have been fate. Kent's father's name meant 'Hilltop', and Bryn had always considered it a good omen; one of the things that had decided him on which farm to buy after they left Wales.

'Thanks, Jeremiah,' Kent said. It gave him a warm glow inside that the old man assumed the baby was his. Indeed, she already had the slightly Roman nose that always seemed to be passed down the family line. But it didn't mean a thing. It neither confirmed nor disproved her paternity. Either Kent or Jack could have fathered the tiny new member of the Evans family. One thing it definitely did prove was that Chloe's allegations about what the wives of serving soldiers got up to while their menfolk were away did not apply here. The baby was indisputably Evans, and for that alone, Kent was grateful.

'What y' want to do now, lad, is father a boy next time, then the future of the farm'll be secure.'

'Oh, I don't know about that, Jeremiah. One's quite enough for now.'

But he did know. There'd be no more children from this sham of a marriage. After the birth, he'd tried to estimate the date of conception, but although he was pretty good at judging when lambs would make an appearance, trying to pin down when he and Chloe had last made love – it wasn't as though he'd put it in the diary – had proved harder and he'd given up. He supposed it was enough to know that the baby certainly belonged to the Evans family, and he already loved the mewling, helpless little scrap of humanity. The feeling was not something he'd had to cultivate; it sprang from somewhere deep within him. Blood calling to blood, as his father used to say about the sheep calling for their lambs out on the hillside. And the same was true for the lambs: they knew exactly which ewe was their mother.

'Aye, I bet you're losin' sleep all reight.' The old man chuckled wickedly. 'I recall our lot: they fair wore yer out before yer even started work of a mornin'.'

Kent smiled. 'That's right. She's got a good pair of lungs on her. And I have to admit, she gives them plenty of practice, and usually at the most inconvenient times.'

What he didn't add was that it was always him who had to get up in the night, attending to both ends with bottles and nappies while Chloe claimed sole occupancy of the double bed – 'To get my strength back,' she insisted. So, no, there'd be no more babies.

'An' what'll yer be calling her, then?'

Here he was on firmer ground. He'd put his foot down over the choice of name. 'We'll be calling her Rachel, OK?' he'd said to Chloe.

'Oh, I don't know—'

'Well, I do. Her name's Rachel – no discussion, right? It means "Little Lamb", and she is. Despite all the sleep I'm losing, that's what she is: a right little lamb, born on my farm.'

Chloe had opened her mouth to object, looked at the expression on Kent's face and closed it again. 'Well, seems I've no choice in the matter, have I?'

'None.'

Jeremiah looked down at Rachel's face and sighed deeply with satisfaction. 'Yer couldn't a' done better. She's a right lamb an' all. Tek good care on 'er, lad. But you'll a' to start saving up now, y' know.'

'Will I?' Kent smiled. 'And why's that?'

'Before yer know it, she'll be gettin' wed. An' that'll cost yer, by gum it will.' And, chuckling away, he carefully handed the white-shawl-wrapped bundle to Kent.

'But between now and then,' Kent said, holding her tenderly in the crook of his arm, 'I'm going to have years of looking after her, watching her grow, teaching her all the things my dad taught me about looking after sheep.'

'He would have been so proud.' Jeremiah nodded his head decisively. 'So very proud.'

TWENTY-EIGHT
2020

No choice. No chance to make a decision – the decision Kent knew instinctively that he would make; had to make. Seven years ago, Chloe's words – just the two: 'I'm pregnant' – had altered everything.

Now, out in the early morning on the cold hillside, the wood pigeon he was looking at was going nowhere. Fox-bitten but – unfortunately – still alive, scaly legs scuffling frantically, wing dragging along over rough grass tussocks, soft dove-grey feathers soaked in scarlet, it had only one way to go and certainly no choice. Kent had none either; he couldn't bear seeing an animal or a bird in agony, and it was down to him alone to do what must be done. He bent and with a deft twist released the pigeon from its suffering. A single feather blew away in the sharp wind towards the wood, and he left the body lying on the grass. Some hungry creature – and there were always more than a few – would find it. Nature's way was a blood-red path. Death, as well as birth, was a part of life, and both were usually accompanied by blood.

It brought back to him his conversation with Chloe the day after his father's funeral. There had been only one thing to do then, and he had done it. It was his responsibility – a child needed parents. His own wishes were immaterial.

He climbed back aboard the quad bike and drove on. The nearest sheep had already heard the roar of the throttle and were streaming towards him. Like Pavlov's dogs, they associated the sound with the arrival of food. Out here in the unremitting cold, food equalled warmth in the belly when there was little goodness to extract from the wind-blasted grass. And with lambs growing inside them, the ewes needed additional sustenance. Like every other living creature, their will to survive, to produce offspring, was hardwired.

Moving slowly across the inhospitable landscape, Kent allowed the bags of sheep nuts to trickle out in a thin ribbon onto the grass, running over a wide area to give all the animals a chance to eat. Instantly, the sheep had their heads down and their noses in the nuts, chewing away with the strange sideways motion of their jaws, leaving nothing behind. The last bag emptied and secured to the trailer behind the quad, Kent let his gaze sweep over the flock. None were quite ready yet to start lambing but he knew only too well that things could alter very quickly. The ewes who had been first served by the tup were the ones to keep a close eye on. Kent needed to be ready to act, to start fetching them down into the barns and lambing pens, especially if any of them experienced difficulties. However, for now he was satisfied that the flock were doing OK. All they required of him was to keep them topped up with supplements, and as regards the lambs, the sheep would do the rest, producing them in their own good time.

Kent continued his survey of the flock, well content with their progress, and rubbed his gloved hands together, trying to revive some feeling in them. A pity he wasn't encased in thick, oily wool like his charges. They wouldn't be feeling the cold like he was. It was time to head back to the farm for a hot drink and a warm-up. Besides, there was other work waiting to be done there. He climbed aboard the quad, and Jess, knowing that they were heading for home, leapt up behind him in her usual place, red tongue lolling madly, her whole world wrapped up between working the sheep and being close to her master. Kent reached behind him with a frozen hand and awkwardly but gently tugged on her ear. She laughed up at him, eyes bright with joy at being out here with him and the sheep and accepting his caress. Rattling away over the tussocks, he headed downhill to the farm.

Running the quad bike into the smaller barn, he stamped his numb feet across the yard to the farmhouse porch, kicking off his boots and shrugging out of his jacket and gloves. Flicking a finger to the bitch, Jess obediently trotted inside and sat down on a nearby pile of newspapers.

Kent smiled and nodded. 'Good girl. Stay.'

He opened the kitchen door. The Rayburn was doing its job beautifully and the blessed warmth met him as he went into the kitchen. He grabbed the absorbent dog towel from where it hung ready on the front rail and returned to the porch, where, using both hands, he rubbed Jess's chest, belly and feathery legs. She stood braced and accepting as he towelled her vigorously – it did a twofold job, drying her out and thawing his hands. The energy he was expending certainly got his circulation going, warming and restoring, and he had no doubt it did the same for Jess. Returning to the kitchen and tossing the towel back onto the Rayburn rail to dry, he pushed the kettle onto the hotplate, before calling in the bitch and closing the back door, shutting out the winter cold. Jess trotted over the quarries, took a long, slurping drink from her water bowl, then jumped into her basket and dropped like a stone, giving a deeply contented sigh as she did so. All she would need later was a bowl of dog food. Already her particular reason to live had been fulfilled out on the bleak hillside.

Kent went over to the sink, took a large nailbrush and, giving it a good squirt of soap from the dispenser, gave his hands a scouring under the hot tap; a ritual his father had drilled into his children every time they'd come in after working on the farm. Mashing a large mug of tea, he took it over to the kitchen table and sat down. There was a laptop to one side and he switched it on, taking a few gulps of scalding tea whilst he waited for it to boot up. Opening up to where he'd left off the previous evening, he continued sipping the welcome drink as he read quickly through the assembled notes. Nodding in satisfaction, he took the now-empty mug over to the sink and swilled it clean. Returning to the table, he pulled a thick file of papers from the top of the adjacent dresser and settled down to what was, at times, the main day job.

He'd always had a flair for languages and had studied both French and Italian at school, taking GCSEs in both and passing with top marks. But he'd seen what an escalating struggle it had been for his father to make a living on the farm and had quickly decided that, if ever he had the chance to run it, he would need a second reliable source of supplementary income. And so the idea of maybe one day earning a living as a translator had been born. However, his dream of becoming a soldier was still strong and he'd signed up for nine years, but his postings abroad gave him the idea that he could study a more obscure language and hopefully become skilled at translating and writing it. He'd chosen Dari, the most widely used language in Afghanistan. Few studied it and, if he could achieve sufficient skill, he would be able to command fair remuneration as a translator. The competition would be minimal. He hadn't found it too demanding. The grasp of the basic grammar had come, if not easily, then certainly not hard enough to stop him studying. It had taken nearly five years to complete the course but, with nine years on his side, he'd felt no pressure to rush and his postings in Afghanistan had complemented his study, which he'd pursued when back home on leave.

He'd intended to pursue a career as a translator when his time in the army came to an end, however Bryn's death coming so unexpectedly had moved the goalposts. Assuming responsibility for the farm had tested Kent to the limit. He had had no idea of the very thin line his father had been walking to keep the farm in the black. And Bryn's personal needs and expenses had been frugal almost to the point of poverty. He had never admitted his struggles, and it had come as a massive shock to Kent to realise the worry and anxiety his father must have been coping with alone. There had been moments when he'd come close to agreeing with Chloe that the farm was a leaking bucket. But his skill as a translator had really proved its worth. After the bombshell Chloe had dropped, money had been very scarce. Kent could barely credit just how much cash a tiny baby – and indeed a growing child – needed. Many times he'd silently thanked God that he'd had the foresight to devote his limited spare time whilst in the army to studying. Without his translating business – and he undertook work in Italian as well – he would have struggled desperately with a very real risk of going under.

As always when he was giving his full attention to his work, he became totally absorbed and unaware of time passing. It was a low whine from the depths of Jess's warm basket that brought him back into the present moment. He had been hard at it for nearly three hours. It was time for her to be fed. He glanced up and across the kitchen; noted her black nostrils flaring as she took in what he too was now aware of: the delicious smell emanating from the far work surface where the slow cooker sat. He'd prepared it earlier with chunks of meat and assorted vegetables, leaving it simmering all day on a low setting. The meat would be ready to melt in his mouth by now; it wouldn't require any chewing. Even the thought of it set his stomach growling with a hunger he'd not been aware of two minutes ago.

'Quite right, Jess. Time I packed it in and fixed us some food.'

Her tail gave a single thud of acknowledgement of his attention, as she lay quietly now, eyes fixed on his every move, waiting patiently for her well-earned dinner. Kent saved his work, closed down the laptop and pushed it to the far end of the table. Opening the Rayburn door, he took out a plate, warm and waiting to be filled. Jess followed every movement with anticipation. She knew she had to wait her turn and, being very well trained, was not about to pester as she watched Kent sit down at the table with a knife and fork and dig in hungrily. She knew and accepted her place in the pecking order and, trusting him to save some for her, was content to simply watch as he broke off a chunk of bread from the seeded loaf and began mopping up the thick juices around the edge of his plate. He forked two or three chunks of meat to one side, leaving them to cool as he cleared his plate, sighing with satisfaction.

'Good stuff, Jess, if I do say it myself.'

Her tail gave a thump of agreement.

'Now, let's get you sorted.'

He took the plastic scoop from its hook inside the pantry, filled it with dry dog food from the big sack and let the kibble rattle into Jess's stainless-steel bowl before spooning over a generous helping of gravy from the slow cooker and the remaining chunks of meat from his plate. There was still plenty of food left in the slow cooker and it would reheat very nicely tomorrow. He could have added more meat and veg to make enough for Lennie was well. He was working tomorrow; a big chap with a big appetite. But he'd tried that before. Thinking that Lennie would fall upon a succulent, tasty meal, he'd offered it to him as a bonus for his hard graft, and been really surprised when the young man shook his head.

'Thanks very much, Mr Evans' – he always called Kent by his full title – 'but Mother will have cooked a meal for me when I get home.'

'And you couldn't possibly manage some before you go?'

'Oh, no. Y' see, she always makes a lovely first course but, oh, man, you should taste her puddings.' Lennie smacked his lips at the thought. 'They are wonderful, just wonderful.' Then he'd wagged a finger at Kent. 'But she won't let me have any if I don't eat my first course all up.'

Kent had been hard put to keep the smile off his face. This wasn't a child speaking but a seventeen-stone – at least – man of nineteen. But the smile, if it escaped, would demean Lennie, putting out between them the unspoken words 'mummy's boy'. And no way would Kent belittle Lennie. He worked as hard as two men, when told exactly what job was needed, and was a very big asset to the farm (especially after Jeremiah had officially retired), easing Kent's workload considerably. So, Kent replaced the lid on the cooker and saved the leftovers to eat by himself the next day. By now, the gravy and meat in Jess's bowl had cooled and he lifted it down onto the quarries. The bitch didn't move a muscle, but her tongue curled around her muzzle as she salivated at the sight.

'Come on, then. Have your dinner, girl.'

She needed no second command. Out of the basket and nose down, she made a quick job of polishing off the food, followed by pushing the steel bowl noisily around the kitchen floor as she extracted every last crumb and drop. Kent stood smiling down at her. She was good company, preventing the farmhouse from feeling empty of an evening when their work was done. Bending down to retrieve the empty bowl, he gave her furry ears a good stroke.

'Well done, lass. You're the best, y' know.'

Jess laughed up at him adoringly, and proceeded to wash down her food with a lengthy drink from her water bowl.

Making himself a coffee, Kent took it through to the living room. The radiators had heated the room but he flicked on the electric fire to get it really cosy. He stretched his arms above his head, flexing his tired back. They were long days and he was grateful for the comfort and warmth that awaited him every evening after work. He picked up the last couple of days' newspapers from the coffee table and flopped down onto the settee, sipping the coffee. The warmth of the room made him feel relaxed, languorous. He could feel his tensions releasing, his eyelids beginning to close.

But he hadn't had a chance to catch up with the news for a day or two and, if you were in business, given the present state of the country it didn't do to be ill informed. A quick glance at the headlines would suffice for now whilst he finished his coffee; then he could indulge himself and have a guilt-free, well-earned doze in front of the fire. He picked up the first newspaper, a tabloid, and then wished he hadn't.

The headline screamed the scary, unwelcome news that there was a black panther at large in Harby, a small village to the east of Redcliffe-on-Trent. OK, maybe there had been a shortage of striking sensations to report, but Kent knew that this wasn't just a ploy to sell more papers. The panther had been seen – in someone's garden, for goodness' sake! – and there was a photograph to prove it. Many years ago there had been reports of a panther roaming around the Belvoir Vale area. It had never been caught but a lot of residents had testified to its existence. Too many people had seen it for the news to be disputed. Obviously, this cat wasn't the same one, not this long after, and Kent seemed to recall that the first cat was said to have been sandy coloured. His father had never said anything about seeing it near the farm but maybe, even if he had, he'd kept quiet about it, not wishing to alarm his wife and children. But a panther could – and would – travel upwards of thirty miles overnight to find a mate or, much more likely, food. Harby was only ten or twelve miles away as the crow flies, over the hillside and fields. For a panther that would be nothing.

Kent groaned. A loose, hungry panther on the prowl was the last thing he needed, especially when lambing season was about to start.

TWENTY-NINE
2020

The helicopter slowly lifted from the lawn of the private garden and hovered above the North Shore Hotel for a minute or two before circling and whirling away up north. Rawson, the pilot, flicked a swift glance sideways at his boss's face – stony and set, not inviting comments. But he was well used to stony silences from Smith, and concentrated on his job. The noise of the rotors and engine precluded much conversation anyway. The light was already going; evening wasn't far off. He wanted to reach the Wild Ark before darkness set in fully.

Smith sat scowling morosely at the patchwork countryside below. He never liked losing a round of golf, but today his disappointment was overshadowed by the news in the paper Phillip Lemmingham had shown him. Of course Lemmingham had no conception of the bombshell he'd dropped, but the unalterable fact was that there *was* a panther at large – no chance of it being 'fake news'; the photograph proved that the woman who'd seen it was telling the truth – had shaken Smith. For most of the journey back he sat lost in thoughts of whether or not the panther was Kala. He had no doubts about her ability to survive, and seek out shelter and food. It would just depend on what food was available in an English January. There could soon be more headlines describing bloody kills. Five kilograms would constitute a filling meal for a panther – mice or rats were merely a mouthful and wouldn't even take the edge off her hunger. And should she become hungry enough, her attention would certainly turn to farm stock – perhaps domestic pets, too. And then the shit would hit the fan. The English were obsessional about their dogs and cats – probably cared more about them than their children. Thank God it wasn't summertime when babies could be outside in their prams. He could almost feel the sweat stand out on his forehead at the thought. There was the possibility, of course, that it wasn't Kala, which would exonerate him from any responsibility for the cat's kills. But he needed to keep up with breaking news and take any necessary evasive action.

To that end, he'd asked for Lemmingham's landline number in case he couldn't be reached on his mobile, ostensibly to fix a future game of golf. Lemmingham had proffered it eagerly, trying to contain his excitement, to keep his elation at his victory under control. He was hooked now; any suggestion of a rematch would be seized upon. And he actually lived in Harby – the dead centre of what was now panther country. If there were any more sightings – or indeed kills – he'd be certain to know. The local grapevine worked a good deal faster and more efficiently than newspapers. And unless the panther really overstepped the line and made a significant kill – and Smith hoped to God it wouldn't – it wasn't likely to make any more headlines. The first sensational story had achieved its objective. Future coverage would require an even more gripping angle. No, Smith's best bet would be Lemmingham passing on the local news.

Smith came out of his reverie, glancing down at the familiar lights of Penrith. He'd be home in a few minutes. Night had fallen quickly; it was almost dark. There was no point in trying to do anything about the unwelcome news tonight. Except for one phone call – he'd do that as soon as he was back in the office and alone.

He turned towards to Rawson. 'Make yourself available first thing in the morning, right?'

'Yes, sir. What time?'

Smith glowered. 'Early – *really* early.'

'Have you finished, sir?'

Smith gave a curt nod. He'd picked at his supper, leaving a good deal on the plate.

Having spent the previous hour in the kitchen cooking for him, Mrs Milton's face reflected her disapproval as she collected up the plate and the wasted food. 'Would you like pudding, sir?'

'Just coffee – *strong* coffee.'

'Very good, sir.' The pudding could go into the fridge then, she thought as she left the room. It would save her making one tomorrow.

'Oh, Mrs Milton…'

Suppressing an expletive, she reopened the dining-room door. 'Yes, sir?'

'Serve coffee in the office. But after that I don't want disturbing again tonight.'

'Very good, sir.'

She returned to the kitchen with relief. He was a difficult man to deal with at the best of times, but just at the moment something was needling him and he was even more of a pain. If it wasn't for the weekends she'd be tempted to look elsewhere for employment. But even as the thought came into her mind, she felt her shoulders relax and she smiled. No, no, of course she couldn't do that. It would be nothing short of an act of betrayal. She was the only female role model now. And the weekends were so special. They made up for all the weekday dross and Smith's boorishness. Petrina began humming to herself as she made the coffee.

Scraping back his chair, Smith left the dining room and walked into his office. On arriving home, he'd immediately checked the landline for messages – nothing. He'd followed that by checking his emails – nothing. Now he gave the latter another quick scan to see if anything had pinged in whilst he'd been having supper. Nothing had.

A tap on the door heralded the arrival of his coffee. He nodded acknowledgement as Mrs Milton placed the tray on the low table.

'I shall be out very early tomorrow morning. I won't be needing breakfast. I'll just make myself a coffee.'

'Very well. Goodnight, sir.'

Smith merely grunted and reached for the coffee cup, dropped in three cubes of brown sugar and sat staring into space, circling the spoon round and round. At the moment he couldn't see a way out. Maybe Gregson could come up with an answer. God damn it, the man was a vet and trained to deal with big cats. If the Harby panther turned out to be Kala, they'd have to work out a way to catch her and bring her back to the zoo. He sipped at the sweet coffee, his mind squirrelling around for possibilities. So far there was no news of any kills, and that in itself was good news. But how long that state of affairs would continue…

Finishing the coffee, he set the cup down on the tray. Going over to the desk, he plumped down in the leather seat and reached for the landline receiver. Gregson answered at the third ring.

'George.'

'You're ringing late – got a problem?'

'Damn right *we* have.' Smith stressed the word 'we'.

'So, how can I help?'

'Tomorrow morning we're taking a flip down to Leicestershire – early.'

'Hmm… how early?'

'You tell me.'

'Let me guess: Isooba has made contact and wants picking up? And one for, shall we just say, the black girl?'

'No on both counts.'

'Oh.'

'What's the best time to catch sight of, shall *I* say, the black girl?'

'Pre dawn, probably. Certainly before it gets fully light.' Then Gregson, realising he'd just shot himself in the foot, scowled and scratched his ear in irritation.

'So, allowing time to get down there, I suggest we take off somewhere around 6.30, OK?'

Gregson silently shook his head. Sometimes Smith's demands, usually concealed within a question, were the very pits. 'Yes, fine. Be with you at the house at 6.30am. Bye.'

Smith put the phone down. Rawson knew he was wanted early but he needed to let him know exactly when. However, right now he needed another caffeine boost. Rawson could wait a bit longer. He poured himself another coffee and plumped down in the leather armchair. But he'd only taken a couple of sips when the phone rang. Heaving himself up with an exasperated sigh, he stomped back to the desk and snatched up the receiver.

'Yes?!'

'Daddy, it's me.'

The change in Smith was amazing. All traces of irritation disappeared and a smile spread across his face, softening his features. 'Raquel, my love – how are you? Everything all right?'

'I'm good, Daddy.'

'That's great to hear. You happy?'

'Oh, yes.'

'And school – any problems? Anybody giving you a hard time? You only have to let me know—'

'Don't be silly, Daddy.' She giggled. 'School's brilliant. I've just earned ten points for my maths – got *all* my sums right. Isn't that great?'

'It certainly is, my little egghead.'

The girl giggled again.

'So, it's just a catch-up with your daddy, is it?'

'We'll be going into the dorm in half an hour, so I just wanted to say hello; ask if *you're* all right.'

'Of course I am, my love. Couldn't be better.'

'Oh, good. You won't forget I'm back soon for half-term, will you? You did promise me a new bike…'

Smith chuckled. 'Mercenary little madam. Quite the chip off the old block, aren't you?'

'Well, you see, I've given it a lot of thought. I'd *really, really* like a blue one.'

'Is that so?'

'Oh, yes, I've definitely decided it has to be a blue one.'

'What if I've already bought a red one, won't that do?'

'Noooo. You are *soooo* naughty, Daddy. I told you I needed to decide…'

'Whoa, hold on there, don't get uptight. I haven't got it yet. You can choose it when you come home, OK?'

There was a deep sigh of relief and satisfaction. 'Brilliant. I do like school, but I love coming back home as well.'

'And I love you being here. It's not the same without you – it's so much quieter.'

Raquel giggled. 'You are funny, Daddy.'

'Anything else, Raquel? You'll be late for bed if you're not careful.'

'Yes, I know – Mrs Reynold is *so* strict about bedtimes. Better go now, then… oh, wait, I nearly forgot. I've made a new friend. She only came a few days ago. And guess what?'

'What?' he asked dutifully.

'Her name's the same as mine – how cool is that? Well, hers is spelled the English way, not Spanish. It's Rachel.'

'That's nice. And you're friends already, are you?'

'Oh, yes. We're bezzie mates.'

Smith smiled. 'Off you go, my love. It's getting late and I don't want you getting into trouble. Remember to ring any time you want a chat. I'm always on the end of the phone.'

'Yes, I know, Daddy. Night-night, then. I love you.'

'I love you, too.' He blew a kiss, and she blew one back before the line went dead.

He stood for a moment, smiling down at the receiver – kids, the biggest worry in life, and the biggest blessing. He beat himself up constantly because she was away at the weekly boarding school in Harrogate. But what else could he have done? He'd spent many sleepless, miserable nights thinking about the problem, kicking against the blow life had dealt out, before finally facing the only sensible way open to him. The decision to send her away had caused him pain – continued to cause him pain – but he had to remind himself that it was for Raquel's own good. When Carlita – his wife; Raquel's mother – had died from cancer last year, he'd known that even with Mrs Milton's help he couldn't give the child the time and attention she deserved and needed. Now, however, she seemed to have settled in very well at school, and was enjoying it far more than he'd thought she would. The weekends, when she came home, were looked forward to and treasured by both of them. *The best of both worlds after the terrible loss of her mother*, he reassured himself. She'd be surrounded by young female teachers, and other girls to play with. That was what she needed: female company. Despite being a millionaire, it was something he couldn't provide for her here at the Wild Ark. He returned the receiver to its cradle. But, if he were honest, he missed Raquel's presence at home far more than she seemed to miss him.

He decided to forego the rest of the cooling coffee and, reaching for the whisky decanter, poured himself a generous slug. It not only gave a warming boost to the body; it strengthened mental resolve. He tossed it back and poured a second, sipping it this time, savouring the pleasure. Tomorrow might prove a turning point for the panther problem. And, of course, it wasn't simply the big cat he had to worry about; there was also the question of the other cargo. But maybe if Gregson could come up with a solution regarding Kala, the second problem would resolve itself automatically. And both could wait until tomorrow. Now Smith needed to tell Rawson what time he'd be needed in the morning.

THIRTY
2020

He'd slept very little, watched the red digits follow one another with monotonous regularity as the seconds, minutes, hours ticked by. When the alarm clock sprang to life at 6am, Smith was already pushing back the duvet. His shower was swift, tepid, and less for cleansing, more for sharpening up his brain and reactions. It helped, but down in the state-of-the-art chrome-and-granite kitchen, he fixed a strong coffee and added three cubes of brown sugar that brought him to pinpoint clarity. He heard a car drive up and park and, seconds later, Gregson tapped on the door.

Seated at the breakfast bar, Smith swallowed the scalding coffee he'd just sipped. 'Come in, George. Coffee's made.'

'Now that's what I call a welcome, especially at this time of a morning.' Gregson shed his padded jacket and poured himself a mugful, then hitched himself up onto a high stool beside Smith. 'So, do you want to fill me in?'

In answer, Smith picked up a newspaper from the bar and slapped it down in front of Gregson. 'Read that.'

There was silence for two or three minutes as the vet did as he was told, reading not simply the headline, but the full article. 'Right area, I suppose.'

'Exactly.'

'Still no sign of Isooba, I take it?'

'None.'

'Hmm…'

'*Could* it be Kala?'

'From the angle of the photograph, I can't say.'

'But it might be?'

'Oh, yes. I mean, a black panther on the loose in the English Midlands – how common is that?'

'So, we're assuming it probably is ours?'

'Odds on, it is.'

'Right.' Smith finished his coffee and slid off his stool. 'Let's get to it, then.' His voice had a steely edge to it now. He'd been hoping that Gregson would weigh it all up and reject the probability.

Outside it was still dark. The two men walked down the long drive to the rear of the zoo premises, passed the extensive big cat enclosures, and came to the very end where there was a large, concreted square of hardstanding. The helicopter was parked dead centre.

Rawson had spotted their approach and came forward.

'Fuelled up?' Smith asked brusquely.

'Yes, sir. All OK to go.'

They climbed aboard and Rawson turned on the engine, set the rotor blades turning, checked his control panel, and took off. The helicopter rose, made a wide circle avoiding the main zoo complex, and, obedient to his boss's instructions, Rawson flew south-east. Flying into the lightening sky, he headed down the backbone of the country for the East Midlands.

Conversation aboard the helicopter was nil. Smith slumped in his seat, his mood bleak, and glowered at the barely discernible landscape below. Just what they could achieve was questionable. One shy creature in scores of square miles… it was a fool's game. But there was that slim chance that they would see some evidence, if not of the panther, then maybe of some debris from the crashed Cessna. He was convinced now that the plane had come down in the storm, and it seemed most likely that it had done so in the Midlands. Gregson, beside him, was thinking much the same thing. As far as he was concerned, there was very little chance of seeing any evidence of the cat – they were sly, cunning creatures. However, only a fool would argue with the boss, and Gregson was nobody's fool. But maybe they would catch sight of some wreckage from the plane. It was strange that there had been no news reports about it but there was no chance now that the plane had escaped ditching. Still, the outcome was unknown – they hadn't heard a thing from the pilot. Gregson was convinced that Isooba was dead. They would surely have heard from him by now if he'd survived. But after speaking to Rawson about the precise direction, timing and effects of the storm, he was aware that the East Midlands was the most likely area for the Cessna to have come down. However, it was more than strange that there had been no coverage of a crash. The only way the plane could have avoided turning into a fireball was if it had somehow become suspended before hitting the ground. If the crate containing the panther had broken apart, Kala could have leapt to safety – a fully grown panther could jump upwards of twenty feet, no problem. But it didn't explain the lack of visual evidence of the wreckage. Still, if Gregson's theory of a suspended drop was correct, that would mean the Cessna was probably buried in woodland.

The helicopter flew on, losing altitude as it dropped down over the Midlands. The sky had lightened considerably and the countryside had become more visible. They had passed over Sherwood Forest and directly below them now was the approach to Newark. Some twenty miles further south in the Vale of Belvoir was the village of Harby, and perched high on a hill overlooking the village was the famous Belvoir Castle, owned by the Duke of Rutland, and surrounding it were the extensive Belvoir Woods. Rawson began circling the helicopter, taking in a wide view of the countryside but keeping Harby at the centre of the circle. It was just light enough now to make out the layout of the village. A small hill carrying a road with a bridge rose above a canal. At the top, almost on a crossroads, was a garage with outside forecourt and pumps. Smith and Gregson, binoculars to their eyes, scanned the area intently.

'Lower, Rawson,' demanded Smith, leaning forwards and peering through the binoculars.

Obediently, the pilot lost altitude, barely skimming the chimney pots of the tallest buildings.

'There, look!' Smith jabbed a finger. 'The name on that sign; that's Daisy Lane.'

'We're definitely on target,' Gregson agreed.

For some time they circled the village closely and then, drawing away, gained altitude, widening the surveillance area to search the more wooded parts. However, they saw nothing. The only movement came from vehicles on the roads and early-morning dog walkers.

Finally, Smith had had enough. 'That's it, Rawson. Get us back home.'

'We'll probably have to wait for news of a kill to give us an indication of where the cat is,' Gregson said. 'Afraid we're wasting our time here just now.'

'Exactly,' Smith growled belligerently.

Rawson, keen to get back and away from the boss's escalating temper, took the helicopter soaring skywards.

Down below, in the dark depths of Belvoir Woods, a male black panther finished raking his claws down the bark of an oak tree before positioning himself carefully, back paws padding the ground firmly, and then directing a pungent spray of urine down the trunk.

THIRTY-ONE
2020

Hunger pangs roused the cub from slumber. Deep within the dark tunnel beneath the fallen tree trunks, he mewed urgently. Batting out with tiny paws, he pushed his sister, who was still asleep, out of the way, exposing the nearest teat, already leaking milk. Latching on, he began to suck. The life-giving milk flowed into his empty stomach, soothing, warming, comforting. Kala purred loudly, her flanks vibrating and dislodging the cub, rolling him over. The hungry cub nosed his way back through the black fur, seized hold of the teat tightly and sucked vigorously. The second cub, disturbed by the movements, stirred and woke up, mewling fretfully. Kala gently nosed her closer and, with tiny nostrils twitching at the smell of milk, the female cub sought out a teat and began to feed. Kala stretched out, eyes closed blissfully, flexing both front paws, claws extending and retracting in rhythm with her rumbling purrs. Totally fulfilled now, she ignored the many still-sore abrasions on her body. Free from any enclosure or cage, she was perfectly happy to adapt herself to the countryside surrounding her. She felt safe here in the sheltering darkness; there was no threat of any kind to her cubs and she knew that out there, beyond the entrance to her den, were water and prey. The two tiny cubs gorged themselves until their stomachs were drum-tight before letting the teats slip from their mouths and immediately falling fast asleep. Kala began licking them with her rough tongue; long, rasping strokes that would not only cleanse their furry bodies but, more importantly, stimulate their digestive systems and encourage the elimination of waste.

When she was satisfied, she eased away from them and nosed the tiny pair close together. They were sound asleep and didn't stir. It was easier with two cubs – their shared body heat would keep them warm enough for her to leave them for a short time. Kala was not only thirsty now; she was also hungry. She needed to leave the den and hunt for food. But at the bramble-shrouded entrance to the tunnel, she lay flat and motionless, taking in the varying smells blown towards her by the strong west wind. *Nothing dangerous* was the message conveyed.

Easing out, she padded, silent as a shadow, placing her pads between twigs, through the body of the wood. Stopping at what was now her usual watering spot, she drank deeply before flicking away the remaining drops of water from her whiskers. Thirst satisfied, she glided westward, head to the wind, eyes mere slits. The bitter wind ruffled cruelly through her black pelt with icy fingers that brushed against her skin, probing the still-raw injuries. But she needed food, and so she padded on through the undergrowth until eventually she came to the northern edge of the wood. The ground here rose sharply uphill, with little cover. Kala dropped to the ground, taking in the smells all around her. Very faintly, she picked out the smell of recent death coupled with the metallic tang of blood. Her stomach responded with a spasm.

Her ears flicked as she caught a high, mewling cry. Not her cubs this time. Overhead, way, way up in the sky, two buzzards, just black outlines, planed in large circles. They too were hungry and out of their natural habitat. The birds had ridden the wind currents down from the Belvoir Woods. Winter months were lean ones; every living creature feeling the sharp bite of hunger. Lifting her head, Kala tested the wind, sniffing the tempting smell, stronger now, that told her there was food waiting out there amongst the sodden grass tussocks. A raindrop dripped from a twig above her, hit the inside flap of her ear and trickled all the way down through her ear canal towards her eardrum. Wrinkling her muzzle with irritation, she risked being spotted as she was forced to lower her head and give it a shake to rid herself of the water. Flattening herself to the ground, alert for any possible danger brought about by her instinctive movement, she stayed still for several minutes but, apart from the two circling birds far above, nothing stirred. Finally, satisfied that no danger had presented itself, Kala moved forward slowly on her belly. Pinpointing the place where her prey lay, she crept, inch by inch, closer and closer, through the tussocks. Then, tensing, she leapt, clearing the remaining ground in one bound. Striking out and dropping down in a seamless attack, she seized the bloodstained dead body of a wood pigeon in her jaws and raced back to the safety of the wood.

Once inside the trees she froze, listening for sounds of pursuit. There were none. Taking a firmer grip on the bird's soft flesh, she held it higher, lifting it clear of the ground between her forepaws, before trotting off through the trees heading for the den, but this time she took a different, more central route. Nearing the middle of the wood, Kala stopped. Her nostrils had caught the smell of man. Cautiously now, she stalked slowly and silently towards the source of the smell. In a rough clearing, she saw what remained of the plane – a crumpled heap of metal. Her questing nose picked up the scent of aircraft fuel and the now-overpowering smell of man. Using the undergrowth to conceal her progress, she clenched her jaws tighter around the wood pigeon and crept up to the side of the plane. A gaping hole allowed a view of the inside, and the smell of blood to drift towards her. Flattening herself, Kala inched forward. Inside, half-lying on the floor almost level with her, was a man. Blood plastered his hair to his head and had pooled and dried around his lower legs. He lay unconscious and motionless within the confines of the twisted metal. Kala's whiskers twitched as she stared with cold, calculating emerald eyes. The man's eyes were shut. But she knew he was still alive, his chest rising and falling with each breath. Even as she hesitated, watching and gripping the dead bird in her powerful jaws, a sudden gust of wind drove through the trees. Up above, a branch snapped, the sound resembling a rifle shot.

The man jerked into consciousness and opened his eyes. For a split second man and panther stared at each other, eyes locked. Then his scream of terror broke the hold. The branch tore away from the tree and came crashing down, missing Kala by inches. Terrified, she took an enormous leap, landing some twenty feet away. Still clutching the pigeon, her one thought being to get away, she bounded into the concealing undergrowth and was gone.

THIRTY-TWO
2020

Mara – what a woman, a real lifesaver, a woman in a million. And she was his wife. How lucky did that make him? Even as the muscles in his shoulders screamed in protest, his heart sang with happiness. Mara had packed his bag, as she did before every trip he took away from her. 'I cook for you with love in my heart, and this way, you carry my love with you,' she never tired of telling him. He knew there would be food in the bag, though exactly what sort was unknown. 'That is my secret,' she always added, wagging a finger at him. 'You will have to wait to find out. That way, it will taste even better.' Mara was a generous woman in all ways. She weighed nearly two hundred pounds. 'There's a lot of me to give,' she had chuckled, 'so I give a lot.' And she did. The last time, he recalled, she had cooked a massive pasty, filled with chunks of meat and gravy. And because she believed in plenty of fresh food, there had also been an assortment of fruit.

For the first time since the plane had ditched, Isooba's stomach rumbled and he felt hungry. A good sign; a very good sign – it could mean he was healing. Really ill people found that they were not only unable to eat; they simply didn't want to. The body dictated its needs at all times. In dire circumstances, the digestive system was not a priority. All energy was required for and directed at overcoming infections and healing injuries. The overriding aim of the body was continued survival.

Ignoring the pain in his upper body, Isooba leaned to his left again and let his questing fingers crawl over the floor, seeking some portion of the bag that was within touching distance. He found it: a corner that afforded him a tenuous grip. Infinitely slowly and carefully, he began to draw the bag clear. It took a long time. For every half-inch of ground covered, Isooba had to release his grip and withdraw his arm from the torturous angle before gritting his teeth and reaching again for the bag. But his persistence paid off. The bag finally teetered on one edge and then collapsed forward to lie right alongside his left hip. With a loud bellow, half of triumph and half of pain, he sank back in his chair and closed his eyes. Witness to his struggle, sweat stood out on his forehead and his underarms were soaking wet. He was exhausted and trembling from the effort. But none of that mattered right now. The reward for his payment in sweat and pain would far exceed his efforts. Now he could afford to lie back, take his time, let the pain drop away and simply anticipate the pleasure to come. As the pain eased he found himself starting to laugh at the prospect of opening the bag and discovering the delights Mara had squirrelled away for him. He felt ridiculously like a child about to open his Christmas stocking. Yet, perversely, he held back, knowing, as Mara knew, that a lot of the pleasure was the expectation. He would relate all this to her, he decided, when he was back home in Africa, in her loving arms.

And then he couldn't debar himself any longer. He pulled the bag up over his thigh and let it lie in his lap. Its contents didn't disappoint. Opening on a high, there was a large bar of his favourite milk chocolate. It lay on top of a thick plastic bag, inside which, individually wrapped in foil, were three roast chicken drumsticks together with three bread rolls spread lavishly with butter. Isooba began munching on the first chicken leg. It tasted magnificent. But one was sufficient. He couldn't even manage a bite from a roll. The remains of the drumstick began rolling around in his mouth, and he acknowledged that maybe he wasn't sufficiently recovered yet to eat any more. With regret he rewrapped the chicken bone in the foil. But the food had done its job and the hunger pangs had gone. He dug into the bag again and discovered more treasures: a bag of freshly home-baked brownies and oatcakes together with a bulging paper bag of fruit. Mara had even packed a short-bladed paring knife – she'd remembered he disliked the peel on apples; what a woman indeed. Love for her warmed him despite the cold weather, and it wasn't the only warming thing. He knew there was a thick sweater in the bottom of the bag – he'd packed that himself. And the thing he was now searching for came to hand: his sponge bag, wrapped inside another large plastic bag.

Taking out the sponge bag, he stretched the plastic one carefully across his seat, wrapping the handles tightly around the arms to hold it in place so it caught the rain dripping down. The drops made a satisfying *plop, plop, plop* as they started to accumulate in the bottom of the bag. The water would assist his survival for several days. And wrapped inside his sweater he could feel something hard and long – he knew what that was. A smile lit up his face and he pulled the flask of coffee free. OK, the contents would probably be lukewarm, even cold by now, but the caffeine wouldn't have lost its kick. He unscrewed the cap and drank deeply, straight from the flask. It wasn't cold – not hot by any means, but certainly warm enough for him to feel the coffee travelling down inside his chest. Sighing with satisfaction, he screwed the cap back on. Then, dipping into the bag again, his questing fingers found something else: also hard, but smaller. He knew what that was too, and joy filled him. Thank God Mara had broken his rule, especially for this one flight where it really mattered. She was forbidden to contact him by phone, because if Smith found out, both of their lives would be worthless. So, to ensure her safety, Isooba always left his personal mobile at home. However, this time she had packed it for him. The message was clear: *Please ring me, if you can.* He yearned for the comfort of her voice, and had to fight the urge to ring straight away and speak to her. But a wave of exhaustion hit him and his hands trembled. He was so desperately tired. Slowly repacking the food into the bag, he drew the zip across tightly, safeguarding it against insects or rodents, before collapsing back in his seat, eyes closing. Keeping calm and conserving his energy and strength was the best he could do now – indeed, the only thing. He couldn't stay awake; he needed sleep, *had* to sleep.

And sleep he did, crashing out suddenly. But, despite his good intentions, it wasn't a restful sleep. His dreams were wild and violent; the dangerous flight replayed with vivid intensity, culminating in a terrifying confrontation between him and the panther. Freed from the crate, the big cat appeared in front of him. In her jaws, she carried the body of a white bird. Above its feathers, her green eyes gleamed fiercely. It was such a real and horrific vision that Isooba jerked awake with a loud scream. But there was nothing in front of him; nothing except the darkness of the night and the wind thrashing the trees. Slowly the panic eased, leaving him weak and helpless. Totally unable to fight the exhaustion that was claiming control, he fell asleep again.

It was hours later when he woke once more. Lying motionless, he was disorientated for several minutes. Then, rubbing the sleep from his eyes, he remembered the successful retrieval of his overnight bag. The plastic bag – half full now – was still safely in place, stretched out in front of him, secured by the handles. He bent his head. There was enough rainwater to last several days at least. Resting his head back, he exhaled an enormous sigh of relief: he was going to be able to get out of here.

And then his hand nudged something. Glancing down, he saw the metal flask. A gulp of the strong, reviving coffee, whether it was hot or cold, was just what he needed. His hands steady now, he unscrewed the cap, lifted the flask and gratefully took a gulp. There was no heat left in the coffee – the flask had lost its insulating sweater that had been wrapped around it – but to Isooba, the drink was liquid heaven right now. He knew that in a few minutes the caffeine would kick in, and his hand curled around the mobile phone stashed safely in his pocket. Then it would be time to ring Mara and tell her how much he loved her and what a lifesaver the bag was proving to be. Resting gently, a smile curving his lips, Isooba felt his confidence in the prospect of getting back home safely to her rise in his chest. All he had to do was ring her, give her his approximate location, and she would take care of everything.

Closing his eyes briefly, he felt the welcome relief flood his body. However long it took for the search party to find him, it didn't matter. He'd made the flight under duress from Smith – the threats against Mara had been sufficient to guarantee Isooba's acquiescence to his demands. The nightmares he'd suffered would probably stay with him for a while, though. It wasn't an ordeal you got away with lightly. But that was all they were: nightmares. The vision of the panther with the dead bird in her jaws was simply a vision. Kala had escaped from the crate, it was true, but by now she would be many miles away; no longer a threat to Isooba. The panther in his dream had been carrying a white bird…

Isooba opened his eyes. He looked to the left where the gap in the wreckage was, at the wet earth beyond. No sign of a big cat. He was just about to laugh at his silly fantasies when he saw the feather stuck to the side of a leaf, just beyond the edge of the wreckage. It was a large wing feather – a white one.

THIRTY-THREE
2020

'Hello, is that Kent? Bryn Evans' son?'

'Yes. Who's speaking?'

'Phillip Lemmingham.'

Kent frowned. 'I'm sorry…?'

'No, no, it's me who should be sorry, and I should have apologised a long time ago. I was a friend of your father's, a few years back. I'm sorry I couldn't make it to Bryn's funeral; down with a virus of some sort – legs made of jelly, not a hope of getting to the church. Out of action for about three weeks, I recall – a devil of a bug. But I asked a neighbour if she'd post my sympathy card for me. Did you get it?'

'Um…'

'Oh, how stupid of me – of course, you can't possibly remember after all this time. 2013, wasn't it?'

'Yes.'

'Should have called you ages ago. But life gets in the way, doesn't it?'

'You could definitely say so.' Kent had been racking his brains to remember who Phillip was, and the penny had just dropped. 'You played golf with Dad, didn't you?'

'That's right.' Phillip chuckled, pleased that Kent had placed him. 'Yes, we were golfing buddies. Of course, that was when Bryn was able to get away from the farm. We didn't play at all later in the winter. He was far too busy then with the lambing season.'

'Hmm, liked a game of golf, did my dad.'

'And I think I'm right in saying that you also play? I seem to recall Bryn taking you for a game as a treat because you'd been working so hard on the farm.'

'Yes, he did. And he paid for me to have a few lessons, too.'

Phillip laughed. 'So he did. Look, Kent, I'd really like to pop in for a catch-up with you. What d'you say?'

'Why not? It gets a bit lonely here these long, dark nights.'

'When would suit?'

'Well, I'm not doing anything this evening – if you're free, that is.'

'Sure. I'm not busy at all now. I could motor over in, say, half an hour?'

'Yes, do that. Look forward to seeing you.'

Good as his word, Phillip drove the Vauxhall into the farmyard and parked up outside the back door. He got out and knocked, setting Jess off barking, and heard Kent shushing the bitch before opening the door.

'Hello, Kent.' Phillip thrust out his right hand. 'So good to meet up with you again.'

'And nice to see you, Phillip. Come on in. Jess is all bark, no bite.'

Minutes later, the two men were ensconced in comfortable chairs in the living room, facing the open fire that extended its hospitality in the cold, dark night. The abundant logs burned brightly, warming the men on the outside, while the generous helpings of whisky Kent had poured into chunky tumblers warmed them on the inside.

'Unforgivable of me, I know, leaving it so long.' Phillip took an appreciative sniff of his whisky, followed by an even more appreciative sip. 'But my life has changed so much since your father's death.' He eased back in the armchair. Just talking to Kent was relaxing him.

Kent nodded. 'Mine too.'

'And I have to own up to the fact that it is probably a selfish reason that prompted me to contact you now.'

'Go on.'

'In a nutshell, I've just retired. Don't misunderstand me, there's nothing wrong about that; I'm very happy to leave the rat race.'

'But...?'

Phillip hesitated, then found himself admitting it. 'But I hadn't banked on feeling... well, lonely. I really miss the crack with my workmates, know what I mean?' To cover his embarrassment, he buried his face in the glass.

Kent nodded. Phillip's words brought back memories of his time in the army; the comradeship of other soldiers. It was the banter and support that got soldiers through the incredibly tough days and nights. Oh, yes, he knew where his visitor was coming from all right. And he also knew that it wasn't an easy thing for a man to put into words and own up to, feeling lonely. 'I know only too well how that feels.'

A look of relief spread over Phillip's face. 'I'd always anticipated enjoying retirement, on the golf course, for instance – and now my old golfing buddy has died. Ironic; we were both so busy earning a living, we didn't make time to indulge ourselves in what we enjoyed. And now, sadly, for Bryn it's too late.'

Kent inclined his head. 'I think that's a lesson for me...'

'Want to tell me?' Phillip finished his drink.

'Let me top you up. You're OK driving?'

'I don't think two are going to put me over.' Phillip held out the empty glass. 'Thanks.'

Kent poured them a refill. 'Have to admit, it was a facer when the adjutant told me Dad had died. I mean, he was only in his sixties. You don't imagine your parents dying at that age.'

'Well, I've just lost my mother… albeit, she was in her eighties.'

'Oh, I'm sorry.'

'Thanks. It wasn't unexpected, though. She was in a nursing home for the last few weeks.'

'And your father?' Kent raised an eyebrow.

'Thankfully, yes, he's still here… there I go again, being totally selfish. Maybe he'd prefer to be with Mum, but I *hope* he's pleased to still be around. He's in a nursing home too and I spend a lot of time visiting him – taking him out for jaunts in the car, visiting country pubs, that sort of thing.' Phillip laughed. 'He can still sink a pint.'

'In that case, I'd say he most certainly is happy to be down here with you.'

'Well, I appreciate his company. He's the last living relation I have.'

Kent nodded his head. 'Must admit, I don't have that many now.'

'Oh?'

'Mother and father both dead.'

'But weren't you married? I thought Bryn mentioned that you lived in married quarters?'

'I *was*…' The expression on Kent's face was more than grim.

'Look, forget I mentioned it; not my business.' Phillip busied himself taking a sip of his whisky.

Kent was only too pleased to change the subject. 'So, you were wondering about playing a round of golf with me, is that it?'

'Yes,' Phillip said hastily, relieved. 'What do you say? Are you up for it? Any time you like; doesn't matter to me. As I've said, I'm retired now; my own boss regarding how I spend my time. I'm finding that is the problem: filling my time. I'd really like a game with you, Kent.'

'Well, right now I could probably fit it in. The lambing season hasn't really begun yet. Very soon it will, and then I won't be able to.'

'Of course. I fully understand. It was the same with your father. We played when he could make it.'

'But what about the state of the ground – is the course open? We've had that much rain even the hillside resembles the Okefenokee Swamp.'

Phillip chuckled. 'You have a point. I went over to Redcliffe Course – I live in Harby, by the way – and was told that it had had to be closed because of the rainfall. The last game I played was over at North Shore near Skegness. But I'm sure we could find a course closer that might be open.'

'Well, shall I leave finding the venue with you?'

'No worries. I'm happy to do a bit of sleuthing, find a decent course that hasn't suffered too much with the rain.'

'Pity I haven't time to try North Shore. It's a good one, isn't it?'

'Oh, yes.' Phillip smiled. 'I actually won that day; first time against Smith.'

'Smith?'

'A businessman from up north, runs a zoo. Wouldn't mind being a pound behind him.'

'Rich, then?'

'And how. He arrived at the course by private helicopter.'

'You don't say.' Kent raised both eyebrows.

'Hmm. A beauty; white with black chevrons. I stood in the entrance to the private gardens and watched it land. So impressive. Even had his initial, X, painted in black on the underbelly.'

Kent frowned. 'X?'

'Yes. His Christian name's Xavier.'

'Now that *is* a coincidence. There was a helicopter flying very low over the farm and hillside earlier; so low it drew my attention. And that had a black X underneath.'

Phillip stared at him. 'I wouldn't think there'd be another one the same, would you?'

'Seems very unlikely.'

'Well, it was way off his patch – more on my patch, actually. I wonder what he was looking for.'

'No idea.'

'I wonder if it could have anything to do with my showing him the newspaper coverage of the panther that's been seen round Harby? Him being a zoo owner, you know.'

'I read about that myself. Is it true, then? Is there a big cat loose?'

'Oh, yes. Mrs Sidcupp is a close neighbour of mine. It was her daughter-in-law who took the picture and her husband forwarded it to the paper.'

'Not good news for me, then.' The grim look reappeared on Kent's face.

Phillip sucked in a breath. 'Ah, I see what you're getting at. Lambing season about to start...'

'Exactly.'

'Smith's face went chalk white when he read about the panther. In fact, I asked him – jokingly, of course – if it was one of his. He wasn't pleased, I can tell you. And I have been wondering since if that's why I won the game. He was winning up to the ninth hole, but after he'd read the article he was definitely rattled. He lost focus.'

'And do you think it's one of his?'

'Well, it's possible, isn't it?'

'Yes, it's possible. I mean, the animal must've come from somewhere. I know many years ago they introduced laws about people keeping wild animals as household pets. That caused a spate of illegal releases and we ended up with a new problem. But that was then, and those animals will be dead now, though they may have bred since they were released. But other than that, where else can you find big cats in this country, apart from in a zoo?'

'But none of the zoos in the country have reported a black panther getting loose, have they?'

The two men stared at each other.

THIRTY-FOUR

2020

When Phillip had left, Kent collected up their glasses, took them into the kitchen and rinsed them under the hot tap. He didn't doubt that there was a panther at large but it still seemed incredible to think that the cat might even now be prowling the local countryside. And out on the hillside, his flock were vulnerable. It made him uneasy. Where the panther had come from didn't matter. What did matter was that it constituted a threat. Even if it killed just one sheep, it would freak out the whole flock and might cause a panicked stampede. And *that* would be a disaster. Heavy with lambs, the ewes would undoubtedly abort, and Kent's fragile finances, mainly dependent upon the coming season's lambs, would take a hit that might tip him over the edge.

He upended the clean glasses on the draining board and left them to dry. He looked out the kitchen window. The moon rode high, clouds chasing across its surface casting moving shadows on the hillside. It was stupid to be thinking of taking the quad out on a recce. If the panther was out there, it would hear the engine long before he got anywhere near, or indeed caught sight of it. And in any case, what could he do? It was almost laughable, really: it was a black cat, and it was a black night out there. But it was no laughing matter. He'd just have to put more time into reconnaissance of the flock during daylight hours. None of the ewes were due to lamb in the next few days, fortunately. And it really was fortunate, because Rachel would be coming home on Thursday for the weekend – a rare event – and he was looking forward to spending quality time with her away from the toxic presence of Sheila, Chloe's mother, the archetypal mother-in-law; disapproving, fault-finding and *still* blaming him for what had happened.

Abruptly, Kent picked up one of the glasses. Returning to the living room, he poured another whisky and slumped down in the armchair nearest the fire. Pleasant though it had been to catch up with his father's old friend, it had without doubt allowed memories to resurface, most of them unwanted. He'd thought he'd buried them, but all it had taken was Phillip's visit for the padlocked iron cover over the well deep inside him to be lifted. And, just like the contents of Pandora's box, once released, the memories refused to be put back. They surged up and Kent seemed powerless to stop them. His hand holding the whisky glass shook a little. It was crazy. Not his fault.

He was already a signed-up serving soldier when he and Chloe had met. She had known from the start; had accepted that if she married him, she was also saying yes to the life of a soldier's wife: to living in married quarters, to long absences while he was serving abroad. But for both of them, he'd thought, it had been love at first sight and for life; the last thing he'd been expecting to happen when, at his mate Ben's urging, he'd agreed to go to the party. Ben's father had just retired and was holding a celebration at a swish venue in Harrogate. Chloe lived with her mother in a small village a few miles further north. Her late father had been friendly with Ben's parents. They'd joked that it had been fate.

'I mean,' Chloe had laughed up at him, her lovely face alight with delight, 'if you hadn't joined us tonight, we'd probably never have met.'

'I nearly didn't come,' Kent had admitted. 'Ben did some serious arm-bending to get me up here.'

Chloe had squeezed his arm tightly. 'You see what I mean? Fate.'

Now Kent took a sip of his whisky, shook his head and muttered moodily, 'And a bloody awful job fate made of it as well.'

He knew she'd seen him as an exciting prospect. Being a soldier, risking his life for Queen and country, lifted him above the men she typically came into contact with. As personal assistant to one of the junior partners in a firm of accountants, she was surrounded by suits; sober and extremely cautious by nature. Security was their middle name. In her mind she'd painted him as a risk-taking hero, glamorising his service when the reality was for the most part gruelling, dirty, sweaty work in taxing heat and nerve-jangling discomfort. That reality had only hit home for her after their marriage. To give Sheila her due, she'd warned Chloe repeatedly, and how Kent wished her words had been heeded. But her continuing to blame him for what had happened was unjust and extremely hurtful. The unwanted memories continued to spool through his mind, faster and faster, one begetting the next, flooding him like a seemingly unstoppable tide.

The one truly bright and wonderful moment had been when Rachel was born. She had changed everything – both for the better and for the worse. With Bryn lying in the cemetery, the full weight of the farm had landed heavily across Kent's shoulders, challenging yet satisfying. And frightening. The balance in his and Chloe's joint bank account had been moving up steadily during his last couple of years as a soldier. He'd made a concerted effort to save, knowing that when he left the army, he'd also be leaving the married quarters and would have to provide a home for them. But that problem had resolved itself with his inheritance, and he'd assumed they'd be comfortably off with the bank balance still intact and acting as insurance for when it was really needed. After Rachel's birth, though, it had begun to dawn on him that the total was dwindling, and not due to the necessary outgoings he himself signed cheques for. To begin with he hadn't wanted to acknowledge that Chloe was running through so much money. OK, a child meant extra expenditure, and he'd reassured himself that the withdrawals would slow down as she adjusted to the cost of providing for the baby. That hadn't happened. It had got worse. But the numbers on his bank statements and the sinking, sick feeling in his stomach weren't the only evidence of a big problem. The marriage wasn't working. And that was the reason he'd hesitated – again and again – to confront Chloe. Perhaps if it had been just the two of them, he would have asked her what the hell she was playing at; where the money was going. But Rachel was growing all the time, birthdays coming and going. It was her future at stake, and Kent was very aware of that. The one time he'd broached the subject and asked Chloe if she could cut back on expenses, she'd gone off on a big one, screaming hysterically that he was the family breadwinner – or should be – and had better get used to the amount of money she needed and try working harder. He'd been so disgusted by her crazy outburst – which had not only shaken him, but had set Rachel off screaming too – that he'd held off from mentioning it again. In the springs when there was a good crop of lambs, the income lifted their bank balance, and that, plus the money he earned from working part time as a translator, placated the bank manager. But it was never sufficient to stem the overall downward spiral. And he was worried.

Rachel was four when the ticking bomb went off. Late in February, snow lay over the farm and the hillside, with more falling, deadening the sounds of the ewes bleating. He'd been out working since 5am. The barns and lambing pens were full of newborn lambs and their mothers, safe beneath powerful infrared heat lamps from the ravages of the east wind and the cold weather. More sheep were on the hillside, their lambs not due for a few days. He'd managed to grab three or four hours of sleep the previous night – not bad in the circumstances. Jess was also putting in the hours, seemingly tireless in circling the remaining sheep outside, isolating the ones at risk and herding them to Kent's instructions. Life was tough, cold and exhausting for man and animals alike.

Kent had thanked Lennie and seen him off after a twelve-hour day before stamping off his snowy boots at the back door of the farmhouse. He'd grabbed the warming dog towel from the Rayburn's rail and spent several minutes towelling Jess down vigorously, warming them both. Then he'd gone inside, fed the hungry bitch and called out to let Chloe know that he was taking an hour off to thaw out and have some food. She'd called back from upstairs, where she was bathing Rachel ready for bed. Kent helped himself to a liberal portion from the simmering pan containing steaming chicken stew. The tempting smell when he took the lid off filled the kitchen. Dropping heavily into the armchair that used to be his father's, plate balanced on his knees, he attacked the hot food ravenously, his appetite sharpened by the intense cold outside. Jess lay in her basket by his feet, nose lifted, nostrils twitching, questing the air with pleasure at the smell of the stew.

'I'll save you a bit, don't worry.' He smiled down at her, reminded again of his debt to her for the unbounded help she'd given him all day. Her tail gave a tiny wag, her warm brown eyes fixed on his face, filled with love and trust. He saved more than a bit, scraping the cooled chicken from his plate into her bowl. As he returned to the Rayburn and refilled his plate with a second helping, Jess gulped down the delightful extra course before nosing the stainless-steel bowl noisily around the quarry floor. He bent to ruffle her ears. 'You deserved that. Good girl.' Then he returned to his comfortable chair and ate the rest of the food with relish. Sighing deeply with satisfaction, he put his stockinged feet up on the side of Jess's basket and closed his eyes. Within seconds, both man and dog were sound asleep.

Kent woke to find a small hand tugging repeatedly at his sleeve. 'Daddy, wake up. Daddy…'

With the greatest difficulty, he forced himself through the layers of sleep, eyelids heavy as sheep nutsacks, protesting at being prised open. 'Whatssamatter, Rachel?'

The child gave a happy gurgle and clambered onto his knee. 'Can't sleep, Daddy.'

'Can't you, darling?' he mumbled, sliding an arm around her and hugging her close. 'Do you think you can go to sleep on Daddy's knee?'

Rachel nodded enthusiastically and snuggled against his chest, small fists clutching his thick Aran jersey. 'Love you, Daddy.'

'Thank you, my little lamb. And I love you too.'

She giggled and buried her face in his chest. Curled in her basket, Jess sighed deeply in her sleep.

'Shush,' Kent said quietly, finger to his lips. 'You don't want to wake Jess up, do you? She's been working so hard today.'

'Love Jess as well,' was the sleepy reply.

'Course you do.' He laid his head back against the padded wing of the armchair. A great feeling of contentment and peace flooded him. Right now, he wanted nothing more out of life; right now he had it all. He and Rachel fell into a restful sleep.

For a second or two when Kent surfaced, restored, from his power nap, he couldn't make out why his left arm wasn't responding. It was numb. Then Rachel moved slightly, allowing his blood to recirculate from shoulder to fingertips. Gritting his teeth against the agonising burning tingle as his arm came to life, he cradled the sleeping child tenderly. The pain she had unknowingly caused him was nothing. His thoughts went to the men in his platoon who hadn't made it back from Afghanistan. It was quite conceivable that their wives and children still shed tears for the husbands and fathers who had been torn from them. His arms tightened around the little girl. Simply sitting here, quietly, lovingly and in the warm, was worth any amount of money, and it was something those men would never again experience. Just thinking about them made him count his blessings. Closing his eyes again – not sleeping now; just listening to her breathing and drinking in their closeness – he felt truly humble that he'd been spared to come home.

With eyes shut, he didn't see the kitchen door open a little and then close again. But he felt the cool movement of air around his ankles; heard Jess stir in her basket as she raised her head briefly before dropping down to sleep again. Turning his head, eyes open now, all he could see was the door leading from the kitchen. It was closed. But he knew it had been opened. Puzzled, he rose carefully from the armchair, Rachel in his arms, and made his way across the kitchen and through to the door leading to the staircase. It too was closed. Struggling a little, he managed to unlatch the catch and, in stockinged feet, began to climb the stairs. There was no sound from the bathroom or the bedrooms and he frowned as, cautiously holding the sleeping child close to him, he mounted the last step. Walking silently down the landing, Kent pushed open the door of the master bedroom with his toe.

Taking one pace into the room, he couldn't believe what he was witnessing. On her knees in front of the dressing table, Chloe was trickling a line of white powder across the glass top. Even as he watched, frozen with disbelief and shock, he saw her draw a wide paper straw from one of the lower drawers. Placing the straw against her nostril, she began to lean forward, bringing her face level with the tabletop.

'No! Chloe, no, don't do it!' The words erupted involuntarily from him.

Waking with a scream, Rachel flung herself sideways in fright, and fell from his arms onto the floor.

THIRTY-FIVE
2020

'It wasn't the beginning of the end – it *was* the end.'

'What the hell did you do?' Phillip shook his head in disbelief.

'We both focussed on Rachel—'

'Well, of course, the poor child. Was she badly hurt?'

'Out cold to start with.' Kent reached for the coffee pot and poured them both a refill.

They were in the living room at the farm, seated in front of a roaring fire, thawing out with hot coffee. Kent had telephoned Phillip earlier that morning to ask if he was free could he come over to the farm? It was important. And did Phillip still have the newspaper article about the panther?

'The answer is "yes" to both questions. What time do you want to see me?'

'Soon as,' Kent had replied.

And an hour later, both men had climbed aboard the quad bike, Jess riding shotgun at the rear, and had rattled off up the hillside. The rain had finally ceased and a watery sun shone out intermittently from behind the racing clouds.

'Reminds me of a golf buggy.' Phillip grinned from beneath his cap.

'Couldn't do without the quad,' Kent replied. 'Even so, Jess can outstrip it for speed. You have to watch out going up the hill. They can turn over pretty quick.'

'Did you bring the tape measure?'

Kent patted a pocket. 'Yes. I stuck it in with Jess's whistle.'

'Doesn't she come to a call? I thought sheepdogs were all about answering to shouts like "Come bye"?' From behind his shoulder, Jess responded with a quick yap at the familiar words. 'Oops, sorry,' Phillip said. 'She's keen, isn't she?'

'Oh yes.' Kent laughed. 'Even knows what I'm thinking before I say the words.'

The hill was beginning to level out and coming to a plateau, he gunned the bike faster, the cold wind rushing past their faces.

'So, why the whistle?'

'The wind can blow away my voice. And it does. I mean, you can see how it's blowing now...'

Phillip nodded, cramming his cap down more firmly on his head.

'Anyway, we're about where we need to be.' Kent cut his speed and pointed over in front. Phillip could see the outline of what looked like a sheep lying down. Kent had told him there'd been a kill, and it wasn't pleasant.

'Just the one sheep was it that copped it?' he enquired, his voice betraying his sudden nervousness.

'Hmm...' Kent stopped the quad bike and put the brake on. 'Just the one – and that's one too many – but there was also her lamb. Well, it was undoubtedly fright that made the ewe abort. OK, the lamb would have been born in a week or two's time, but even so, it would likely have been dead when she dropped it.'

'At least it wouldn't have suffered, then.'

'No. She did, though.'

'Oh.' Phillip's face had lost colour.

'If you'd rather not see the ewe, that's OK, just wait here.'

'No, no. I'm coming with you. We need to measure, don't we?'

'Yeah. But it's not a sight for a weak stomach.'

'Kent, my stomach's fine. Just fine.'

The two men left the bike and walked across to where Jess was already sniffing at the dead sheep. Her ruff was standing up and she was growling. The sheep's wool was stained a vivid red, her head thrown backwards and a raw gaping hole where her throat had been. From below her tail, the bloody afterbirth trailed away from her body, telling the sorry story of a birth gone wrong – of the aborted lamb, there was no sign.

Phillip, despite his bravado, clapped a gloved hand to his mouth at the pitiful sight laid out on the muddy grass before him.

Kent, meanwhile, had walked to the far side of the carcass and was scanning the ground. 'See, here, Phillip… look. What do you make of it?' He pointed at the imprint in the mud of a huge paw print.

'My God! What a size.'

Kent nodded his agreement. 'It's bloody big. Even allowing that all this rain may have allowed it to spread a bit.'

'Let's measure it. You got the tape?'

Kent pulled the hefty metal case containing the measure from his pocket. They bent down and carefully laid the tape alongside the spoor.

'Five and a half inches, I reckon,' Phillip said.

Kent nodded. 'That's what I make it.'

'Let's get a photo of it. Proof, y'see. I think we need to.' Phillip knelt down with his mobile and took several snaps from different angles. 'Do you notice anything else?'

Kent was frowning down at the paw print. 'Like what?'

'Like, it's got four pads at the front but there are only three marks where the claws had a grip. Look, see what I mean?'

'I can now you've pointed it out. Looks like there's a complete claw missing. All the other three have dug into the mud. When we get back to the farm, we can check this photo on your phone against the one in the newspaper article. See if it's the same.'

'Right.'

Both men made their way over to the quad bike. Jess was circling the sheep, ruff still fully raised and giving deep growls, her eyes wide and staring.

'Seems scared, doesn't she?' Phillip looked at her with concern.

'She is, you're right.' Kent reached over and slapped the side of the bike. 'Here, Jess, leave it. Come on, girl.'

Slinking along almost on her belly, Jess went over to him. She was shaking. Kent took her head between his hands. 'It's OK, girl. I'm here, you're OK. Now, get up.' Again he patted the rear of the vehicle. The dog sprang up and immediately flopped down, tongue lolling, flanks heaving as she panted with fear.

'Let's get all of us back, shall we?' He started the engine and drove away from the dead sheep. 'I'll leave Jess at the farm and pick the body up later. But there's just something else I want to check out on the way back.'

'Of course,' Phillip said, more shaken than he wanted to admit.

Steering the bike carefully downhill now, Kent pulled up part way down, just below the wood. Applying the brake, he stood up and looked across the rough tussocks, and then shook his head. 'It's not there, but I'll just get off and make sure. You stay here with Jess.'

Phillip nodded, turning round in his seat and taking hold of the bitch's scruff.

Kent flat-palmed the dog. 'Stay.' He didn't need to say more. The bitch was only too pleased to remain lying down. He walked over the grass coming to a halt a short way away from the edge of the trees. He bent down and inspected the ground before nodding to himself.

Returning to the quad, he climbed back on board. 'Right, home it is.'

'What were you looking for?'

'There was a wood pigeon that was suffering. I had to wring its neck. I left it lying here because I knew something would find and eat it.'

'And?'

'And yes, the body's gone. Plus, we have a partial print close by.'

'The panther's?'

Kent nodded, solemnly. 'It was the panther.'

They travelled back to the farm in silence.

The open fire and the hot coffee had worked miracles – lifting both body temperatures and spirits. Jess had stopped shaking and calmed down on reaching home. She was curled up now in her basket near the Rayburn sound asleep.

As they talked out the panther situation, Phillip had spread out the newspaper article and they'd compared the image on his mobile to the printed one. In size, it was almost identical but both men agreed it wasn't the same animal that had made it. In the newspaper article four claws could clearly be seen. There was definitely only three showing on the mobile. They were at a loss to explain it but conceded in the end that one explanation was another cat could possibly be at large. Or, alternatively, the cat in the article had met with an accident and lost one of its claws.

And the talk had then turned to Rachel and her impending visit. Kent, seeing the slight frown on Phillip's face, had unburdened himself as to why she no longer lived at the farm permanently.

Phillip's expression had turned from a frown to one of distress as Kent filled him in on the background. He accepted a second mug from the coffee pot gratefully. 'Thanks. And did you have to take Rachel to hospital, then?'

'We did. And you know what hospital A&E's like, we waited absolutely ages. But thankfully, they did a scan and some tests and were satisfied there was no lasting damage. They thought perhaps it wasn't so much the fall and the bump on the head that caused her to go unconscious but the actual fright itself. Thought she might have simply fainted. But of course, they covered all aspects just to be sure.'

'Yes, they'd have to.'

Kent hesitated. 'But that, as I said, was the end. I mean… the end of our marriage. When we'd established Rachel was all right, we waited until she'd been put to bed and then Chloe told me it was over. She wasn't going to live with me anymore. She'd decided she would take Rachel and go back up north and live with her mother. There wasn't a lot I could do about it. Rachel was only four at the time. She needed someone around all the time to look after her. There was no way I could run the farm and be there for her. So, there wasn't much else I could do but agree with Chloe.'

'But she was an unfit mother, surely. I mean, she was a drug addict, wasn't she?'

'I don't know what actually defines an addict, or how long Chloe had been taking the vile stuff. She wouldn't tell me. Nor would she tell me where she got it from. I pleaded with her to give it up… for Rachel's sake if not our marriage.'

'And?'

'She laughed in my face, told me to "Get real; everybody takes it these days".'

'I asked her to get some help, sort the problem out.' He hesitated, shook his head slowly. 'She said there was no problem. The only problem she had was *me*.'

It was Phillip's turn to sadly shake his head. 'I really don't know what to say…'

'Nothing you can say. Thanks for the listening ear, though. That's helped me a lot. I'd bottled it up, never told anyone and didn't realise how it had festered inside, eating away like acid. I'm glad to spill it out. Thanks.'

Phillip rose to his feet. 'Glad I've been of some help. Anyway, I know you've work waiting, so I'll push off now.' He raised a hand. 'Don't bother to see me out.' Then he turned at the door, grinned. 'I take it Jess *will* let me out? Or is she like the old saying, "She'll let you in, but just try getting out again"?'

Kent, well aware Phillip was deliberately trying to lighten things, grinned back. 'She's one of those in reverse, nobody gets in unless they're allowed.'

'Take care, Kent. I'll see you again.' He raised a hand in farewell.

Closing the kitchen door behind him, Philip crossed the yard and hastened to his car. The bleak wind screamed around the barns and farmhouse, even finding its way down inside his turned-up collar, chilling him in seconds, and he was glad to climb in and slam the car door closed.

He was filled with sympathy for Kent and the situation the man was in and could understand the farmer's massive relief at finally feeling able to tell someone else his troubles. He supposed it was something along the lines of allowing the man to express himself and then, possibly, coming to some kind of acceptance. Not for the first time, Phillip found himself grateful that he had been spared some of life's hardest lessons by remaining single.

Driving along the A52 towards home, another thought struck him. He'd promised Smith to let him know when there was any further news of the panther, either a sighting, which was not likely, or possibly a kill. Well, now there had been. And he himself had seen the unmistakable evidence of the panther's presence – that paw print, the size of it.

He felt a rise of excitement at the thought of telling the zoo owner. And, suddenly, he couldn't wait until he reached home. Swinging off the main road onto the lane leading up to Langar, he pulled into the narrow dirt lay-by and reached for his mobile. Punching in Smith's number he waited for the man to answer.

'Oh, hello. It's Phillip Lemmingham here. You all right?'

'Sure am.'

Phillip nodded. 'Good, good. I have something to tell you. You remember, I promised to keep you updated about the loose panther?'

'It's been seen?'

'Well, there hasn't been a sighting, no, but there has been a kill—'

'Whereabouts?'

'I've actually just come from there. It's a farm, Hilltop Farm at Redcliffe-on-Trent. One of the farmer's sheep has been killed, up on the hillside, just west of the wood. I took a photograph of the spoor at the side of the dead animal—'

'You're sure it's the panther's spoor?'

'Yes, yes, I'm sure it is the panther. I mean, the paw print is massive.'

'Is the sheep still out there, or has the farmer moved it?'

'No, no, it's still lying there. He said he'd move it later today.'

'And that could be extremely dangerous. If I were you, I'd stay away from there. Well away.'

'I intend to. It gave me the creeps the first time I saw that poor sheep. All that blood and gore. I certainly don't intend going back up the hillside, I tell you.'

'What's this farmer's name, do you know?'

'Yes. It's Kent Evans.'

'Thank you, Phillip. Thank you very much. Any further news, keep me updated.'

It was only after Phillip had returned the mobile to his pocket that he realised he'd now probably contravened data protection regulations. He'd disclosed Kent's name and address. But then, the act was only in place to ensure people were kept safe, wasn't it? He hadn't given away any information that was really crucial, not like the farmer's bank account numbers, no insurance number or anything of that nature. There'd been nothing vital whatsoever really.

So, no harm done.

He engaged first gear and drove off.

THIRTY-SIX

2020

Isooba felt himself start to tremble. It began in his fingers, progressed to his hands and continued until he was shaking all over with fear. Could it be that what he'd thought of as a nightmare had actually occurred? It seemed impossible. The big cat was surely many miles away. But – his eyes remained focused on the feather – supposing it *was* true? That meant the cat knew where he was, and had probably sussed that he was trapped here – dinner waiting to be eaten. The trembling increased until even his teeth chattered. He clenched both hands tightly together. Think, that was what he had to do; control the nerves, control himself and think. It was what placed man above the animals, and it was the one thing left to him that he *could* do right now.

Had the cat really come back and found him? Even if it was accidental, as he suspected, she would certainly return. Hunger would force her to extremes. Maybe she'd picked up on the scent of the chicken leg he'd been eating. And that thought led to another. Mara; she had so thoughtfully packed the food – and the mobile phone, his lifeline. With cold, trembling fingers he fished in his coat pocket and drew out the mobile. He had no idea of his exact whereabouts but he'd been following the River Trent just before the accident, and before that he'd managed to slip past the air traffic control tower at East Midlands Airport. He remembered passing over a village that lay to the right alongside the river but then rose very quickly uphill, culminating in an old quarry. The wood was only a minute or two's flight time from there. He was sure Mara would be able to trace his location.

It was daylight now. The panther wouldn't risk making a move until dusk fell at the earliest. He was perfectly safe for now. That thought eased his fear and, to his relief, the trembling lessened and soon stopped. But it had left him feeling very weak, light-headed and weirdly uncoordinated. What he needed to do was eat some more of the food Mara had packed for him. Leaving his mobile on his lap, Isooba carefully unzipped the big bag and took out a second roast chicken drumstick. He bit down into the succulent flesh and tore chunks off it, and very slowly, he felt a little strength returning. Unscrewing the lid of the flask, he finished off the last of the cold coffee, then, dipping the flask into the rainwater that had collected in the plastic bag, filled it to the top and replaced the stopper. It would be the easiest way to drink it, and when the light began to go later in the day, he might be glad he'd had the foresight to fill it. At the thought of the coming night, his nerves started to kick in again and his hand holding the flask shook. Deliberately, he thrust the thought away. He'd be out of here by nightfall. He trusted Mara; knew she would do what needed to be done to summon help for him.

Somewhat restored, he put the flask back in the overnight bag and picked up his mobile again. This time his fingers had stopped shaking, and he called Mara's mobile number. Holding it to his ear, Isooba waited. It was ringing. A smile curved his lips as he anticipated her picking up the phone and then hearing her sweet voice. But as each ring went unanswered, the smile died. Finally, forced to acknowledge that she wasn't going to answer, he hung up. However, there was always the option of a text – not so good, but he needed to contact her. Going into his messages, he began the text with the words 'Crashed, trapped' and went on to give her all the directions he could to help her track him down. Finally he added, 'Love you forever, Anan.' He deliberately didn't mention the panther – it was more than enough that one of them knew about the additional threat to his life.

Sliding the mobile back into his coat pocket, he pulled his coat closer around him for warmth and closed his eyes. He was so very tired. And even if he did fall asleep, he was quite safe – until it started to get dark...

THIRTY-SEVEN
2020

Inside the helicopter, Smith put down his mobile. He turned to Gregson sitting beside him, a wide smile stretching across his face.

'Well?' Gregson raised an eyebrow.

'Oh, yes, very well, I'd say. That was Lemmingham. There's been a kill.'

Gregson whistled. 'Really?'

Smith nodded. 'I thought he'd prove useful to us.'

'And do we have the location of this kill?'

'We do indeed, George.' Earlier that morning Smith had decided he couldn't stand not knowing the whereabouts of Isooba's plane and its cargo any longer. There had been no news reports of an airplane coming down but he needed to know. He didn't want to wake up and find the police on his doorstep. It was worth another try, not to locate the panther this time, but to find the plane – if it had indeed crashed in a wood. And his aim was the wood within the Belvoir Castle estate. He'd called in Gregson and Rawson. They'd flown south to the East Midlands and were now above Sherwood Forest. However, the unexpected but timely phone call he'd just taken from Lemmingham altered everything. He leaned forward and spoke to the pilot. 'Forget Belvoir. I want you to head west and then circle around the land beyond Bingham and over the eastern outskirts of a village sited on the banks of the Trent. It's called Redcliffe-on-Trent.'

'Very good, sir.' The helicopter rose and whirled away towards the far-off spread of Nottingham on the horizon.

Smith sank back into his seat and patted Gregson on the forearm with satisfaction. 'According to Lemmingham, the land is owned by a man called Kent Evans. He's a sheep farmer.'

'You don't say.'

'Yes, I do.'

'Sounds ideal hunting ground for a hungry panther.'

'Exactly. And wait for the best bit… situated in the middle of Evans' land is a wood, George, a *wood*.'

'Now that's what I call really promising.'

Both men started to laugh.

A few minutes later they'd flown over the Saxondale island, a relatively new rerouting of the old Fosse Way and the A52; one that had produced far more accidents than its predecessor.

'They call it progress, George.'

'Keeps a few more in work. First in the designing and building…'

'…and then at the hospital.' Smith finished his sentence.

'Let's just hope that the panther won't add to their case numbers.'

Smith nodded. He pointed to the left where there was a wide expanse of grassland sprinkled with the woolly backs of grazing sheep. Raising his voice, he shouted to Rawson to go much higher. 'And further on, right over the Trent. I want to get the whole layout clear.'

The helicopter soared and carried on flying west until they came to Redcliffe-on-Trent. Below them the wide river surged, swollen by the recent heavy rain, passing by soaring, heavily wooded red-clay cliffs and then bending away to the north-east where it would continue on, cutting through the ancient town of Newark. Both men were looking out of the helicopter, tracking the course of the river.

'Hope to God Isooba didn't come down that side of the Trent,' Gregson remarked. 'We'd have the Devil's own job of finding him.'

'Don't think he would have,' Smith said. 'He was a good pilot; lots of experience. That's why I employed him. No, my money's on my gut instinct right now.'

'Which is…?'

'The wood near the kill. So, let's find it.' Smith called out to Rawson. 'Take her back to the hillside where we saw sheep grazing. But before going up the hill, I want you to maintain altitude and circle the farmhouse. Seems to be the only one round here.'

'Very good, sir.'

The helicopter whirled sharply right and the farmhouse could be seen up ahead above the village, tucked into the side of the hill. Dutifully, Rawson flew in a wide circle whilst the other two men studied the layout carefully.

'Take some snaps, George.'

'OK.' Gregson took in the wide sweep of the farmyard followed by a few photos of the barns and outbuildings before, as each circle brought the farmhouse closer, adding numerous shots of the drive leading up to the old house and then the farmhouse itself. 'That do?'

'Oh, yes.' Smith smiled. 'That will do nicely. And when we get up to the kill, I want you to take a good few more.'

Far below them, a figure appeared in the farmhouse doorway, looking upwards to where they were circling.

'One more photo, I think, George.'

Gregson snapped him.

'Time to go, Rawson.'

'Sir.' Rawson flew them out of sight on the far side of the hill.

'What d'you reckon, George? Think that was Kent Evans?'

'I'd say so, yes. I noticed just the one other man who was obviously working in and around the barn.'

'Hmm, so not overstaffed, then.'

'Not much money in sheep farming these days.'

They were interrupted by a polite, throat-clearing cough from the pilot.

Smith craned his neck. There was a big wood coming up, bounding the far south side. 'Oh, yes, the wood… and I can see the kill now. Rawson, set her down to the north side of the wood, close as you can.'

'Yes, sir.'

Gregson continued to take photographs as the helicopter circled, losing height before almost delicately closing in on the ground and landing with expert precision. Smith reached behind him for a pair of green wellington boots and swapped them for his loafers. Gregson followed his example. They climbed out onto the saturated grass, which squelched unpleasantly, sinking under their weight.

'Not easy, walking in this lot,' Gregson complained, tugging his boots clear of the mud.

Smith nodded. 'I'll follow you. We'll have a look at the dead sheep first. Oh, and be careful not to obscure the paw print. Lemmingham told me he was sure it was made by a panther. I need to see it for myself.'

They plodded around the perimeter of the wood, coming round on the north-east side. The bulky body of the sheep was easily spotted and they approached it in a wide arc, being careful where they placed their boots. Coming closer, Smith's face screwed up in distaste at the sight. The bloody afterbirth had soaked into the ground, leaving a reddish-brown stain that led back to the dead ewe.

'So, where is the lamb, eh? She's obviously given birth, but there's no sign of it.'

'Good question.' Gregson was standing beside the animal. 'I'd say the panther separated her from the flock, gave chase and brought her down, probably with just one swipe of a paw. Her throat's completely ripped out.'

Smith nodded, his gaze wandering from the ewe's rear end and over the blood-soaked fleece to her almost severed head. 'And look,' he said, pointing, 'there's the evidence. That's what Lemmingham was on about. Says he measured the spoor and it was over five inches, and he took photographs to prove it.'

Gregson nodded, took a tape measure from the pocket of his waxed jacket and laid it alongside. 'Yes, I'd agreed with that.' He then bent down beside the sheep and took photographs of the paw print, and of the sheep's injuries and the positioning of its body. 'I'd guess the lamb wasn't due yet. The sheep aborted and I expect the lamb was stillborn. I also think that, judging by the trail of the afterbirth, the panther took the lazy option, snatched the lamb and bounded off with it.'

'To where?'

'Well...' Gregson waved a hand vaguely towards the wood. 'I'd say the cat felt exposed out here on the hillside and made for the nearest cover.'

Both men stood and looked at the dark, sombre mass of trees. The wood extended all the way along the boundary of Redcliffe Golf Course. It had a brooding, intimidating atmosphere; a place best avoided.

Smith licked his lips. 'And do you think the cat is still in there? Or would it have moved on? I mean, it was seen and photographed in a garden in Harby. That's where Lemmingham lives.'

Gregson shook his head. 'You've missed the obvious mistake.'

'Oh?'

'The newspaper photo showed a very large, complete paw print, yes?'

'Yee... ss?'

'And this one isn't, is it?'

'I don't follow. What are you getting at?'

'Well, look.' Gregson pointed at the ground. 'See? This particular print proves the panther has a claw missing.'

'Missed that, didn't I?'

'Hmm, but what does it suggest?'

'Well, that's obvious. There must be more than one panther at large in the East Midlands.'

THIRTY-EIGHT
2020

Far above them, the wind rose to a roaring crescendo. The trees at the edge of the wood took the full westerly force, bending almost double, branches rattling and crashing together. The wind tore a gap in the grey canopy of cloud and a single ray of sunshine threw a shaft of slanting light across the hillside. It illuminated the patch of ground where the sheep lay – and glinted off something made of metal lying in the grass.

It was Gregson who noticed. 'What's that?' He pointed to the slim metal tube half covered by the thick grass.

'Don't know.' Smith bent and picked it up. 'Looks like a whistle, but I'm not about to give it a go – no telling where it's come from.'

Gregson nodded. 'I can see what it is now. Even if you did blow it you wouldn't be able to hear it. That's a dog whistle. It would only produce an extremely high-pitched sound, too high for a human ear. But it would certainly be heard by a dog.'

'What's it doing out here?'

'Likeliest scenario is that it belongs to the farmer – for his sheepdog.'

'Hmm, I'm guessing you're right. We'll take it. Might come in handy at some stage.' Smith pocketed the whistle. 'Now, are we going into the wood? Is it *safe* to go in?'

'We're looking for the plane, remember, not the panther.'

'Yes, George,' Smith said testily, 'I *know* that, but you've just said the panther most likely took cover in there after it took off with the lamb.'

'And I'm pretty sure that's what happened. However, it's daylight, right? Panthers hunt at dusk, and that's a long way off. No doubt Kala has got her head down and is sound asleep, especially now she's got a full stomach. So she's not going to be prowling around looking for prey right now, is she? Later, yes, she most certainly will be, but not now. I'd say we're pretty safe, even if she has found herself a den in the wood.'

'OK, you're the expert. I'll take your word for it.' Smith set off marching over the treacherous tussocks into the wood. 'There's a bit of a path we can follow; seems to lead through the middle but it's really gloomy and extremely muddy. Better watch your step, George. Wouldn't do to have an accident.'

The two men picked their way cautiously along the narrow path, avoiding the trailing brambles and ground ivy roots that threatened to trip them up with every step. Above their heads, the wind lashed the branches, creaking and snapping as it screamed eastwards. Both men looked warily up at the trees.

'Bound to bring a few down, this strength,' Gregson muttered. 'Best keep an eye open.'

They struggled on for several minutes, their progress disturbing some roosting wood pigeons that took off in fright with a sudden sharp clapping of wings, startling them. The sounds added to the eeriness of the dark wood.

The low-level menacing atmosphere was beginning to get to Gregson. 'Look, I don't think we're going to find anything.' He took a further step and suddenly his feet began to slide from under him in the waterlogged, clutching mud. He grabbed for a handhold on a trailing vine of ivy hanging from a branch as he sought to keep his precarious balance. 'I vote we give it five more minutes and then call it quits. What d'you say?'

Smith grunted. 'We're not even halfway. I'm not giving up yet.'

'But it's a damn dangerous place to be in with this gale. We'll be lucky not to get brained if a branch comes down.'

Even as Gregson spoke, a forceful gust rampaged through the trees, bending the topmost branches at impossible angles. A tearing screech that set their teeth on edge lent credence to his warning. To their right the top of a thick sapling snapped off, falling to earth with wicked speed. The end, sharp as a sword, hit the centre of the path barely two yards in front, burying itself deep in the mud. It remained upright, quivering violently from the impact.

'Bloody hellfire,' Smith said. 'That was close…'

'Too sodding close,' Gregson gasped with feeling.

Gingerly, both men moved forward, avoiding the obstacle. In front, away to the side, it appeared that another branch had suffered the same fate. But this one was enormous and still partially attached to the main trunk of a huge old ash tree.

Smith came to an abrupt standstill. He pointed through the tangle of brambles and ivy leaves. 'Look, George.' His voice rose in excitement. 'Could that be the remains of the plane? I know it's almost impossible to see from here – we'll have to get closer, risk it – but I can see what looks like metal glinting…'

Gregson nodded. 'I can definitely see something catching the light, reflecting a bit. And whatever it is, it's big – definitely not a whistle this time.'

'Could it be the Cessna?'

Gregson shrugged. 'Until we get closer, I can't say.'

'Then let's get closer. Come on.'

Smith stepped off the path and began to force his way through the restraining brambles and foliage. After a moment of hesitation,

Gregson followed him. The brambles hooked into their hair and coats, scraping painfully against flesh.

'This had better be bloody well worth it,' Smith snarled as he snatched away a sharp barb that had clawed his cheek, leaving behind a long trail of blood.

Gregson, who was also struggling, raised a hand. 'Listen... did you hear that?'

'What?' Smith jerked his head round but only succeeded in encountering more barbs. 'Is it the panther?' He began batting away vigorously at the persistent undergrowth.

'No, not the panther. Calm down; just listen.'

Both men stood stock-still.

'You're hearing things.' Smith gritted his teeth. 'If it's not the panther, what the hell else could it be?'

And then he too heard a weak cry, almost blown away by the wind.

Gregson nodded. 'You heard that.'

Again they were silent, and the cry was repeated.

'Is it a cry for help?' Smith asked.

'Doesn't sound like "help"; more like "here".'

'Hmm...' Smith nodded. 'Yeah, I'd say it was as well. But it doesn't make sense. Why call out "here"? Sounds almost like a child's game of hide-and-seek.'

'It's definitely not a child's voice.'

They continued to listen. The next time the cry was weaker.

'OK, it's not carrying far, but it's definitely a man's voice, don't you agree?' Gregson said.

'Yeah, I do.'

'But it's a man who wants to be found, rescued, pinpointing where he is.'

'And you know what, George? I think it's Isooba.'

'You think he's crashed and got trapped, maybe?'

'Could well be.'

'Reckon we'd better see if we can find him – if we can get through these sodding brambles.'

Gregson unwound his thick scarf from his neck and double-wrapped it around his face, leaving only his eyes peering out over the top. Picking up a small broken branch from the ground, he began to force back the brambles. Smith also seized hold of a decaying branch and broke it off. Together, they gained ground.

'No wonder nobody else has found him. If it is Isooba he couldn't have found a more difficult place to land if he'd planned it.'

'Oh, I don't think he planned it. I'm damn sure he didn't,' Gregson said, gasping and puffing as he slashed away at the trailing undergrowth. He stopped to catch his breath, holding up a finger. 'You hear anything?'

'No. But I'm going to give him a shout. See if he answers.'

Smith did so. They remained silent for a few moments but there was no further cry to be heard. Smith bellowed again, louder this time, but the only sound was the soughing of the wind and the tree branches rattling and creaking ominously overhead. Then, as Smith prepared to shout again, they heard another cry.

'I'm here!'

The two men stared at each other.

'Right,' Smith said. 'Let's go get him.'

He started bashing away at the intervening foliage. Gregson gripped his own piece of wood and joined in. Spurred on by the cries that got louder as they drew closer, they finally broke through the bramble barrier and found themselves looking at the pitiful shattered remnants of what had once been a plane. Concertinaed and crushed into the ground, it was scarcely recognisable.

'By God, nobody could have withstood that crash and lived.' Smith stood in frozen disbelief, gaping at the once-beautiful Cessna. It beggared belief that the crumpled metal could have flown high above the earth, magnificent in its mastery of the sky.

'Don't forget, the panther escaped, didn't she? So if she survived, Isooba might have as well.'

Smith nodded slowly. 'You're right.' He pointed to what appeared to be the cockpit. The pilot's seat was still bolted in place, its back facing them.

Even as they stood, hesitating, a man's quavering voice called out. 'I'm here… I need help… please.'

Slowly Smith walked along the side of the crumpled plane and leaned over, looking down at Isooba. 'So, you crashed my plane…'

The relief in the pilot's eyes drained away, replaced with terror as he stared wildly back at Smith. 'The storm, sir, the storm… I had no chance to land.'

Smith folded his arms across his chest. 'So, you crashed…' he repeated, and smiled coldly. 'But now I've found you. I'm guessing you didn't have a clue who you were calling to for help, did you?'

The terrified man shook his head. 'No…'

'And if you *had* known it was me, you'd have kept bloody silent, wouldn't you?'

Isooba, lying defenceless at Smith's feet, simply shook with fear.

THIRTY-NINE
2020

'What do you think, Gregson? Have you ever seen a more pathetic specimen?'

Under Smith's sneering, denigrating gaze, Isooba shrank back further into the pilot's seat. Smith in a bad mood was seriously scary, but coupled with Gregson…

Isooba closed his eyes. In his mind a vivid memory replayed: when after a previous flight he'd landed the Cessna back at the Wild Ark, and the vet's fury when he'd opened the crate behind the pilot's seat and found that the pregnant lioness inside was dead. The reason why Smith and Gregson got on was obvious. Each had a towering temper, and lost it at a split second's notice. Combined, they were like something out of a horror movie. Isooba had been forced to help move the dead lioness from the aircraft over to the tiled and echoing prep room behind the aquarium block. He'd watched with revulsion, bile rising in his throat, as Gregson savagely gutted the cat, tugging out four small dead bodies from her gaping womb, his temper rising exponentially with each cub extracted. Finally, all four bodies were laid out on the stainless-steel counter. Gregson had then grabbed two by their tails, gone through the keepers' entrance into the crocodile enclosure, and walked up to the edge of the water. As his shadow passed over the surface, Isooba had watched in fascinated fear as a ripple slowly broke the smoothness of the water. The vet gave a whistle. A long, dark shape began to rise until it was just visible: first, two nostrils surfaced, followed by two reptilian eyes, and then the body, covered by an almost walnut-shell-like crusty skin. Captain Hook. Gripping the first dead cub's tail tighter, Gregson had swung the body back and forth. The crocodile remained motionless, his expressionless eyes fixed on the body. Then Gregson raised his arm high and flung it. The cub arced out, landing with a small splash near the waiting reptile. In a sudden swirl of water, there was a lunge, and great jaws opened and enclosed the dead cub before snapping shut. Captain Hook sank below the surface, taking the cub with him. A couple of minutes later, Gregson had repeated the action and the second cub went the way of the first. This time it never even hit the water. With jaws spread wide and vicious teeth waiting, the crocodile had grabbed the body in mid-air.

The memory faded and Isooba half-opened his eyes. He expected to see both men standing over him, maybe with a gun pointing at him. He knew Gregson usually carried one. But Smith appeared to be on his own. However, Isooba heard movement behind the pilot's seat. Barely daring to breathe, awaiting the impact of a bullet in the back of his head, he froze.

Then Gregson spoke. 'Never mind *him*,' he said disparagingly. 'Look here, can you see these?'

'What?'

'The bags of cocaine. They're still here. Clearly nobody else has seen them.'

There was a delighted guffaw from Smith. 'Damn right. We could still be in the clear.'

Isooba closed his eyes – he didn't need to see anything right now. He could play dead – he was already on the way – and simply listen. However this scenario played out, the more information he had the better. But cocaine? First he'd heard of it. So, his cargo had not simply been an illegally imported wild animal, but Class A drugs as well. That made him a drug runner. God, Mara would never forgive him. She hated the dirty trade; had voiced her opinion about drugs enough times. He groaned. He'd thought things had sunk as low as they could, yet now they'd dipped again. Keeping his eyes closed, he lay motionless, listening to the dialogue between the two men behind his seat. It seemed that, fixated on the cargo, they had totally forgotten about him. But that suited him fine – any delay to him facing the Pearly Gates was a big plus and he accepted it gratefully. Thinking back to the crash, he recalled Kala escaping from the crate. She'd sneezed a couple of times, and a second or two before she'd leapt away from the wreckage, he'd been aware of a fine white powder drifting up from behind him. At the time he'd been far too concerned with the big cat's escape to bother about any finer details. But now he understood what that must have been: a ruptured bag of cocaine. He knew she'd injured her paw while struggling to break open the wooden slats – he'd seen the blood run out onto the floor of the plane. But supposing one of her claws had penetrated a plastic container? He didn't think they would be especially strong, and Kala's claws were very powerful. He shivered. He really didn't know who frightened him most: Smith and Gregson, or Kala. But he knew for certain he'd be facing one of them, and right now his chances of survival felt very slim.

After the guffaws of delight from behind Isooba died down, Smith become businesslike. 'Couldn't have had a better outcome. However, we now need to work out how to shift this little lot back to the zoo.'

'Preferably without Rawson being aware he's carrying cocaine, eh?'

'Exactly. What do you suggest?'

'Well,' Gregson cleared his throat, 'there's a lot of it and it weighs a ton. Plus, we have nothing to carry it in.'

'Is there anything back in the chopper?'

'No, doubt it. But…'

Rustling. Isooba frowned, trying to make out what Gregson was doing behind him.

'It will mean a couple of trips at least, can't carry it in one go, but,' there was a grunt and more rustling, 'here you go – we can use my Puffa jacket. Zip it, tie the sleeves together and Bob's your uncle.'

'Yeah, good thinking. Could work. Let's get to it.'

More movement and scuffling behind Isooba. He could only hope that they'd remain focused on shifting the heavy cargo. Right now, they seemed to have forgotten about him. If only that could continue. He decided to stay motionless and silent. It was all he could do. His hopes of Mara trying to contact him were starting to fade. He wasn't even sure she had received his message. And now Smith had located the aircraft, time was running out fast. Keeping his eyes closed, Isooba tried to assess what was happening in the rear of the Cessna. It seemed to take quite a time, accompanied by grunts and oaths together with the sound of bags falling onto the metal floor, before he heard Smith give a heartfelt cry.

'Hallelujah. OK. Let's shift this back to the helicopter.'

'I've had a thought. We could tell Rawson we're having a lunch break, empty all the food and stuff from our hamper, leave it free to pack with the cocaine. What d'you think?'

'I think that's a damn good idea. It will mean at least another hour before we can take off, but that won't matter. He's flown in bad visibility before now.'

'Come on, then.'

Isooba saw Smith hoist the bulging jacket by one of its knotted sleeves. Gregson followed suit and they clambered out of the wreckage. They were well loaded down. It would take them a good deal of time to get back through the wood, across the open hillside to where the helicopter must have landed. Isooba watched, more openly now, as they struggled through the brambles and undergrowth, slowly slipping and cursing their way back through the wood. From what he'd just heard, they were going to eat before returning for the rest of the cargo. Well, he could indulge as well. A condemned man was supposed to eat a hearty meal before being offed. Inside his overnight bag there was plenty of good food waiting, prepared and packed with love by Mara. And it would hopefully restore a little strength to his body – much-needed strength, he acknowledged reluctantly. He drew the bag nearer and unwrapped the remaining chicken legs. If this was to be his last meal, they fit the bill and tasted wonderful. Dipping into the bag for something else, he felt the bag of fruit and withdrew an apple and the paring knife Mara had so thoughtfully provided. He peeled the fruit, then slid the knife down the side of his boot. It wasn't much of a weapon but it was all he'd got and he might very well need it before the day was out. Then he lay back, chewed the juicy apple and waited for the return of Gregson and Smith.

He awoke with a start. From somewhere nearby came the sound of breaking twigs. How long he'd been asleep, he had no idea. Was it long enough for the men to be returning, or was something equally unpleasant and unwanted, like Kala, approaching? His heart went into overdrive, sweat gathering on his forehead and running down his face, hands slippery as he tried to grip the arms of the seat. Then he heard voices.

'What a bloody caper. I'm ripped to bloody bits.' It was Gregson.

'Stop moaning. Without a jacket on you're bound to get scratched.'

'Well, I have got it on now. But I'll get bloodied up again on the way back through this sodding wood. And it's cold.'

'We need the jacket for the cocaine, so stop griping, get it off and start shifting the rest of the cargo, OK?' Smith's voice had an edge of steel to it now.

Isooba sank as low as he could into the pilot's seat. It didn't do to argue or disagree with Smith. He treated all his staff with disdain and contempt, but Gregson wasn't simply another staff member; more on the way to being a partner. Smith needed his expertise as a vet, but clearly he was still the boss and expected to be obeyed. A silence followed, broken only by grunts as the two men dug down into the bowels of the wrecked crate, heaving up the bags that lay beneath it. The operation seemed to take forever, and all the while Isooba lay motionless, barely breathing, praying that they would just finish the job, hoist the heavy load out of the aircraft and take it back to the helicopter. Rawson had always seemed a reasonable chap, but even though an ally was exactly what Isooba needed at the moment, Rawson might just as well be on a boat sailing along the Trent for all the good he could do.

'Right.' Gregson stepped away towards the side of the Cessna. 'Seems about it. One or two bags have burst but we've nothing to collect the spillage in, so let's get off. It'll be dusk soon.'

Smith gave a mumble of agreement. For a beautiful moment, Isooba thought he was going to escape their notice.

'Oh, hang on. I nearly forgot. We've got company, haven't we?'

Isooba's hopes crashed.

Smith's shadow loomed over him. 'You dead yet?'

A boot thumped hard into Isooba's ribs. He kept his eyes closed but let his mouth drop open a little, enabling him to take very shallow breaths which gave him oxygen without requiring much movement from his chest.

'Well, has he gone?' Gregson's tone was past impatient. 'Come on, we have to carry this lot to the chopper.'

'You brought your gun with you, didn't you?'

'What? You're expecting me to finish him?'

'Yeah, finish the job and let's get off.'

'And when the body's found, it will bring down the coppers like a flock of bloody vultures. Don't you see? As it stands, he died in the crash. You put a bullet in his skull, it's no longer an accident, it's murder.'

'Hmm… yeah, OK, guess you've got a point. So, we just leave him, eh? Until somebody finds him?'

'Oh, I don't think it will be some*body*…'

'Eh?'

'We don't need to kill him. You're forgetting: Kala's around. When it gets dusky, she'll be out on the prowl. And by that time she'll be hungry.' Gregson began to laugh. 'Know what I mean?'

'Oh, yes, I know what you mean. What a way to solve a problem. Neat, that, very neat…'

Both men laughed like drains as they walked away through the wood.

FORTY
2020

After Phillip had left, Kent poured the last dregs of the coffee. Facing him was one of the worst jobs on the farm: removing a dead body. Not that it was a rare or unusual occurrence; far from it. Sheep were incredibly accident-prone, foolhardy creatures, and as a consequence Kent was accustomed to the removal of dead ewes. But this time it was very different. He'd never had a sheep mauled and ripped apart by a panther before, and it wasn't something he could keep quiet about. The police would have to be informed, probably before he attempted to retrieve the body. Following that unpleasant realisation there came another. The press would be on it like wasps on ripe plums, and with lambing time only days away, the intrusion was bound to present problems and extra work at one of Kent's busiest times of the year, when his working hours very often continued throughout the night. He wondered what his father would have thought of the situation. But Bryn was long gone and Hilltop Farm was now Kent's. He drained the coffee. Whatever the problems, they were his to deal with.

The landline rang.

'Kent Evans.'

'Mr Evans, this is Westwood School. My name is Jaqueline Bolton, speaking on behalf of Cordelia Lytton.'

Kent gripped the receiver tightly. Rachel was a weekly boarder at Westwood Girls' School in Yorkshire. Cordelia Lytton was the headmistress. 'Is there a problem?'

'Yes, I'm afraid so, Mr Evans.'

Kent's stomach flipped over. 'Is Rachel all right?' His anxiety rocketed. He'd felt stressed before because of the panther attack and all the fallout that would shortly come down on the farm, but where Rachel and her welfare and safety were concerned, all his senses instantly went on red alert.

'I can assure you, Mr Evans, that your daughter is perfectly well.'

Kent gave a deep sigh of relief. 'Thank God for that. I was imagining all sorts…'

'But as a school, we *do* have a problem – a health problem.'

'What sort of a problem?'

'Rachel is to return to you for the extended weekend, is she not?'

'Yes…'

'And is that still the plan?'

'Yes, definitely. She's looking forward to coming.'

'Good, good. Well, as you're aware, normally Rachel stays with her grandmother near Harrogate.'

'That's right. Is there a problem with Sheila?'

'No, not at all. I have spoken to Mrs Clarke and she is aware of the situation. As Rachel's grandmother, she has confirmed you are a person children will be safe with. The reason I'm calling is that the school is closing today. Is it possible you could collect Rachel as soon as possible, please?'

'But why – what's prompted the closure?' Kent said, perplexed.

'Regrettably, we seem to have an outbreak of measles. Oh, don't worry – Rachel hasn't contracted it.'

Yet. Kent bit back the retort. 'Right.'

'That's why we need to act swiftly and send the girls home before they are exposed to the disease.'

'I see… and does Sheila approve of you allowing me to collect Rachel and bring her to the farm?'

'Yes, Mrs Clarke is in full agreement, and she is unable to take Rachel because she never caught measles as a child, so if she were to catch it now it could be very serious.'

'Well, I've had it. I remember quite clearly; it was when I was about five or six, soon after we came here from Wales.'

'Oh, that's good. It answers my next question. So, shall we expect you quite soon?'

'I shall have to speak with my farmhand first, but then I'll leave straight away.'

'Thank you so much. I'm sorry it's short notice but the medical officer only issued his instructions an hour ago and we're trying to contact all the parents – quite a job, as you will appreciate.'

'Yes, I'm sure. But I'll be leaving in fifteen minutes and will hope to be at Westwood later this morning.'

'Thank you again. We'll see you then. Goodbye.'

Kent was left holding the receiver and listening to the dialling tone as Miss Bolton abruptly ended the call. His first thought was one of relief that he'd had the measles and was in a position to fetch Rachel home. He squashed the thought that by now it was possible that she could be incubating the virus. She would certainly need a lot of time and care if she became ill. Strange that Sheila hadn't had the disease as a child, but of course when adults went down with it, it wasn't a soft option, and at her age it wasn't something she should risk. He grabbed his coffee mug and took it through to the kitchen. It would be wonderful to have his daughter home for a few days, but it would also pose a few problems. He shrugged them off. Rachel being home was always a blessing. He didn't see her half as often as he'd like.

After Chloe had left, taking the child with her, the farm had been all he had left. But it had still seemed a very empty place without them. Rinsing the mug, he paused, looking out of the kitchen window at the hillside stretching away before him. Chloe could never have foreseen the disaster in front of her when she'd first experimented with cocaine. She'd blamed him – of course she had blamed him for her decision to take the vile stuff. It wasn't her fault; how could it be? 'With you abroad most of the time, what do you expect me to do? I've got to have a bit of fun, haven't I?' Her reasoning would have been more credible if she had begun taking the drug whilst he had been in the army. Yet he'd not noticed any signs at all during his home leaves. It had all gone down the pan when his father had died so suddenly and he'd come home from Afghanistan and found Jack and Chloe in bed. An unpleasant thought occurred to him. Could Chloe's habit have anything to do with Jack? He had no idea where she had got the drugs from. Surely to God Jack hadn't supplied her with cocaine? Certainly, when he'd found them together, Chloe had seemed as high as a kite; totally unrepentant and focused on her own pleasure. She had also been pregnant.

Mulling it over now, Kent shuddered at the thought that Rachel could have been affected. But she wasn't. Thank God she wasn't. So did that tell him that at that time, Chloe hadn't been addicted? Yes. His hands clenched on the edge of the Belfast sink. He had returned from the army just in time, it seemed, to protect the unborn Rachel from catastrophe. But he'd been unable to save Chloe. He was sure it had been only a recreational activity at the start. She'd been blithely playing with danger, confident she could remain in charge, but she was no match for the power of the drug. Sheila had blamed Kent, and his long absences from home, for the state of her daughter's health. She wouldn't hear anything against Chloe. Of course she wouldn't; it was a case of blood bonding. All her sympathy had been for Chloe, although initially she had urged her to stop using the drug. But Chloe had produced a grandchild for her to dote on, and, to give Sheila due credit, she had been a caring and responsible grandparent, providing everything Rachel needed. Until today.

Kent became aware of the cramp in his white-knuckled fingers and relaxed his grip on the sink. Replacing the mug on a hook on the Welsh dresser, he grabbed his coat and flicked his fingers to Jess. She was out of her basket and waiting at heel as he opened the kitchen door. He went across the yard to the main barn. 'Lennie, you there? Need a word.'

'Sure, Mr Evans.' Lennie appeared, wiping his hands on his old jeans.

'I've just had a call from Rachel's school. Seems they've got an attack of measles. I have to drive up straight away and collect her. She needs to stay here for a while. She was coming for an extended weekend but now it has been brought forward. It's going to make things a bit awkward work-wise, see.'

'Don't you worry about that. I can work all the hours you want me to, or help with Rachel, whatever you need. I had measles when I was a nipper.'

Kent double-clapped him on the shoulder. 'You're a great help, and it looks like I shall need a fair bit. I really do appreciate your loyalty, Lennie.'

Lennie beamed. 'I like helping out, Mr Evans.'

'Well, I need you to hold the fort while I drive up to Yorkshire.'

'When will you be back?'

'Hmm, not sure. I doubt they won't have had a meal at the school, so I'll probably stop off somewhere and have lunch with Rachel. She's well overdue for a bit of spoiling. Depends what she wants to do.'

'I'll stay until you get home, don't worry about anything. And I'll feed Jess.'

'Right. Thanks very much, Lennie. If it gets late, help yourself to some hot food out of the slow cooker, and make yourself all the hot drinks you need. And I'll see you soon as, OK?'

'Sure thing, Mr Evans. But could I make a telephone call, please? It's my mother, you see; I should let her know I might be late home.'

'Of course. We don't want to cause her any concern.'

'Thanks; she's sure to be home to answer the phone. She's not working right now. The old lady she helped to look after died about three weeks ago.'

'Oh, I see. Well, I must get going. Bye, Lennie.'

Kent took the Ford estate; plenty of room in case Rachel started feeling poorly and needed to lie down on the way back. Heading towards Grantham on the A52, he turned off onto the A1 and floored the car up north. It was a swift, easy journey, one he'd made many times before – Bawtry, Doncaster and onwards before turning west into a more rural area. He motored on through Dalton, the village where Sheila lived, and briefly considered calling in before dismissing the idea. Miss Bolton had asked him to collect Rachel ASAP. Swinging sharply north, he drove the last twenty-odd miles using the third of the shortcuts he'd perfected that took him to the outskirts of Brenton. Half a mile farther on was an impressive old manor house with ornate iron entrance gates that were set wide open. A large board at the side proclaimed, 'Westwood Private School'. Kent looked at his watch – an hour and thirty-five minutes. He'd made very good time. Allowing a couple of cars to turn out of the driveway, he drove through the gates and up the tree-lined drive.

Inside, one of the staff was standing in the hall by the main door. Kent was shortly shown into the headmistress's study.

Miss Lytton rose as he walked in. 'Mr Evans, do come in. So good of you to collect Rachel. It's an unfortunate situation but we have to adhere to the rules.'

'No trouble whatsoever. It will be lovely to have her at the farm.'

'Well, my next request may very well prove troublesome.'

'Oh?'

'Very few of the girls have developed symptoms. Rachel has shown no signs, I'm pleased to say. And her best friend, Raquel; the Spanish spelling,' she tinkled a laugh, 'also appears to be free of symptoms. They sleep in the same dormitory and none of the other girls in there have displayed signs either.'

'And your request, Headmistress?'

'Obviously, we have contacted all parents,' she half-turned to a side window and waved a hand, 'as you can see from the number of cars, but we do have a slight problem with Raquel. Normally, she is transported to and from home by her father's helicopter.'

Kent found his eyebrows starting to rise, and hastily drew them together in a slight frown instead. He knew this was an exclusive school, he couldn't have afforded the fees – it was Sheila who had decided that only the best would do for her one and only grandchild. But he had never asked her how much the fees were. She insisted on taking care of the payments herself. And after today, he'd never dare ask.

'I'm afraid we were told by Mr Smith's housekeeper, Mrs Milton, that he flew off early this morning and has been unavoidably delayed, so he won't be home until this evening. And unfortunately, Mrs Milton's car is at the garage being repaired.'

Kent nodded. 'And where do I fit in?'

'Well, subject to your agreement of course, we have provisionally agreed that since the Wild Ark Zoo – Mr Smith's business – is not open to the public today and therefore there should be no risk of spreading the virus to other children, if you could drive both girls up there prior to taking Rachel home – your daughter has expressed a desire to go with her friend to visit the zoo – it would solve the problem. I would think it shouldn't take more than forty minutes' extra driving time. Mrs Milton has given her consent, after speaking to Mrs Clarke.'

This time Kent made no effort to stop his eyebrows rising. His first thought was *What a bloody cheek!* But just then there was a knock on the study door.

'Come in,' Miss Lytton instructed.

The door opened to admit a teacher accompanied by his daughter and another girl.

'Daddy!' Rachel flung herself at him.

'Hello, sunshine.' Kent's arms were around her, returning her hug.

There was a discreet cough from the headmistress. 'This is Raquel Smith.'

'How do you do, Mr Evans?' Raquel said politely.

Over the top of his daughter's head, Kent nodded to the child. 'Hello. It seems that you need transport to get home?'

'Yes, yes, I do. My daddy's not home today. But I've asked Rachel,' Raquel flashed a quick smile at her friend, 'if she'd like to visit the zoo.'

'And I bet she said yes, didn't she?'

Both girls fixed him with beaming, expectant smiles, nodding vigorously.

'Please, Daddy,' Rachel wheedled. '*Please* say I can visit.'

Kent knew a corner when he was backed into one. Knowing that he should get back to the farm and his other responsibilities, he tried the only excuse he could think of. 'But,' he turned to Miss Lytton, who was wearing a slightly smug smile, 'shouldn't the girls be kept apart? I mean, that *is* the reason you've had to close the school.'

'As I have already explained, neither girl is showing any signs of illness. And they've been together most of the time, so I think we can discount them suddenly infecting each other, don't you?' Her smile widened. 'It's a neat solution to the problem.'

Kent could only nod and give in. 'Yes, a neat solution.' Then he remembered his conversation with Lennie. Rachel was due a bit of spoiling. 'Very well, then. If it's been agreed and both girls are keen—'

There was a joint cry of 'I'm keen, I'm keen…'

He spread his hands in surrender. 'OK. But I'd like you to ring Mrs Milton again and tell her that you've authorised it.'

'Only too pleased.'

'And,' Kent said in a desperate last try, 'I'll need the address and postcode. Though I certainly don't want to contravene data protection…'

'Of course. Not a problem. And thank you so much, Mr Evans. What do you say, girls?'

A united 'Thank you' from the children, who by this time were jigging up and down with excitement.

'I can see why you think they're both in excellent health,' Kent said, shaking his head ruefully as he followed the teacher to the door. 'Just hope I'm up to the job…'

FORTY-ONE
2020

Kent glanced in his rear-view mirror. Both girls, belted up, were sitting on the back seat, heads together, their giggles filling the car. He smiled. If Miss Lytton had got it wrong and one of them had been infected, by now it was a pretty safe bet they both had it. But kids took things like measles as they came: dying one day, bouncing back in the next few, displaying spots proudly like badges of honour. He felt a grin stretch his mouth. What the hell; it didn't matter. At worst, Rachel would have to return to school next week, but at best, it would mean he could keep her at home a while longer. And he had no objection to that.

'So, Raquel, you're Spanish, are you? Or is it simply that your name is spelt the Spanish way?'

A dark curly head lifted and turned towards him. 'My mummy was Spanish, and my grandma. But I was born in England.'

'Uh-huh. Well, Smith is certainly an English surname.'

'Daddy says it gives him…' the child hesitated, struggling over the word, 'anonymity.'

Kent agreed. 'Certainly does; it's just about the most common one in England.'

Raquel nodded. 'We're nearly home now – look.' She pointed ahead to a roundabout. 'You have to turn off left; the zoo's not far now.'

'Are there signs for it?' Rachel asked.

'Lots and lots... and arrows pointing.'

'I'm sure we'll find it.' Kent approached the roundabout, and sure enough a prominent sign declared, 'Wild Ark Zoo – 5 miles'. He took the second left and drove down a B road that shortly branched off down a country lane with a further sign that told him that a mile and a half in front he would find the zoo.

'Are there lots of animals in your daddy's zoo? And do you have lions and tigers?' Kent widened his eyes in mock fear. 'You know, *really* scary ones?'

Raquel laughed. 'Of course we do. That's what the visitors come to see. Daddy says they like being scared.'

'He's probably right.'

'I like llamas and alpacas; they look *so* cuddly,' Rachel said.

'Sorry, Rach, but we don't have any of those.'

'People keep them as pets now, don't they?' Kent suggested.

'I like them because they remind me of the lambs at our farm,' Rachel said.

'You see, Raquel, she's a real softie.' Kent smiled at his daughter in the mirror, and the look of love he gave her took away any sting from the words.

'No I'm not,' Rachel protested. 'It's OK for you, Daddy, you can see the sheep and lambs every day. I have to wait for school holidays. I miss them.'

'It's fine, sweetheart; I know you do, I'm only kidding. You were born on the farm and, as old Jeremiah would say, it's in the blood. But you're going to be at home for a while now, until Miss Lytton cracks the whip.'

'Like a ringmaster?' Raquel queried.

He chuckled. 'No. Sorry, I could have put it better. It's just a saying. It means when it's time to return to work.'

'But we don't have to work now.' Raquel clapped her hands. 'And I can't wait to show Rach the zoo.'

'Well,' Kent said, pointing to a big sign coming up on the right-hand side, 'you won't have to wait much longer.' It was an impressive sign; not one you could miss. Kent turned off the road and stopped in front of a huge pair of wrought-iron gates set back and flanked by trees. The sign above the left-hand gate showed the head of a black panther, muzzle wide open displaying vicious white fangs above a pair of glaring green eyes. A trickle of saliva ran down from its rough red tongue in a very lifelike fashion. 'And do you have one of these big cats here?' Kent queried.

Raquel nodded, smiling ear to ear with pride. 'Oh, yes, Mr Evans.'

'It looks *really* scary.' Rachel leant forward, her hand gripping Kent's shoulder tightly.

'Oh, don't worry, Rach, it's quite safe; the cats are all locked in, they can't get you.'

'Hmm, but it's more a question of how *we* get into…' However, before Kent could finish his sentence, the big gates began to open on their own, soundlessly, spookily, tempting them in. 'Well, I'll be d—'

Raquel crowed with glee. 'There are cameras, Mr Evans. They know up at the house that we're waiting to get in.'

'So it seems.' Kent engaged first gear and drove in, following the tarmac as it curved in an elongated 'S'. Clearing the second bend, the zoo came into view. There was another pair of double gates, plus a single one behind which was a single-storey building sporting a sign saying, 'Office'. There didn't appear to be anyone around. The road twisted sharply away to the right.

'Could you drive on that way?' Raquel pointed. 'It leads up to my house.'

Obediently Kent drove on… and on… He was about to ask how much farther they had to go when, up front, set at the back of a wide circle of gravel, the house emerged, surrounded by tall poplar trees. But 'house' was far too understated a term; it was a mansion. As they approached, the solid mahogany door opened and a small dark-haired woman came out onto the top step. She was olive-skinned, certainly not English, and her expression was joyful. Kent pulled the car round and parked at the bottom of the circular run of steps. The woman dashed forward to meet them, flinging her arms wide as Raquel alighted.

The child, in her turn, squealed in delight. 'Petrie! I'm back.'

'Bless every hair on your head, my little one.' The woman swept the little girl up and crushed her close in a fierce embrace.

Kent got out, shivering as the sharp cut in the strong east wind found its way through his jacket, then remembered that the zoo was much farther north. He motioned to Rachel to stand close. Her hand crept into his and squeezed it. He squeezed back. The reunion before them was very touching. He recalled Raquel's words: 'my mummy was Spanish'. *Was.* Presumably Mrs Smith had died.

The housekeeper gave Raquel a smacking kiss before releasing her. Then, dabbing at her eyes with the corner of a brightly striped apron, she said, 'Welcome, welcome to Wild Ark, Mr Evans, and thank you so much for bringing Raquel home for us. I'm sorry my own little car was in the garage,' she spread her hands, holding one out towards Kent, 'so, you see, I could not fetch her. But I have had measles.'

'Please,' Kent said, coming forward and shaking her outstretched hand, 'it was no problem. Do call me Kent.' He was pleased now that he'd gone the extra mile and agreed to ferry Raquel home.

Raquel grabbed hold of Rachel. 'This is Petri – well, Mrs Petrina Milton,' she giggled. 'And this is Rachel, my bestest friend from school.'

Petrina engulfed Rachel in a tremendous hug. 'So pleased to meet you. I look after Raquel when she's home, and I know you are a good friend to her when she is away at school. Thank you.'

'Hello,' Rachel said shyly.

Mrs Milton collected herself. 'Now, come along. I have hot drinks waiting in the kitchen. Follow me.'

And so they did. Or, rather, they followed the welcoming smell of fresh coffee emanating from down the hall. The kitchen was a massive room running almost the whole back of the house. The heating system – totally undetectable, but which Kent decided had to be underfloor – was doing a fantastic job. Despite its size, the kitchen was toasty, and as well as coffee, another delicious spicy smell filled the room.

'Please sit wherever you wish. I'll just pour the drinks.'

'Come on, Rach,' Raquel patted the deeply upholstered sofa, 'sit with me.'

Kent found himself dragged along, Rachel still clutching his hand, and the three of them packed onto the comfortable seat. Minutes later, he was sipping the most delicious coffee he'd ever had. 'Wow. You can certainly make coffee. It's fabulous.'

Petrina accepted the compliment. 'But don't forget, Mr Evans—'

'Kent, please.'

'—Kent. I am Italian. It is my birthright to make good coffee.' She laughed. 'But not for children. They have hot chocolate.'

'It tastes lovely, thank you, Mrs Milton,' Rachel said.

Petrina smiled. 'And now would you like a nice hot meal?'

Both girls nodded.

'It wasn't time for lunch, so we didn't have any at school, Petrie,' Raquel explained.

'I didn't think you would have. I've made lasagne Verdi for supper tonight, but I think it would be just the thing to have right now, don't you?'

The nods continued.

'And you, Mr Kent? Could you manage a hot meal?'

'Indeed I could. I was up at five o'clock this morning and it seems an age since I had any food.'

'Then come and sit at the table. I shall dish up straight away.'

The lasagne tasted even better than it smelt. They all did justice to Petrina's faultless cooking. But Kent, sitting back in his chair, stomach full, gave a glance at his watch, mindful of time's march. 'That was great, thank you. However, I need to think about getting back fairly soon.'

'But, Daddy,' Rachel protested, 'I haven't seen the animals yet.'

'Oh, I think we can spare an hour…'

Raquel undertook her duty as their tour guide with enthusiasm and soon they were being shown the rhesus monkeys, the marmosets, and their big brothers the gorillas, followed by many meerkats and some tapirs.

'I'm sorry, Raquel, but we don't have time to go around all your animals, I'm afraid,' Kent warned.

'Then we won't bother with the tropical bird houses or the aquariums. But you *must* see the big cats. My daddy says they're the star attraction.' Then she blushed. 'He says I am as well.'

'If that's what he says, then you certainly must show us.' Kent smiled at the excited little girl. He felt a stab of pity for her. She obviously adored her father and there seemed to be a special bond between them, no doubt because her mother had died.

Raquel led them along wide, cleanly swept paths through the beautifully landscaped grounds. The zoo was vast, far bigger than it appeared from the entrance, and certainly impressive. It was a place you could easily spend an entire day visiting, walking around, taking in all the animals and birds. Today they were only getting a taster. Kent had the feeling that this wouldn't be the only visit Rachel would want to make.

'And these are the big cat enclosures. We have four. The cats have to be separated, otherwise they would fight with each other.'

Kent and Rachel nodded solemnly. The first enclosure was for the lions (one male with an enormous mane, and three lionesses); the second was occupied by a pair of young tigers; and the third, much smaller, was for a pair of lynx. Parts of the enclosures were under cover and had one-way windows embedded in the stone walls, through which the animals' dens and sleeping area could be seen. A strong, rank smell of cat permeated, adding to the dangerous jungle atmosphere as they watched the big cats from their privileged viewpoint. They were perfectly safe, but seeing and smelling the wild cats at such close quarters was decidedly scary.

'And there's one more enclosure to show you.' Raquel led them further along. 'It's the one for the black panther. You know, from the picture on the entrance gates?'

They nodded. Rachel slid a hand into Kent's as they followed her friend to the last of the big cat quarters. Stopping in front of the strong, heavy mesh separating them from the panther's outdoor space, Kent read out loud the notice displayed:

Panthera pardus: the black panther.

FORTY-TWO
2020

Traffic was light on the way back. Kent took advantage again of the several cross-country shortcuts he knew before reaching the A1 and flooring the accelerator.

The visit to the zoo replayed through his mind and he recalled how he'd felt observing the black panther. Rachel had continued to hold on to his hand as they'd entered the undercover viewing room and approached the window. In each of the other enclosures, the cats had been inside – none prowling about outside in the bleak cold; they were all bedded down and sleeping. But in the fourth, lying so close to the window that you felt you really could reach out and touch its head, was a black panther. Probably because it was so close, it had seemed enormous. Its dense black fur was so beautiful it almost entreated you to stroke it. Kent had never been so close to a wild cat before, and had caught his breath in wonder at the power and magnificence of the beast.

'There,' he'd whispered to Rachel, 'what do you think of *that*?'

Rachel had been equally entranced, nodding mutely, her eyes wide with wonder, glued to the magnificent animal. And then she'd pointed with one shaky finger. A foolish fly, no doubt roused from winter sleep by the pungent smell and the warmth given off by the big cat, buzzed dozily around the cat's head. Landing on its ear, it crawled around. Disturbed, the panther woke up. Slowly opening emerald-green eyes, it lifted its head, rolling it back above powerful shoulders. Unaware that it was being watched through the one-way glass, the cat yawned. Its muzzle, gaping wide to display gleaming wet fangs, pointed directly towards them, barely three feet away. It was so close they could see the rough papillae coating the top of its red tongue.

Rachel had gasped, and Kent had felt an age-old instinct kick in that made his own shoulders rise in preparation to protect his offspring. By now both were completely hypnotised by the spectacle in front of them. The fly buzzed clumsily around the cat's head again before smacking into the glass right in front of their faces. Then, dizzily, it tried to fly off. With unbelievable speed, the panther lunged towards the window, straight at their faces, and snapped its jaws closed. The fly disappeared. Rachel had let go of Kent's hand, screamed in pure terror and flung herself into his arms. It had been an experience that could only happen once; the odds against them being there right at that second were astronomic. Even Raquel, who was used to the big cats, had been considerably shaken and Kent had found himself with two crying children to cope with. Even now, as he reduced his speed, came off the A1 and drove down the A52 towards home, he could still feel the shock of it.

On getting into the car, Rachel had burrowed down on the back seat under the car rug, buried her face in a pillow and fallen asleep. She'd slept for most of the journey back home. Casting a look in his rear-view mirror at her pale, barely visible face, Kent felt a wrench of conscience; totally unjustified, but that didn't help at all. He knew it had been a horrible experience that, like some of the bad experiences in his own life, one she would probably never forget. But you could never go back, never undo what had happened. He cursed Miss Lytton to all hell for putting him – and Rachel – in that untenable position. And it hadn't just had a bad effect upon his daughter. He knew, just knew that that night he would have that terrifying dream again. The animal's slavering jaws snapping shut would surely act as a trigger to what he had witnessed and then buried in his subconscious all those years ago. He'd thought – hoped – that the nightmares had finally passed, but he'd lay money on the memory reactivating them again tonight, bringing him screaming back to consciousness, but not in time to prevent himself throwing up.

Rachel was still asleep when he drove into the farmyard. He cut the engine and closed the door as softly as he could behind him. Going across to the main barn, he said, 'I'm back, Lennie. Everything OK?'

Hearing his voice, Jess barrelled across between the lambing pens and pressed herself firmly against his leg, eyes full of love, seeking his face and approval.

He reached down and fondled her head. 'You're a good girl, so you are.'

'Ah, Mr Evans.' Lennie heaved himself up from the rail he was putting into place to form part of a lambing pen. 'You're back early.'

'Yes; put my toe down coming back, see.'

'Is Rachel with you? Has she caught the measles yet?'

'Yes she is, and no she hasn't,' Rachel said as she entered the barn and heard his questions.

Kent swung round. 'You all right, sunshine? Had a good sleep?'

'Yes thanks, Dad. I'd like a drink. I'm thirsty.'

Lennie's face split into a beaming smile. 'Ha, now, you come alonga me. I've something for you, from Mother.' He cast a quick enquiring glance at Kent.

'Yes, you go on, Lennie; I'll get the car unloaded and be right in.'

Kent watched them race across the farmyard; one with light, fast, twinkling steps and one with clumping great big ones. He gave a sigh of relief. The sleep had obviously done her good. And being around Lennie was the perfect antidote to stress. Lennie didn't do stress. He listened to the problem or situation and then mentally stepped away from it. His usual comment was 'Don't worry. It will fix itself. Give it time.' And mostly, it did – whatever 'it' was.

When he entered the kitchen, Rachel was sitting at the table, having a long drink and laughing at something Lennie had said.

'From Mother,' Lennie said, pointing to the glass and then to a bottle three quarters full. 'She made it herself, in case the little lamb had caught the measles and was feeling poorly.'

'It's home-made lemonade,' Rachel put in, 'and it's great.'

'Well, pass on my thanks to your mother, Lennie.'

'Oh, don't worry. She's comin' up tomorrow to see you, she said.'

'Oh, what about?'

'Dunno, really. See Rachel, I suppose.'

'And I can thank her too; that was scrummy.' Rachel drained her glass and rinsed it under the tap. 'But now I'm going out to play. OK, Daddy?'

'Yes, I suppose so, but Lennie and I are busy right now.'

'That's OK. I want to see the sheep. I'll take Jess with me.'

Kent nodded. 'But don't go too far. Be sure and stay within shouting distance of the farm.' For a moment he was tempted to transfer his anxiety for her safety onto the little girl, but he caught himself just in time. She'd had a big enough shock today; fanning the fire and warning about the possibility of a panther prowling around the area could do no good. It was still daylight; would be for a couple of hours. Even if the beast was nearby, it wouldn't venture out into full view on the hillside. Big cats were secretive, nocturnal animals. 'And put some warm gear on: scarf, hat, etc.' His last words followed her up the stairs as she raced off to change out of her school uniform.

'I will.' Her reply floated down.

'Ah, don't go fretting yoursen, Mr Evans; she'll be fine now she's back home.'

'I hope so, Lennie.'

'Course she will. Is there anything else you want me to do? Or shall I carry on assembling the pens in the big barn?'

'No, you carry on. There's nothing that can't wait until tomorrow.'

Lennie stomped off happily across the yard. Kent watched him go. He hadn't told Lennie about the panther yet, for the same reason he hadn't told Rachel. Of course Lennie saw no danger in the child playing out as she normally did when she was home. As far as he was aware, she could come to no harm. But Kent knew he would have to come clean soon and tell him about the big cat.

That line of thinking reminded him about the dead sheep. He needed to report it to the police and then drive up and collect the carcass. After that, there would be police at the door for certain; maybe reporters and photographers too. There was no way he could shield Rachel. She would be sure to find out. But he'd be damned if he'd stir the mud today. No, let her enjoy her first day back at home. The sheep was dead and the panther likely far away by now. It could wait.

Rachel hurtled into her bedroom, threw her school bag onto the floor and bounced up and down with delight at being home again. Then she tore off her school uniform, unbuttoned her blouse and, shivering, pulled off her thin vest. It was meant for centrally heated premises; certainly not for wearing at the farm. Delving into the chest of drawers, she pulled out what she called her 'proper' vest – a five-rating thermal one – plus a woven shirt and a thick woollen jumper and corduroy trousers. They were clothes for wearing at home, her real home on the farm, in cold weather like this. Dressing quickly, she dragged on a second pair of socks – wellington boot liners – and hastened downstairs.

The men had disappeared but Rachel wasn't bothered. She had enough cosseting from her Granny Sheila. It didn't sit well with her; never had done. But she was grateful to her grandmother for providing the lifestyle she enjoyed, mainly being able to attend Westwood School during the week. Weekends of smothering were the price she paid willingly, and sometimes she even enjoyed them. But the farm was where she came alive. It wasn't something she could explain but whenever she returned it just felt right. And now she was here, maybe for quite a while until Cordy – the universally used nickname for the headmistress – saw fit to recall her.

Mindful of her father's instructions, she piled on thick outer clothing, tucking her single long plait underneath her scarf and jamming on a woolly bobble hat before sorting out her wellingtons. Jess lay in her basket near the warm Rayburn, watching her every move, waiting for Rachel to flick her fingers. She loved it when Rachel was home, and stuck to her side, practically rounding her up. Rachel in turn loved the dog's company and felt no need for a human playmate; the lure of the freedom outdoors, with only the dog at her side after days of close-knit community sharing, chimed a special note inside her. Finding her boots, she thrust her feet into them and, turning, flicked her fingers. 'Come on, Jess. Let's go.'

The dog was out of her basket and at her heels in an instant.

Rachel opened the back door, slammed it behind her and raced across the freezing yard. Catching sight of Lennie, she raised a fist and punched the air. 'I'm off.'

He grinned and returned the gesture. 'Tell the sheep I love them,' he called.

'Me too,' she yelled, giggling as she ran, skipping, through the gateway and out onto the hillside.

She had to slow down long before she was even a quarter of the way up the hill, her breath coming in gusty gasps. It took a great deal of effort to reach the plateau where she stood, bent over, getting her breath back ready for the next steep climb. Then she was off again, at a more sensible pace now, Jess nosing the ground in large circles around her. Finally she reached the top, flung herself down on the thick tussocks of grass and let her breathing slow to normal while Jess, content just to be with her, nestled close by her side, muzzle resting on her knee. Shielding her eyes against a thin yellow beam of late sunlight, Rachel could make out a matchstick man moving across the farmyard way below. She was about to yell out a greeting to Lennie (although the figure was only small from up here, it was still large enough for her to know that it wasn't her father, and in any case, at this time of the day he'd be in his study, working hard on a translation), then realised she'd disobeyed her dad and moved out of earshot. Standing up, she looked away from the sun over the hill and could make out the woolly blobs of the sheep much further away. The wind gusted across the hillside, cutting straight through even her thick coat and making her shiver. She pulled a face. Today the sheep had wandered away to the east; too far for her to walk. Still, she consoled herself, by tomorrow they would be nearer and she could come and see them in the morning. And it didn't seem that any lambs had been born yet; it was a bit early in the year. But she was here for a long holiday and there was plenty of time.

She gave a skip of pure happiness and was about to turn and race Jess down the hill when two figures caught her eye, emerging from the wood higher up. They appeared to be struggling, each carrying a long handle of what seemed to be a large, bulging sack. One caught his foot and stumbled. He swore loudly and the bag lurched to one side, hitting the ground heavily, before he managed to save himself from falling by grabbing hold of the other man. Swinging the bag higher between them, they struggled on over the rough ground. Jess had also caught sight of them and, sniffing the air with flared nostrils, growled low in her throat.

'What do you think they're doing, Jess? Stealing something? Do you think they could have picked up a lamb?' Rachel, eyes wide and worried, clenched her hands together. If it was a lamb, she ought to do something about it. Her daddy needed all the lambs for the farm. He'd often said so when he had brought in a sickly one from the barn that needed bottle-feeding: 'We can't afford to lose a single one, Rachel. They're precious.'

There was no time to go back to the farm for help. It would take far too long, and by then the men would have made off. It was all down to her right now.

'Come on, Jess.' Making up her mind, Rachel raced off after them.

FORTY-THREE
2020

Raquel burst into tears again.

'Now, now, don't cry, little one. What is it?' Petrina wiped her floury hands on her apron and put an arm around the child's heaving shoulders. 'You're not still thinking about what happened earlier, are you?'

'Yes.' Raquel struggled to overcome her emotion. 'Well, no, not about the panther; about Rachel.'

'Oh, don't upset yourself. She'll have got over it by now, like you have.'

The dark curly head shook. 'Not about the panther,' Raquel repeated. 'I don't think she'll want to come and visit me again. She won't be friends any more.' A fresh burst of sobbing overcame her.

'Hush.' Petrina sat down on the kitchen sofa and lifted Raquel onto her lap. Rocking her gently, she waited for the tears to subside.

It was what Raquel's mother would have done. Since Carlita's death, Petrina had been only too aware that there was only herself to offer the child comfort. She discounted Mr Smith. For all the hands-on parenting he did, he might just as well not be Raquel's father. A more selfish man she had yet to meet. Oh, he wanted the child's company when there was no other on offer, but his real relationship was with money. And it seemed that making money only increased his desire for more. He was not mean – anything Raquel mentioned that she wanted, he would buy immediately. But the one thing the child truly needed – his undivided love and attention – was in short supply. Indeed, as Petrina told her friend Lisa, if it wasn't for Raquel, a different job, different lifestyle, would have claimed her already. However, a promise wasn't made to be broken, and she had truly meant it when she'd promised Carlita that she would take care of Raquel like her own. Carlita had clutched at Petrina's sleeve and drawn her closer to the bedside. The cancer in her liver already far too advanced for anything to be done, she'd known her death was inevitable. Petrina's promise had given the dying woman peace in her last hours. It was sacrosanct, at least for now, until Raquel was old enough to manage without her care. But the child was only seven years old. It would be years before that promise was fulfilled. Yes, she could break it, think about *her* needs. But she wouldn't – *couldn't* – do that. Petrina was a Catholic; there would be no peace in her soul if she abandoned Raquel.

'Tell Petrina all about it,' she whispered as Raquel burrowed against her, the sobs dwindling away, replaced now and again by a hiccup.

'Rachel's my friend at school.'

'Yes.'

'And I want her to be friends away from school, too. I want her to come and play with me here at home. Now I don't think she'll come again. The panther really frightened her.'

'I know. But when she gets home, she'll get over her fright. She'll realise that although it *did* frighten her a lot, the panther couldn't have hurt her. I'm sure she'll want to come and visit you again. I mean, you don't have to go into the cat house again, do you? You can play outside or even indoors if you want to. Now cheer up.'

Rubbing her eyes, Raquel slid off Petrina's lap. 'Can I help you make the pastry?'

'Of course you can, my little one. Just pop on an apron, and don't forget to wash your hands first.'

Petrina felt a satisfied, almost maternal glow inside her. By making these scones she wasn't just doing her job, she was helping to bring up a child – one who really needed her; just her. That alone made everything else in her life immaterial right now. Then, with Raquel suitably garbed in an outsized apron, hands washed and plunged into a bowl of flour beside her, Petrina felt secure enough to ask a potentially upsetting question about Rachel's mother.

'Maybe she could come too – you know, next time Rachel visits us.'

Raquel's head shook slowly. 'She can't.'

'Why not?'

Raquel stopped kneading the pastry. She lifted her face and gazed at Petrina. 'Because she's dead too. That's what makes us best friends.'

Her long blonde pigtail had escaped from her scarf and tossed around in the fierce wind as Rachel dashed after the two men. Jess, unsure of just what was happening, chased around, barking loudly. The rise of the hillside was finding the men out. Their progress had slowed under the unwieldy weight they were carrying.

The distance between them narrowed. Rachel reached the spot where the man had stumbled. There was a half-buried branch sticking up from between the tussocks. Glancing down to place her steps carefully and avoid it, she noticed three bags lying where the man had dropped his burden. They stood out against the grass: clear plastic filled with some white substance. She reached down and picked them up. They were quite heavy, yet surprisingly soft and squashy. So the men had not stolen a lamb. She'd misjudged them. The odd bundle obviously contained more of these strange packages.

'Hey,' she called out, 'you've dropped some.' Struggling to carry the slippery bags, she tore off her bobble hat. It was made of wool and could be stretched. Stuffing the packages into the hat made it a lot easier to carry them. She resumed her pursuit; not, now, to intercept them, but to return the three bags. She shouted again. This time they stopped and turned. She came to a halt and took one of the bags from her hat. Waving it high in the air, she yelled, the wind carrying her words, 'You've dropped some stuff.'

The men looked at each other. The taller one waved an arm and snapped at the other, 'Get her!' His voice was harsh, filled with menace.

Rachel felt a sharp stab of fear. Dropping her arm, she stuffed the bag back into her hat, turned and ran. Fear gave her the advantage, lending speed to her flying feet. Halfway down the slope she risked a swift glance behind her. There was only one man running after her, and she was drawing away from him. But she heard another bellow from the tall one.

'Grab her – don't let her get away!'

The man behind her redoubled his attempt to close the gap. 'Come here, you!'

Utterly terrified now, Rachel found a further burst of adrenaline and careered down the hillside, skidding and sliding in parts but managing to keep well ahead. The farm gateway was only a short distance away and, sobbing and screaming, she hurled herself the last few yards and all but fell into the yard.

'What the…?' Lennie, hearing her cries, lumbered out of the barn and swung her up into his arms. Rachel clung to him, still screaming hysterically and jabbing a finger behind her towards the hillside. 'Don't let him get me; please, please don't let him get me!'

'I've got you, little lamb. You're safe. Steady now.'

She buried her face in his old jacket that smelled strongly of sheep and sobbed with fright and relief.

'Let's get you inside, eh, find your dad?' Lennie carried her across the yard and through the back door into the kitchen. 'Mr Evans, Mr Evans,' he shouted, 'Rachel needs you.'

Kent came through at a run. 'What on earth's the matter?' He caught sight of Rachel's tear-streaked white face and held out his arms.

Letting go of Lennie's coat, she clutched Kent desperately. 'The man… the man…' she sobbed. 'He's going to get me. He said so.'

Kent's face hardened. 'What's all this, Lennie? What man?'

'Don't rightly know, Mr Evans. I was in the barn an' I heard her come screaming into the yard. She was pointing back up the hillside and saying, "Don't let him get me." That's as much as I knows.'

Kent nodded. 'Get the quad and get out there. Take Jess. See if you can find him. If you have trouble, set Jess on him. I can't leave Rachel in this state.'

'Don't you worry about me. You look after the little lamb. I'll take care of that bas…' Lennie caught himself just in time as he saw Rachel's eyes, wild and wide, on him. He patted her head. 'Steady now; your dad's here and he'll look after you.' Then, turning to Kent he said, in a grim voice totally unlike his usual gentle one, 'I'll sort it.'

From the safety of Kent's arms, Rachel watched Lennie stomp off across the farmyard, whistling to Jess as he went. A minute or two later, the quad bike hurtled out of the barn and off up the hillside.

'Come on, my sweetheart, let's get a flannel and wash your face,' Kent said, and carried her upstairs to the bathroom.

The cool water soothed her scarlet cheeks and removed the salty tearstains. He held her close and rocked her gently.

'There now, that's a lot better, isn't it?'

'Yes, Daddy.'

'Right, I think a mug of hot chocolate is called for, don't you?'

Rachel nodded and, wrapping her arms round his neck, allowed him to carry her back downstairs, sit her in his fireside armchair and fix her drink.

'Now,' Kent said when she'd finished sipping, 'are you OK to tell me what happened?'

She nodded. 'I ran up on the hill with Jess. I wanted to see the sheep. I got right to the top, but the sheep were out over the other side so I couldn't get to them. It was too far.'

'And...?'

'And then I saw them – two men, carrying a funny sort of bag thing with very long handles. It looked heavy. They were struggling up the far side of the wood with it.'

Kent nodded encouragement.

'I thought they'd found one of our lambs and were stealing it. You said all our lambs are precious and we can't afford to lose a single one.'

Kent groaned softly. 'OK, then what happened?'

Rachel told him the rest.

'So where are your bobble hat and the bags?'

'They must be in the yard. I dropped my hat when Lennie picked me up.'

'Come on, let's go and see if we can find them.'

They saw the hat straight away from the back doorstep.

'Stay there, Rachel, I'll get it.' Kent was back in swiftly. 'You're quite right. There are three plastic bags stuffed inside.' He tipped them out onto the kitchen table, and recoiled.

'What is it, Daddy? What's the matter?'

Kent took a deep breath and scooped them up again. 'I'll just put these away in the barn for safety. They're not ours. They belong to someone else.'

'But, Daddy—'

'No buts, Rachel. Out they go.' Then, thinking on his feet, he said, 'We mustn't risk damaging them. Y' know, like ripping the plastic open. OK?'

'Yes, Daddy.'

'Now, I suggest that while I do that, you go and watch television.'

'But what's inside the bags?' she persisted.

'I don't know, and it isn't any of our business.'

Obediently, Rachel slid down from the armchair and went through to the living room. Kent passed a shaking hand over his eyes. He'd lied to her; had to. He knew only too well what was inside the plastic bags. When Chloe had left, taking her vile drugs with her, he'd thought it was all over and that he would never again see drugs inside the farmhouse. He'd been wrong.

Those plastic bags were filled with cocaine.

FORTY-FOUR
2020

Daylight was fading. Inside the wood it was a dark dusk. The birds had already gone to their night perches, their heads beneath their wings. The larger nocturnal animals – foxes, badgers – were stirring below ground, nostrils quivering, picking up the scents borne on the wind. Hunger and thirst, their constant companions in this deepest, toughest part of the winter, insisted that each must leave the safety of their dens. Thin, bones prominent, their pelts and skins barely held their bodies together. It was imperative that they venture out to search for food.

Inside her tunnel beneath the fallen trees, Kala too was stirring. Her green eyes wide, pupils dilated to the maximum to trap whatever light was available, with muzzle lifted she quested the air currents. They carried the information she needed to assess the level of danger outside. Tonight she was even more zealous, remembering the noises and danger that had stalked the woods earlier. Eventually, satisfied that nothing was approaching, she dipped her head and began licking one of her cubs as it lay tucked snugly into her warm belly, her furry hind leg covering it. Her rasping tongue dragged at the skin and fur covering its head, lifting the little creature up with the force behind it. The cub mewed in protest, tiny paws flailing helplessly, but Kala took no notice of its protests and continued with her meticulous grooming, covering every inch from head to genitals and down to the tip of its tail. The cub's wriggling and mewling awakened its sibling, who took up the chorus and they formed a duet for a few minutes until, having completed the first cub's toilet, Kala repeated the process with the second. Well before she'd finished, the first cub sought out a teat and attached itself firmly, both front paws kneading determinedly, encouraging the precious flow of milk, sucking with a life-or-death effort – which of course it was. Without Kala and her mothering care, the cubs wouldn't survive. Just as eagerly, the second cub followed its sibling's example, clamping pink gums around another teat and sucking greedily. Kala purred gently, her own paws contracting and extending claws in pleasure, lay back, and the three cats sprawled in contented peace – one large female and one small one, plus one small male. The cubs were still blind, still vulnerable, but growing bigger and stronger all the time.

Although Kala appeared relaxed her instincts were keen. She was still feeling unsettled. Earlier in the day her sleep had been disturbed, starting with the sound of a helicopter circling above the wood. She'd listened as it flew lower, finally landing, its noisy rotors chattering to a stop. But the subsequent silence had been broken a short while later by men struggling through the brambles and undergrowth, twigs snapping beneath their feet. They'd been heading away from where she was holed up, so Kala had been content to remain where she was, dry and safe, protecting her cubs. The sounds had faded, she'd known they were no longer inside the wood, and she'd slid into a comfortable doze.

But later, she'd been awoken again. The men were back, snapping twigs and branches, shouting to each other. She lay motionless, apart from her large, rounded ears which twitched back and forth, catching all the noises, her lips drawn back from her fangs in a soundless snarl. Again she'd monitored the sounds of their withdrawal, but then her nostrils dilated, twitched and conveyed another message. There was another animal moving about; not the same smell as the prey scattered over the countryside beyond the wood, but a predator – one that could pose a threat to Kala and her family. All her senses were on red alert as she heard barking and a shrill, small human voice calling. Kala remained where she was, unsettled now, sensing possible discovery and danger. The voices and the sounds of running feet faded, and after a while she began to relax. She nuzzled her cubs, more to reassure herself than to soothe them – they were satiated and fast asleep. But then she'd heard the familiar roar of an engine and, aware of the speed at which it could travel, her fur had bristled, her tail fluffed, her eyes dilated. She waited, wrapped protectively around her babies; heard raised voices before the drumming roar of the helicopter drowned them out. As the noise grew deafeningly loud, Kala flattened her ears and snarled. The rotors made a heavy, continuous clattering in the cold air as the engine increased to maximum. Then the helicopter lifted and flew high into the sky, and the noise dwindled. Processing the sounds, assessing the threat, Kala lay curled around her cubs. The last sound she heard was a quad bike bouncing and clattering down the hillside, and then, at last, all was silent and peace had returned. Except Kala wasn't at peace. She knew what she had to do, but it wasn't time yet – not dark enough. However, the threat had subsided for now and she had succumbed to her weariness and gone to sleep.

Much later, with daylight fading, the sound of wood pigeons clattering into the trees above her den to roost had awoken Kala from her rest to face the demands of motherhood. But pleasurable though all the grooming and suckling was, the instinctive, wild part of her brain remembered the noises and the very real possibility of danger. However, her stomach growled with hunger. It was time to hunt. The last food she'd consumed had been the aborted lamb. But she was feeding cubs now. She needed a substantial meal.

Easing gently away from the dreaming cubs, Kala silently left the den and glided through the wood. Stopping first for a much-needed drink, she then prowled to the edge of the wood. Lying flat, concealed by the brambles, she surveyed the hillside, silvered now by the moon that was riding through the clouds in the night sky. But she didn't need to rely on her sight, excellent though that was; her nostrils told her all she needed to know. Away to her right, still lying in a partially dried and crusting pool of blood, was the body of the sheep she'd separated from the flock, chased, brought down and killed. Remaining motionless, she spent some time checking out the surrounding area. She was about to move forward through the undergrowth when a movement to the east of the corpse alerted her. She was not alone in seeking food. A furry red body slunk along low to the ground through the rough grass. Kala sniffed the air. A strong smell filled her nostrils and curled her muzzle into a silent snarl. The kill was hers by right. The interloper was not going to take it from her. Waiting, waiting until the very last second before the unsuspecting fox reached the dead sheep, she then launched herself forward in a charge of black fury, covering the ground between them at phenomenal speed. For a moment the fox froze in shock and fear. Before it could react, Kala leapt and seized the back of its neck, snapping its spine with one savage bite. It died without a sound, blood pumping from a severed artery, urine soaking its pelt with a rank stench, and then it was lying limp on the ground where she dropped it. Stiff-legged, she walked away from the dead fox and began to feast on the sheep.

Having assuaged the worst of her hunger, Kala squatted, all four paws on the ground, and swung her head, assessing the hillside. No scent of a possible further predator reached her nostrils. Nothing moved. Satisfied, she rose, straddled the remains and, raising her head high, lifted the sheep into the air. In her natural jungle habitat she would have deployed her massive strength and carried the carcass up into a tree. Now, dragging it between her front legs, she padded silently away, out of the dangerous moonlight and into the black wood.

FORTY-FIVE
2020

Unable to believe his luck in escaping a bullet through his skull, Isooba stayed exactly where he was, scarcely breathing, nervous sweat soaking his shirt under his arms and pouring down his face. But as the sounds of twigs snapping and undergrowth being forced aside died away, reality hit him. They had gone; they'd *really* gone, and he didn't expect them back. One or two of the cocaine packages had apparently burst over the cabin floor, but not enough to warrant a return by Smith and Gregson. He was *alive*! He lay back in the pilot's seat, sobbing like a child, totally spent. And, as his sobbing slowly ceased, he was unable to keep himself from crashing out, the need for sleep overcoming his willpower to stay awake to face whatever came next.

It was almost dark when he regained consciousness. But high overhead, a bright, silvery moon shone down through the trees, enough for him to see his flask lying beside the seat. Unscrewing the top, he drank greedily, feeling the blessed relief of water cooling his throat. A pity the flask wasn't still full of coffee. A drink of that right now would have given him the kick he badly needed.

He knew that, despite the food he'd eaten, he was weakening. His head was splitting, and spikes of pain shot along his ribs where Smith had booted him. Reaching for his overnight bag, he grabbed a couple of the cakes Mara had baked for him. He was feeling curiously light-headed and sick, and yet at the same time he was hungry. Cramming them into his mouth and chewing furiously, he welcomed the sticky sweetness, knowing that his blood sugar must be very low now.

But he had to hang on. One massive danger had been overcome. If he could evade Kala's ravenous jaws – and he was sure that by now she would be ravenous; one wood pigeon was just an appetiser to a cat of her size – all he'd need to do would be to stay alive; just hang on until someone found him. And since Smith and Gregson had forced their way through the wood, smashing off branches and cutting back brambles, they must have left a trail. It would be noticed sooner or later – had to be. Isooba's job was to keep going until then.

He finished the cakes and picked up an apple. His fingers felt for the paring knife he'd slid inside his boot. Despite the circumstances, a grin split his face. 'All home comforts, eh?' he murmured. 'Well, all I'm going to get until I get home to Mara.' As he peeled the fruit, taking care not to cut his fingers in the gloom, his thoughts were all for his wife and when he might see her again. Crunching the crispy apple, relishing the sharp tang on his tongue, he gave a grunt of exasperation. What the hell was he thinking of? He'd been so focused on surviving his encounter with Smith and Gregson that it had driven everything else out of his head. Maybe by now Mara had found his text message. She might even have sent a reply. He'd left the phone switched off since he'd tried to contact her, many hours ago now. There was no means of recharging it here in the middle of the countryside. But it was safe to turn it on again now that Rawson would have flown the men home to the Wild Ark.

With shaking fingers, Isooba fumbled in the gloom until he found the right button to turn on the mobile. Two beeps, and then the screen lit up with a text from Mara. His SOS had got through and been answered. Elation burnt through him like a treble whisky. His headache seemed to vanish instantly, as did the pain in his ribs. Nothing registered except the words Mara had written:

God hrd my prayers! So relieved. Bless U, my love. Hve told English police to find U. They R checkg location. Hold on, Anan. Big love, Mara.

He gave a wild cry of joy, then read and reread her message several times, tears rolling down his cheeks, this time of happiness and hope. To save the battery he switched off the phone again and, hugging it to his chest, closed his eyes and once more let blessed sleep carry him away before his pains reasserted themselves.

Kala heard him. She froze, mid-chew, blood staining her whiskers, claws buried in the sheep's flesh. But there were no more cries. After two or three minutes, she lowered her head again and resumed tearing at the carcass. It had been some time since she had eaten a full meal, and she intended to take advantage of the largesse in front of her. Finally satisfied, she dragged the remains of the sheep into the undergrowth, left it there and padded silently back to her den. Her food intake would provide a rich supply of milk for her babies. They were still asleep, twitching gently as they dreamed. Carefully, Kala curled her lithe body around them and fell asleep herself.

It was nearing midnight when she awoke. She scented the air, and listened then eased her way to the entrance of the den, where she halted, checking with eyes, nose and instinct for possible predators. Nothing was stirring. Padding cautiously to her usual watering hole, she drank deeply. Then she was away through the wood, bounding at full speed over the hillside heading east. Her wounds healed, her muscles rippling with the delight of extended movement, she covered the ground rapidly, slowing only when she came to the boundary trees and hedge above what had been the old railway line between Nottingham and Grantham. Axed decades before by Richard Beeching, it had fallen into neglect. It cut through the countryside and continued east for several miles. The metal rails were long gone, as were the supporting timbers, leaving only occasional flint stones to hint at times past. The sides of the railway cutting rose some thirty feet or more, the banks overgrown with bushes and scrub. Pockmarked by rabbit holes, some larger excavations into the red-clay sides indicated that foxes and badgers had been digging out tunnels and caves.

Kala slowed and trotted along, searching for what she so urgently needed. At one point she froze and became just one more black shadow amongst the thick undergrowth, watching vehicles pass along the bridge spanning the railway cutting. At ground level, the bridge formed a long black tunnel. Edging closer, she snaked along, her belly skimming the stony floor, the arch high above her and the brick walls extending ten metres or more in front. She reached the other end of the tunnel and halted in the concealing darkness. A narrow gorge ran away at an angle, choked and cloaked by almost impenetrable brambles and stunted hawthorns. In turn, this led into a disused culvert. Constructed more than half a century ago, its sides were made of brickwork, through the mortar joints of which some determined roots and weeds protruded. The entrance was more than half blocked by a dislodged boulder. Kala approached it cautiously. The culvert had been built to last, and although some of the brick facing had crumbled away over scores of years, despite the storm and the winter weather it was still firmly intact and, most importantly, dry inside. She inspected every foot of it and discovered a second opening at the far end. Largely obscured by a long-ago fall of shale and earth from the outside bank, and with deeply rooted undergrowth ensuring stability, it was just accessible – an escape route if needed. The culvert offered all the space the cubs would need as they grew. Satisfied, Kala retraced her way through its length to the entrance. It no longer provided a service for human beings but it was ideal for her purposes.

Squeezing between the brick side and the boulder, she trotted back down the old railway line. The line led from the outskirts of Bingham, close to Redcliffe in one direction, and in the opposite direction through the countryside towards Grantham. At this end, though Kala was unaware of it, she was very close to Harby, with the Belvoir Woods just a handful of miles away. Exiting the cutting, she bounded across country back to her cubs. On the hillside above the wood she stood checking that she was unobserved before making her way down through the trees. Her old den had given her the safety she'd so urgently needed to give birth. But it was no longer safe.

Entering the den, she found that the cubs were still fast asleep. She bent her head, opened her jaws and clamped them securely around the loose pelt at the back of the male cub's neck. Backing out of the den, she carried the cub, still asleep, high and safe in her mouth. His weight was nothing to her and did little to slow her progress. She returned to the railway line, the boulder by the culvert entrance, and took the cub inside and laid him down. For her, the next part of the operation was the hardest: she must leave the male and return to fetch his sister. They both needed her. Kala did not waste a second. Her powerful muscles propelled her back to the wood and the old den. Her jaws closed around the second cub's neck, and she carried her, swinging slightly and whimpering, yet secure, to her new den.

She was within a few yards of the hidden entrance to the culvert when it suddenly began to rain hard. Big drops splashed onto her dark pelt with a vengeance and she had to pad through puddles that were already filling up. Beside the boulder there was a large depression in the ground. It was already forming a perfect watering hole. Flicking the water from her paws, she crept deep inside the culvert and placed the little female beside her brother. Lying down, sides heaving with her exertions, she licked and licked both cubs, reassuring, cleansing, soothing them. They mewled a little but, needing only their mother, were indifferent to their new surroundings and soon fell asleep.

Only then did Kala allow herself to rest. Satisfied now, she felt no unease, only contentment and peace. There would be no intrusive noises, no men and no predators to find them here. They were all safe.

FORTY-SIX
2020

Phillip awoke from an afternoon nap that had lasted far longer than he'd intended. It was getting on for 5.30 – time he lit the oven; it took ages to warm up these days.

Going into the kitchen, he noticed the rain clouds picking up in the west. The forecast said they were due for a deluge during the night. He stood pondering the weighty problem of what to have for dinner. Living by himself, it was entirely his choice. He went out to the garage and lifted the lid of the chest freezer. The first pack he lifted out was frozen lamb chops. They'd do… then he hesitated. Perhaps not – an image of the dead sheep lying, covered in blood, on the wet grass came into his mind, killing his appetite instantly. No, definitely not. He thrust the pack back and took out a vegetable lasagne instead. It was enough to convert you to vegetarianism, seeing sights like that. He didn't know how Kent coped with all the tough situations he had to face. Once again, he felt a satisfying warmth inside at the knowledge that his life's work had been completed successfully. His time was now his own, and he was determined to include Kent in his next game of golf. He wondered briefly about Kent's wife. Obviously she had gone up north and taken the child with her, but was there any chance that she and Kent would get back together? Phillip shook his head at his own foolishness. He was just an old romantic.

He opened the oven and slid in the lasagne. There was time to start the crossword while his meal cooked. The landline rang just as he closed the oven door – a strange time for anyone to be ringing him, unless of course it was one of those infernal sales pitches or, worse, a scam. He certainly wasn't expecting a call.

'Phillip? Smith here. How are you? Good, I hope.'

Even before the man identified himself, Phillip recognised his voice.

'Yes, I'm fine, thanks. And you?'

'Oh, yes. Now, could I ask you a question?'

'OK, shoot.'

'I believe there's a golf course quite near you – you mentioned it once before, when we met at North Shore?'

'Yes.'

'It was flooded, I think you told me?'

'Yes. The course I usually play on is at Redcliffe-on-Trent.'

'That's the one.' Smith chuckled. 'Now, the farmer whose land runs parallel to that – you did tell me his name but, stupidly, I've forgotten it.'

'Yes, he's a friend of mine, actually.'

'And his name?' Smith persisted.

Phillip hesitated. There was something about Smith's voice: an edge to it, probing, almost intrusive. He didn't like it. 'Why do you need to know? I mean, I'm not sure… the data protection regulations—'

'Come, Phillip. This is between friends, isn't it?'

'But why do you need to know? Is there something I can help you with?'

'You can help by giving me his name.'

'I really shouldn't have said anything before. I've always played by the rules, and I wouldn't want to break any laws.'

'Well, let me just ask you if he has a child, a girl? Do you know that? If this man's a friend of yours, I think you would know the answer.'

Phillip's immediate urge was to close the conversation. He hadn't liked the demanding nature of Smith's question – sugar-coated, of course, but now his instincts were on red alert. No way was he going to answer. A child's safety could be in jeopardy. 'Look, I'm sorry, but I really feel I can't give out any information.'

'I'm sorry too. You see, I think I might have something that belongs to your friend.' Smith's voice was persuasive now.

'If you tell me what it is, maybe I'll know if it's his,' Phillip parried.

'Very well.' Smith gave an exaggerated sigh. 'It's a whistle – a dog whistle.'

Now Phillip, far from being reassured, was even more disturbed. The only reason Smith could be in possession of Kent's dog whistle was if he'd been in the vicinity of the farm at some point. He could think of no other explanation. He'd have to have words with Kent; ask if he'd lost a whistle and, if so, just where he'd lost it. Maybe Smith *had* found it somewhere else. It was possible. However, his insistence in expecting Phillip to pass on the little girl's details heightened his concern. His palms began to sweat, and the receiver felt slippery. In mentioning the village by name he'd said too much already. 'Look, I'll ask the farmer myself, OK? Then if he has no objection I'll get back to you. Must leave it at that. My dinner's cooked and waiting. Must go, bye.'

He put down the receiver, his hand shaking. Then he remembered that he'd already mentioned Kent by name when he'd updated Smith on the panther's kill, and how he'd sweated buckets afterwards, thinking of the information he'd trotted out and the regulations he'd breached. He was all kinds of a fool. Thank God Smith had forgotten Kent's name. But had he, or was that just a ploy to learn about the child? What the hell was it all about? It certainly wasn't just about a whistle. Then in his mind he heard Kent's voice: *The wind can blow away my voice.* He'd been talking about Jess's whistle that he'd placed in his pocket together with the measuring tape. Had he lost it when they'd been bent over measuring the print in the mud? Maybe, maybe not, but if he had and Smith had found it, that meant that Smith had been up on the hillside. And that was certainly Phillip's fault because he'd told him about the kill.

He took out a handkerchief and wiped sweat from his forehead. He'd never live with himself if any harm came to Kent or his daughter because of his loose mouth. When he'd eaten, he'd phone Kent and tell him about Smith's questions. At least then if anything did blow up he wouldn't be caught unawares. He should be alerted that he needed to keep a close eye on his daughter. Going over to his drinks cabinet, Phillip poured a generous whisky. He was not in the habit of drinking at this early hour but he was in need of a strengthener.

'Three bags; there were only three bags. OK, they were worth several thousand, but are they worth the risk of going back and getting caught?' Gregson was doing his best to calm Smith down. The man's temper was in the stratosphere.

'You don't get it, do you?' Smith slammed a fist on the top of his desk. 'It's not just the value of the drugs; that child *saw* us. She could identify us to the police. Have you thought of that?'

'So what you're saying is, we have to shut her up? And how do we do that, eh? Kill her?'

'Until we find out her name, we don't know for sure that she lives at the farm, do we? She could just be a child from the village.'

'That's true.'

'And I could have said anything to Lemmingham as an excuse, and I had to go and say something so bloody stupid as a dog whistle. Places us right there on the man's land.'

'Maybe he won't join the dots.'

Smith ignored him. He was furiously searching his pocket. 'And you're not going to believe this. It's ironic. You know what? I've only gone and lost the fucking whistle.'

The whisky helped. Phillip went to the kitchen and dished up his meal. Sitting down, he began to eat. The food was good but he barely tasted it. His thoughts squirrelled around, rerunning his last conversation with Kent. Although Rachel no longer lived at the farm, Kent had said that he was expecting her to visit in the next day or so. How ghastly if any harm came to her, and in the very place where she would feel the safest. Phillip gave up picking at his food and pushed his plate from him. It was no good putting off making the call. He was dreading Kent's reaction. The risk was definitely attributable to Phillip's loose talk. Not having realised the threat was no excuse. For the first time he understood the principle behind the annoying data protection laws. For goodness' sake, he should have known better. He groaned.

Picking up the plate, he scraped the uneaten food into the bin, chastising himself for wasting it, and was about to put the plate in the washing-up bowl when there was a very loud knock on the front door. And 'knock' was an understatement; it was more a loud banging – the sort that demanded immediate attention. Phillip hastened to open the door. Two uniformed police officers stood there. Shock hit him in the solar plexus like a physical blow.

'Mr Phillip Lemmingham?'

'Yes?' With an effort he managed to get the reply out through dry lips.

An ID card was flashed towards him. 'I am DC Dunstone and my colleague is DC Ireling.'

Phillip nodded apprehensively. 'What's happened?'

DC Dunstone answered. 'It would help if we could come in, please, sir.'

'Oh, yes, of course.' He showed them through to the lounge. 'Please have a seat. Can I offer you some tea, coffee?'

The policeman shook his head. 'No thank you, sir.'

'So,' Phillip said, spreading his hands, 'what is wrong?'

'We need to ask you some questions regarding your work.' Before Phillip could protest that he was now retired, Dunstone continued. 'We understand you were employed as an air traffic controller. Is that correct?'

'Yes. Before I retired, I worked at Nottingham East Midlands Airport.'

Both policemen nodded and it was noted down in the younger man's notebook. Phillip licked his lips. He had no idea why they were here, or where this was leading. The policemen exchanged a glance, and then Dunstone spoke.

'We are investigating an incident that occurred on Sunday – your last shift, we understand?'

'Yes. I worked until about seven o'clock.'

'And were any other controllers working alongside you?'

'Well, of course there were others, but the man next to me was a new recruit, Mickey. He was taken ill with the flu – a lot of the workforce had caught it – and knocked off early.'

'So, that left you on your own during the last part of your shift?'

'Yes.'

DC Dunstone leaned forward. 'Is it possible that a plane could have flown past – under the radar, perhaps – and not been logged?'

Phillip was very pleased he was sitting down. The officer's words pierced him like a blade. He actually felt physically ill. 'What you're saying...' He swallowed hard. 'You mean... did I miss seeing a plane?'

'Well, basically, yes, sir.'

'I have never been accused of this before, never. Not in all my twenty-seven years on the job. My record is above reproach—'

'I'm sure it is, sir. But we have received a telephone call that seems to indicate that there may well have been a plane – almost certainly flying illegally, below radar – that came down somewhere in the immediate locality.'

'You're talking about a crash?'

'Yes, sir. It would seem so.'

Phillip shook his head in disbelief. The hurt inside was unbelievable: so much for his pride in completing a blameless work record. Coming on top of his anxiety about passing on Kent's information to Smith, it rocked him to the core. 'I… I'd like a drink of water…'

'Stay where you are, sir. I'll fetch you a glass.'

Phillip leaned forward, putting his head in his hands. He'd never fainted in his life but right now it seemed a distinct possibility.

FORTY-SEVEN
2020

The officers had left eventually. Phillip had seen them out to their car through the driving rain. He'd come clean; told them about passing on Kent's personal details during his game with Smith, and about Smith's continued interest in Kent and his little daughter. If anything bad happened now it would still be Phillip's fault alone, but at least the police would be on the alert. The only thing he could do now was to put Kent in the picture. And it wouldn't do to tell him over the phone. That was the coward's way. It had to be a face-to-face job, however much he shrank from the idea.

Phillip reached for the phone. 'Hello, Kent. Is everything well?' He nodded with relief. 'Good. However, I've something to tell you, and I'm sorry but it can't wait. Can I drive over now?'

Twenty minutes later he was knocking on the farmhouse door, hearing Jess give several warning barks.

Kent opened the door. 'What a night. Come on in, Phillip. It must be serious to get you out in this weather.'

'If I hadn't come, I wouldn't have slept tonight.'

'Really – that bad?'

'Yes. And I've only myself to blame.'

Kent ushered him through to the living room, where a bright fire blazed cheerfully. 'Now, you'll have a whisky, yes?'

'Yes, I could do with one, thanks.' Phillip accepted the chunky glass and took a quick swallow.

'So, what's so urgent?'

'First, is Rachel here? You said something about her coming to stay.'

'She certainly is. Her school rang me this morning. They asked if I could fetch her straight away as they were being closed down because of an outbreak of measles. We got back earlier this afternoon.'

'And is she all right?'

'I haven't noticed any symptoms yet.'

'No, no, that's not what I mean. I have to tell you, Kent, she's in danger. Well, I *think* she's in danger.'

'From whom?' Kent frowned and poured himself a small whisky.

Phillip was about to tell him when there was a knock on the kitchen door. Jess voiced another series of warning barks.

'Excuse me.'

Kent left Phillip sitting by the fire, nursing his drink, and went through to the kitchen. Phillip could hear him quietening the bitch and then opening the door. There was a prolonged murmur of voices and then Kent reappeared, followed by a black woman. Phillip set down his glass and stood up to greet her.

'Phillip, this is Mrs Isooba—'

'Mara, please; call me Mara.'

'Hello, Mara.' They shook hands.

'She's just driven in from East Midlands Airport.'

'That's right, my flight landed earlier this evening – from Nairobi.'

Phillip nodded, at a total loss now.

Kent said, 'Phillip has just retired from his job as an air traffic controller at East Midlands.'

'Ah!' Mara exclaimed. 'Were you on duty on Sunday afternoon?'

Phillip nodded. 'I was.'

She clutched at his sleeve. 'My husband, he was flying a plane around then. Did you see it? His plane,' she caught back a sob, 'it crashed.'

Phillip shook his head. 'I think what I have to tell Kent includes you too, so I'd better tell both of you now.' He glanced across towards Kent.

'First of all, let me get you a stiff drink, Mara,' Kent said. 'And come closer to the fire – you're shaking with cold; get yourself warmed up.'

'Thank you.' She sat down near Phillip and accepted the whisky gratefully. The glass clattered against her teeth as she took a sip. 'Please, Phillip, go on. I need to find my Anan, and I need to do so urgently.'

Beginning from the moment when he'd officially finished his last shift and congratulated himself on twenty-seven years' unblemished service, Phillip continued until the point when he'd said goodbye to the police officers half an hour ago. Kent and Mara sat in silence, listening intently.

'Thank you.' Mara dabbed at her tears. 'My Anan, he was flying a plane for this man, this Mr Smith. He is very good pilot. It was transporting something illegal, I think. He refused to tell me. Wouldn't say any details, you understand? "For your safety, Mara," he said. "You don't know, you can't say, you not involved."'

Both men nodded. They understood.

'So, how did you miss seeing the plane?' Mara asked Phillip. 'That was your job.'

'Like the officer said, it was flying illegally, below radar so it wouldn't register on our screens.'

'There was a massive storm going on,' Kent put in. 'Anan could well have got into difficulties.'

'Yes.' She nodded. 'That is possible.'

'But how come you think his plane came down near here?' Phillip said.

'Because my Anan send me a text message. After airport, he describe the River Trent and say he followed it; had to increase height to clear houses and a quarry, a hillside with sheep; then he flew low over woods and… he crashed. But he's not dead, not dead.' She blew her nose in a defiant gesture and took a gulp of whisky.

'But,' Phillip said, very gently, 'planes that crash—'

'Oh, I know. They crash and burn.' She fixed her gaze on him. 'But his plane, it didn't burn; he say not.'

'And you told the English police all this?'

Mara turned a tear-stained face towards Kent. 'Yes. They say they trace location, find him.'

'That would be through the mobile phone network,' Kent agreed.

She nodded. 'They say they ring me, let me know. But soon as I report all of these facts, I cannot wait. I get on plane. I *must* find him. Will you help me, please?'

Kent and Phillip exchanged a glance, then nodded in unison.

'Absolutely. But do you have any idea whereabouts the plane crashed?' Phillip said.

'No.'

'So, really,' said Phillip, 'we are in the hands of the police on that.'

Mara nodded miserably. 'Yes.'

'When did you get the text – today?'

'Yes, it came through and I read it, but then Anan's mobile was switched off. I couldn't speak to him, only leave a message.'

Kent rose, went over to the heavy velvet curtains and drew them aside. 'It's still lashing it down out there. To be honest,

Mara, even if we get up a search party, there's no way we'll find your husband in the dark. The police could use a heat-seeking helicopter, of course, if they have some idea of where to look, but I think that's why you haven't had a callback yet: they haven't got a trace on your husband's phone yet. Reception's a bit in and out up there. And he could have switched it off to conserve the battery.'

'In his message,' Phillip asked, 'did he say he was in any immediate danger?'

Again the men exchanged a swift glance. Neither of them was going to say anything about the panther.

'He was trapped, he said that, but he did not mention injuries, no.'

'Has he any food – water, even?'

A beam lit up Mara's entire face. 'I pack him lots of food, yes. In his overnight bag.'

'And do you think he can access it – if he is trapped, I mean?'

'Oh, yes. I *know* he has. You see, I pack the phone at bottom of bag, then flask of coffee and then the food. So I know if he has found the phone, he also found the food.'

'Well, in that case, I'd say he can last until tomorrow at least,' Kent said, pointing to the grim weather outside. 'We stand a chance in daylight, I reckon, but tonight…' He shook his head.

'Yes.' The smile left Mara's face. 'You are right.'

'Unless the police ring you during the night, of course; give you some idea of where he is.'

She nodded.

'In the meantime, I suggest you stay here, have some food and get some sleep.'

'But,' she began to protest, 'I couldn't—'

'Yes, you could,' Kent interjected. 'Look, if the police contact you during the night, we need to know. If the plane ditched somewhere on my land,' he waved a hand towards the window, 'I'm the one with the best knowledge of the area.'

Phillip nodded. 'That's true enough.'

'So, let's get you some hot soup – you must be hungry. Or, if you prefer something more substantial, my farmworker's mum came up earlier and brought us a fish pie. And believe me, her cooking is legendary. Then when you've eaten, I'll show you to the guest room and you can get some sleep, eh?'

'You are so kind, thank you. Yes, I agree, we cannot find my Anan tonight; it's not possible. But in the morning, yes, we go looking for him?'

'Yes,' Kent assured her.

'And now,' Phillip said, getting to his feet, 'I'll push off home. But do ring me at any time if you hear from the police and I'll be straight over to help.'

'We will.' Kent went to the back door with him. 'Drive safely, Phillip. It's a pig of a night.'

'I will.' Phillip lowered his voice. 'And… we're keeping quiet, are we, about the panther?'

'Oh, God, yes. The poor woman's in a bad enough state as it is.'

'Let's hope it's long gone, then. Goodnight.'

Kent watched him slosh through the puddles that pocked the farmyard and, as the car fired up, headlights sweeping the gateway, waved him off.

In his office at the Wild Ark, Smith lifted the whisky bottle again and waved it at Gregson, who nodded and held out his empty glass.

Smith poured them both another drink. 'So, what's the best we can do right now? I'd say we need to recover those three bags of cocaine. It's not so much their value; more that they link us to this whole bloody mess. Remember, we left Isooba there to die. But there's always an outside chance that the panther will sod off, isn't there? I mean, she's pregnant. How will that pan out? Does it make her more likely to stay put, or take off?'

'Difficult question. Wherever she is, I'd lay money on her not going very far. Don't forget, she's had the trauma of the plane crash and she may be injured for all we know. And she's heavy with cubs. No, I'd say she'll stay somewhere in the vicinity.'

Smith frowned, swirling his glass. 'I'm beginning to think we should have finished Isooba while we had the chance. Not necessarily shot him – we could have just bashed his head in.'

'Oh, yes? And when they found the plane, and the body – which they will, given time – a post-mortem would prove that the head wound was inflicted some time after he crashed. Anyway, by now, even if Kala hasn't finished the job, I'd say he's well on the way to developing gangrene or sepsis.'

'So, are you saying we should finish him or not? Dead men tell no tales, you know.'

Gregson, frowning, took a swig of whisky. 'Be safer if he *was* dead, wouldn't it? He links us with the illegal animal importation *and* the drugs. Let's eliminate that link. If Kala hasn't finished him, we could, say, use a branch to smash his skull, leave it lying there; that way they'll think it was brought down in the wind after the crash. Job done.'

'Don't forget the child. She's a witness. *And* she's got the bags of cocaine.'

'Look, we could do for Isooba, then try and locate the bags. If the child lives at the farm down from the wood, and it's an odds-on certainty that she does, we could raid the farm, demand they hand over the cocaine and be away again in the chopper before they can stop us. They won't be able to prove anything.'

'Hmm...' Smith stared at the spirit in his glass, mulling over what Gregson had said. 'Yes, I reckon it makes sense. At least we'll be covering our tracks. There'll be no hard evidence left.' He lifted the glass and drained the whisky, then, going over to the window, shook his head in disgust. 'Can't do anything about it tonight; not in this blasted weather. So, tomorrow morning?'

Gregson nodded. 'And to make the odds even better, I shall be taking the Beretta with me. Just to be on the safe side. I mean, Kala could turn up, and, like you said, dead men don't talk.'

FORTY-EIGHT

2020

Kent was on the train again, returning from a posting abroad. He could feel the blessedly cool air through the partly open window, the clattering rhythm rolling him gently from side to side; very soothing after the traumas he'd endured in Afghanistan.

But then the anxiety began to build. It was an anxiety that increased as the train sped onward, mile after mile, towards its destination. They were approaching a level crossing. Kent could see the road running away on either side, the wide gates held high and open to allow the train access. And just beyond was a row of cottages fronting a side road, down which a leather-clad youth was walking a black pit bull. The dog strained on the end of a metal chain; the youth leaned back, trying to hang on to it. Down the sloping garden path from one of the cottages came a young girl on a scooter. No older than five or six, she was wearing a pale pink dress, her fair plaits flying in the wind as she furiously propelled the scooter using one foot. Kent could see her very clearly. A gleeful smile on her face, she sent the scooter flying along the path towards the gateway... the open gateway.

And then everything went into slow motion. The pit bull straining along the pavement, the child going far too fast on a collision course, the accident a split second away. And Kent – transfixed with horror, stomach churning and witness to it all – was stuck aboard the train, unable to do a thing to prevent the disaster. The child overshot the path, zooming out into the road. The scooter rammed into the big dog. The child began screaming. Then the dog was on her. Big jaws snapped at her throat; blood fountained out, staining the pink dress with scarlet; and her screams were cut off. In seconds, it was over, and the train was already away down the track.

Kent woke with a jerk and instinctively flung himself sideways, leaning over the side of the bed, prepared to vomit. It didn't happen. He sat with fists clenched, taking deep breaths. This was his recurring nightmare, always followed by his stomach emptying violently, uncontrollably… until this morning. As the sweat slowly dried on his forehead, he lay back against the pillow and replayed the memory of the panther, its jaws snapping at his and Rachel's faces, the strengthened glass a barrier between them. He'd dreaded the nightmare returning; known that the previous afternoon's events would prompt it – and they had. But the fact that they hadn't been injured by the snapping jaws had broken the sequence of events in his subconscious. He knew he'd never have the nightmare again.

He lay still for a few moments, recovering, before remembering that he had a visitor. Mara Isooba was staying in his guest room. He looked at his clock – it was barely half past six. Outside his bedroom window he could hear the relentless drumming of the rain – it seemed to have been raining for the whole of the winter. He dressed quickly and hurried down to the kitchen.

Mara was already up and making tea and coffee. 'I didn't know which you preferred, Mr Evans.'

'Kent, please. And I like tea, thanks. Did you hear from the police?'

She shook her head.

'Never mind; we'll get out on the hills shortly. If your husband crashed on my land I'm quite sure I can locate the plane.'

'You think so?' Mara's eyes filled with tears.

'Yes,' Kent said firmly. 'Now, help yourself to some breakfast, and when Lennie shows up we'll take the quad bike and quarter the land.'

Behind them the kitchen door opened and Rachel walked in, rubbing her eyes sleepily. 'Hi, Dad... oh...' She spotted Mara.

'Ah, yes. Mara, this is my daughter, Rachel. Rachel, this lady is Mrs Isooba from Africa.'

'Hello,' Rachel said shyly.

'Mrs Isooba is staying in the guest room for a little while.'

'Are you hurt?' Rachel peered up into Mara's face. 'You're crying – what's the matter?'

'Just grown-up stuff; nothing for you to trouble over.' Mara took out a tissue and dabbed her eyes. 'There, see, no more tears. Your father is helping me.'

'To do what? Can I help?'

'Mrs Isooba's husband has got lost, Rachel; he may be somewhere on the farmland. Lennie and I are going out to look for him soon.'

'Can I come too?'

'No, little one.' Mara shook her head. 'I don't think so.'

'You stay with Mrs Isooba at the farm.'

'But can I go out to play soon? I want to play with Jess.'

Kent smiled. 'Yes, of course you can.'

There was a tap on the back door and Lennie came in.

Kent did the introductions. 'We'll be going up the hill straight away. Mrs Isooba's husband is missing. We're trying to find him.'

Lennie was about to open his mouth to query this but Kent dived in quickly.

'Tell you all about it on the way, OK?'

'Sure, Mr Evans. Good job the rain's easing off now.'

Mara grasped Kent's hand. 'Find him for me, please?'

'We'll do our very best. If he is out there somewhere, we will find him. I have my mobile with me. If you hear anything from the police, ring me straight away. I've written down the number for you.' He gave her a piece of paper. 'And if you can't get through, keep on trying; the reception can be variable.'

'I will.' Mara nodded. 'Soon as I hear.'

'Good. OK then, we'll get off.' Kent drained his mug. 'Be a good girl, Rachel, and help Mrs Isooba. I'll be home as soon as I can. Right, then, Lennie, get the quad out, please.'

Although it had eased in the middle of the night, towards dawn the rain had suddenly grown heavier – much heavier. A small rivulet ran along the length of the stricken Cessna. Fat drops struck the fuselage like machine-gun fire.

The noise woke Isooba. His eyelids fluttered open. Clouds had obscured the moon and it was pitch black. As consciousness returned, so too did pain. Hot stabs shot through his brain, creating bright points of light inside his eyes. His head felt about to burst from the pressure inside. He groaned. He was cold – more than cold, he was shaking uncontrollably all over; except for his legs, which remained inert. Despite being surrounded by water, his mouth and throat were on fire, sandpaper dry and rough. He groped around and found his flask. Tipping it between his lips, he felt the water slide, cool and soothing, down his throat and drank deeply. It provided some temporary respite from at least one of his torments. But all the time his eyes scanned around him – pointless, really, because he could see next to nothing in the dark. However, the darkness would provide the panther with all the cover she needed to go hunting, and he could very well be her prey. What was it they always said – flight or fight? Well, in his circumstances flight was impossible, which just left fight. He smiled, a bitter, twisted little smile – he had nothing to fight with, except a four-inch paring knife. Against the claws and fangs of a ten-stone cat it would be laughable.

He had no idea of the time; no idea how close dawn was and how much of the night he'd survived. Then he remembered his mobile phone. He'd checked it before crashing out and had fallen asleep holding it close to his heart – it held love from Mara. During the night, it had slid from his feeble grasp, but it was now resting safely between his knees. Fumbling for the power button, he pressed it and the mobile sprang to life, glowing in the dark like a guiding candle. 6.30. Morning wasn't far away. With trembling fingers, he tapped in Mara's mobile number. There was no connection. Isooba pushed down the desolation he felt and lay back once more, clutching the phone to his chest – he was going to leave it on now. Although the battery must be almost flat, the light was comforting in his dark bubble of pain and fear. And he could keep on trying, see if he could get through. OK, the battery wouldn't last for much longer, but hopefully it would be long enough.

Pain flared all over his body. Despite the cold, his face felt scorching hot. Although dizzy and light-headed, he was still rational enough to realise that he was probably dying. It was more than likely that blood poisoning had set in. He felt very bad indeed. But there was nothing he could do. Unless someone found him today, he knew that, even without the threat of being mauled by the panther, he wouldn't last another night out here.

The light from the phone was only strong enough to illuminate his immediate surroundings… but then it seemed to be joined by a further bright light; one that glinted to his left. He squinted. The flow of water along the plane had floated something towards him, and now whatever it was had hit a piece of jutting fuselage and got stuck. Cautiously, ignoring the flaring pains in his left arm and ribs, he reached sideways. His fingers managed to close around the object and he lifted it up into the light from the mobile. For a moment or two he pondered what it could be. Then he recognised it. He had a similar one himself, back in Africa. Mara was very keen on dogs. This was a dog whistle. His spirits lifted a little. He now had two items that could help him to seek rescue. Placing the whistle between his lips, he blew it, hard. There was no sound – he hadn't expected to hear any. This was a whistle that only dogs could hear, their hearing being so much more acute than human beings'. But if there was a dog anywhere nearby, it was odds on that it would come to find him. Even so, it was an act of faith. He had to believe that the whistle still worked, because there was no way he could check.

Having done all he could, Isooba, clutching the phone against his chest, was content to wait out his fate. But, with the whistle still clamped between his lips, every few minutes he continued to blow hard upon it. He just needed to hang on.

FORTY-NINE
2020

Kent finished fastening his waxed jacket, shoved his mobile phone into the inside pocket and glanced out of the kitchen window. The quad bike was waiting by the yard gate, engine ticking over, Lennie in the driving seat. The rain had eased.

He swept Rachel up into his arms and gave her a kiss. 'Be back as soon as I can, my sweetheart. Hold the fort; you're in charge.' He set her down.

With a wide grin, she straightened to attention and snapped up her right arm, fingers extended stiffly, fingertips to temple. 'Aye aye, Cap'n.' Then she rather spoilt the image by dissolving into giggles.

Turning to Mara, Kent said, 'Stick with it, Mara. Man the phone.'

Bereft of words, Mara nodded.

Jess watched Kent open the porch door and pull on his wellingtons and gloves. Then she was at his heels.

Kent paused. 'No, Jess.'

Wide-eyed with bewilderment, the collie stared up at him.

He pointed towards the little girl. 'Stay with Rachel.' His tone said, *Don't argue – just do it.*

The bitch dropped her ears, totally downcast.

'Come, Jess.' Rachel bent down and flicked her fingers.

Obediently, Jess went to stand beside her. Rachel fussed her silky ears and was rewarded with a lick on her hand.

'Right, then.' Kent closed the kitchen door behind him and went over to the waiting quad. 'OK, Lennie, take her straight up, then head left. We'll cover the far eastern boundary to begin with.'

Rawson knew better than to voice an enquiry about returning to the East Midlands at this goddamned early hour. He wasn't privy to much of what his boss did, but he was damn sure it wasn't legal. But what he didn't know, he couldn't be blamed for. He wanted to keep it that way. However, he was sure that the fine white powder that had peppered the floor of the plane last night after Smith and Rawson had clambered out, dragging their weighted bundle with them, had been some sort of drug. Still, he consoled himself that the wages Smith paid were higher than anybody else would fork out. That alone told him a great deal. So, he simply kept his mouth shut, and kept the fuel topped up and the helicopter ready to fly at a moment's notice. And since only he could fly, if there was major trouble, it could very well provide just his own escape route. Whilst not belonging to him, of course, the chopper was his pride and joy, and he kept it immaculate inside and out. He'd hoovered up all the white powder straight away when they'd landed, leaving it pristine. No sense in taking any risks. It wasn't his business – none of it was his business. He was paid to fly the helicopter; paid a very good wage, but not sufficient to risk ending up in jail. The white bodywork gleamed from all his efforts and the big black cross painted underneath reminded him that, although he felt proprietorial towards the aircraft, that 'X', standing for Smith's Christian name, Xavier, declared his boss's ownership of the vehicle.

They were coming now, Smith and Gregson, walking abreast past the big cats' enclosures. They were talking and laughing

– Gregson lurched towards the metal fence as he guffawed at something Smith had said. One of the tigers was also watching. It had just been released from its overnight quarters. It sprang up from where it had been lying unseen beside the fence and lashed out with an orange-and-black striped paw, claws extended. Totally ineffective, of course; the fence held it back efficiently. Rawson shivered. A different story entirely if it had been on the loose.

Rawson watched them walk across to the chopper, Gregson carrying a small backpack. He stood stiffly and, in answer to Smith's query about the chopper's readiness to fly, responded, 'Yes, sir.'

Smith swung himself aboard, followed by Gregson. They strapped themselves in and Smith gave the order to fly south, back to where they'd been yesterday. 'But don't land. I want you to circle that farm, the one at the bottom of the hillside.'

'Very good, sir.' Rawson took off.

As Lennie gunned the quad up the slope at a pace that would normally have warranted a telling-off, Kent filled him in on the situation.

'So we have to find this man?'

'Yes, and quick. I don't know if he's badly injured but it's likely. However, if he's managed to get mobile at all, he may have tried crawling to safety. Keep a lookout for a heap, a mound, something of that sort on the grass.'

'What about his grub, Mr Evans? He's going to be pretty hungry by now.'

Despite the seriousness of their mission, Kent smiled. It was so in keeping for Lennie to project his own first-and-foremost need onto the other man. 'I understand from his wife that she packed some food for him.'

'Oh, good, that's good.' Lennie nodded. 'So, if he's not injured he'll be all right, then.'

'Well, I wouldn't go that far…'

'Not to worry, Mr Evans, we'll find him. Even if I didn't find who frightened Rachel. It will all work out.'

They'd reached the top of the hillside now and were progressing along the left side.

'Just a minute, Lennie, throttle back. I'd forgotten there's a dead sheep somewhere near here. I meant to collect it but…' Kent scanned the expanse of grassland. 'Pull right here; about fifty yards, or less, maybe.'

They travelled on.

'OK, stop now. This is about where it was. And there's something lying on the ground.' Kent jumped down and walked across to it. It wasn't the sheep. He could smell it way before he got to it. The odour of fox was unmistakable. The pathetic little heap of red fur stank appallingly, coated in blood and urine, its ripped-out throat obviously the work of the panther.

Lennie had clambered down and joined him. 'Weren't no dog did that.'

'No. It wasn't.'

'An' where's the sheep?'

'Where indeed? It's saved me a job but I'd rather have removed it myself later.'

Lennie scratched his head. 'Don't quite know what to make of it.'

'Like you always say, it will all work out; it usually does.'

'Aye.' Lennie smiled. 'That's what I allus says. An' it's true.'

'Come on then, let's get on. We've got a man to find; never mind a sheep.'

It was much better right now to keep Lennie in ignorance of the true predator.

Rachel had polished off one bowl of cereal and again reached for the box of cornflakes. She poured out a further helping before lifting the milk jug high and letting the icy milk cascade in a welter of bubbles into the bowl. 'I just love doing that. We aren't allowed to at school.'

'My, you are hungry, little one, aren't you?'

Rachel nodded. 'I eat a *lot* more when I'm home at the farm. I help out, see, with the jobs. And I run around a lot; that's what makes me hungry.'

'The fresh air will do that,' Mara agreed.

'When I've eaten my breakfast, I'm going out to get started. First, I'm going to see if there are any lambs yet in the big barn. It will soon be lambing time, you know.'

Mara, sitting on the other side of the table watching the child shovelling spoonfuls of food into her mouth, nodded. 'You will stay close, won't you?'

'Well…' Rachel finished off the second bowl, went to the sink and slid it into the hot water in the washing-up bowl. 'When I've checked the barn, I'm going to play with Jess. Daddy said I could.' There were the beginnings of a pout on her lips. 'I *always* play with Jess when I'm home.'

The sheepdog, hearing her name, cocked her head on one side.

'See, she knows I'm talking about her.'

'That's fine,' Mara hastened to smooth the waters; she was a guest here, 'but do take care.'

'Oh, I do. I love Jess. I won't let any harm come to her.'

'Yes, I can see you love her, but I really meant for you to take care, child.'

Rachel reached inside the closet for her thick coat. She did up the buttons, jammed on her bobble hat and gloves, then, reaching into her coat pocket, took out a yellow tennis ball, its fuzzy coating worn very thin. Jess was instantly attentive. She knew they were going to play.

'You don't need to worry, Mrs Isooba,' Rachel reassured her. 'You see, we look after each other.'

And Mara was left staring after them through the kitchen window as Rachel, cavorting in delight at her freedom from school, raced the dog across the yard to the big barn. Suddenly bereft, Mara watched and waited. She fingered the mobile phone in her pocket. There was still no news from the police. Taking the mobile out, she tried calling Anan again. It was too much to hope that it would connect this time, but there was nothing else she could do. But to her incredulous delight, it rang, and a few seconds later she heard her husband's croaking whisper.

'Anan, my big love! Thank the good Lord. Where are you? Oh my, speak to me.'

'I'm still trapped, Mara; I can't last much longer. I think my legs are gone…'

'Oh, God, oh, God… Hang on, Anan. We are trying to find you. Tell me where to look. I'm at the farm near the hill with the sheep. Where are you?'

'In the wood… at the top somewhere. The plane crashed… hit the biggest tree… came down in the wood near the middle.'

'I'll tell the others; they're out there now, looking for you. And the police will be able to track you now your phone is working. We're coming, Anan, we're coming. Keep your phone on, my love. I ring off now, let others know where you are. All my love, Anan. Please, please wait; don't die, don't die…' She broke off, sobbing.

'Hush,' Anan croaked. 'I'm not going to die, not now, no way. I love you, Mara.'

The phone disconnected and Mara was left clutching it tightly, tears running down her plump cheeks. Taking great breaths, she fought to get a grip. It was up to her now. She must ring the police and Kent, let them know Anan's whereabouts and that his phone was working. Snatching up the piece of paper Kent had left with her, she held the phone to her ear as she looked out across the hillside. Somewhere up there was a wood – and somewhere within it, Anan was still alive. As she waited desperately for Kent to answer, she watched Rachel and Jess on the gentle lower slopes, the child throwing the ball, the dog chasing joyfully after it and dropping it back at the girl's feet. And then suddenly, it all changed. Rachel threw the ball again. Jess darted up the hill after it and then skidded to a halt. As Kent answered his mobile, Mara saw the dog race away, bounding over the grass tussocks, and disappear over the brow of the hill. Rachel, waving her arms, raced after her.

'Mara, what is it?' Kent said. 'Have the police got in touch?'

'No, no – we must let them know straight away. I get through to my Anan; he tell me he is in your wood. The plane, it crashed near biggest tree in middle of wood. He is very bad… injured…'

'Don't upset yourself. I'll find him. I'll ring the police now, then I'll go straight to the wood. I'm on the far boundary at the moment. It'll take me a few minutes to get there. I'll ring you back soon.'

Once again, Mara was left holding a silent phone. She had had no time to tell him that Rachel had run off after the dog. And she couldn't now. He would be focused on letting the police know and finding her husband.

Anne Brown, Lennie's mother, knocked on the back door of the farmhouse. Whilst she waited, she glanced at the Citroën parked near the barn. It wasn't a car she recognised. Kent drove a Ford estate when he wasn't driving the tractor or the quad bike. The door opened a few inches. A frightened black face peeped round.

'Oh,' Anne said, startled. 'I was expecting to see Kent.'

'He's up there,' Mara opened the door wider and waved a hand, 'looking for my husband.'

Anne took one look at the tear-filled eyes of the troubled woman. 'Perhaps if you let me in, we could talk about it?'

'Oh, yes, yes, come in, my manners…'

'I'm a friend of the family; have been for years. My name's Anne Brown. My son works for Kent. His name's Lennie.'

Mara nodded. 'Yes, he drive the… quad?'

'That's right. Have the men taken it up the hill?'

Mara nodded again, vigorously. 'Yes. They go to find my Anan. His plane, it crashed. He's somewhere in a wood…' Her words trailed away.

'How about I make us a nice mug of tea, eh? And you can tell me all about it. Is Rachel still in bed? I'd like to see her.'

At that, Mara broke down sobbing. 'She's gone.'

'What do you mean, gone?' Anne took hold of Mara's arm. 'Where is she?'

The helicopter flew over Lincoln, the cathedral easily visible, and then Newark, the skies lightening all the time.

Gregson, who had been dozing, stirred and turned to Smith. 'Which are we going for first, then?'

'When we circle the farm, if it's deserted, we'll go for that. Collect those three bags; if we can find them that's tangible evidence.'

'But we flew over that wood first, didn't we?'

'Hmm… yes, we did. But we need to get the drugs back – that sort of evidence is incriminating on its own,' Smith said.

'But what if there *is* somebody… if there's resistance?'

'You've brought the Beretta, haven't you?' When Gregson didn't reply, Smith reached under his jacket, withdrew his own Browning and laid it across his knees. 'See? We deal with any resistance.'

'Somehow, I don't think we'll encounter any. Look, we're over the wood now,' Gregson said. 'And would you believe it – there's the farmer and his man on their quad bike. Seems you were right to go for the farm first.'

Kent ended his call to the police. As he'd suspected, they had been alerted by Isooba's phone being switched on and a trace had already been made. 'OK, Lennie, head back west now to the start of the path leading into the woods. It seems pretty sure that the plane came down somewhere in that area. If we can find it, we can find the pilot.'

'What did the police say? Are they coming?'

'Yes, and they've already got a helicopter search started.'

Lennie's face lit up. 'D'you reckon they've got heat-seeking equipment, Mr Evans?'

'I think it's a fair bet.' Kent quickly punched in Mara's number. It rang out, then went to voicemail. 'Kent here, Mara. Just a quick message. The police have traced your husband. They're on their way and have sent a helicopter. Speak later.'

Even as he finished speaking, Lennie nudged his arm. 'Look, Mr Evans. There's a helicopter coming over. D'you think it's them?'

FIFTY
2020

Kent looked upwards. Sure enough, a helicopter was flying in from the north. 'I don't know, but it's possible. Anyway, let's get moving.'

'Yes, Mr Evans.' Lennie looped the quad in a wide circle and headed away from the boundary back towards the woods. They skirted areas dotted with trees and shrubs and were approaching the main wood as the helicopter flew directly overhead. 'Don't it make a racket, eh?'

'Yes.' Kent squinted up at it. 'It's pretty low. I don't know what a police helicopter looks like, really, but…' He shook his head. 'I don't think that is one.'

'It's got a big cross underneath.'

Kent was instantly alert. 'Has it?'

'Yes. A black cross… ah, no, it's going over the hill now. Can't be them.'

Kent didn't answer. He called Phillip's mobile, drumming impatient fingers on the side of the quad whilst he waited for him to answer. 'Phillip? Kent. No time to explain. Just checking – who did you say has a helicopter with a black cross painted underneath?

Was it Smith?' He nodded. 'Right. Well, looks like he's here at the farm. Can you get over ASAP?' He ended the call. 'Lennie, that helicopter wasn't the police. They should be showing up here soon. I want you to get off the quad. Stay here by the entrance path till they come.'

'But—'

'I've got trouble at the farm. I have to get back – now!'

Leaving Lennie open-mouthed, Kent slid into the driving seat and roared away.

'Wait! Jess, wait…'

Rachel's call went unheeded. The collie was lightning fast and away up the hill in seconds. Rachel raced after her. By the time she was halfway up, the little girl had to stop, panting hard and bent over with a stitch. She gave up on wasting breath by calling and, face set determinedly, renewed her pursuit. Stopping once more on the top of the hill, bent over, hands on hips, gasping for breath like a landed fish, Rachel felt her anger growing. Her grandfather she'd been told had been a fair man, but he had also been very strict, and he'd trained Jess from a tiny pup to do what she was told. The smooth running of the farm depended on it. Rachel couldn't understand the bitch's disobedience. She'd never run off on her own before. But she had to find her.

Straightening up, she set off again. There was no sign of Jess on the open hillside, so that left the scrubland and the wood. Racing as fast as she could on the flat, Rachel reached the wood. She stopped and called Jess's name. From deep in the wood there came an answering bark, followed by a series of excited yaps. With increased determination, Rachel plunged into the wood, following the path that wound through the trees. The wood was gloomy, the tops of the trees meeting overhead and blocking out the weak morning light. Several times she stumbled, catching her foot in the trailing brambles and proud tree roots that criss-crossed the path. It was also very wet and muddy. Tiny rivulets of rainwater had run down from the higher ground, tracing a complex pattern in the mud and making the ground very slippery underfoot. She ran with an arm raised in front of her, shielding her face from the cruel, whipping branches as the increasingly loud barking drew her on. But it was scary the farther into the woods she went; the trees drew closer together and it grew darker, making it difficult to see the obstacles in front of her.

A sudden clapping of wings overhead startled her. Rachel cried out, heart hammering, hand flying to her mouth as several disturbed wood pigeons took flight. Then there was more crashing, this time at ground level, and Jess appeared, forging her way through the thick undergrowth.

'Oh, Jess, Jess…' Rachel flung her arms round the dog's neck in relief and joy at finding her. 'Why did you run off? Why?'

Of course there was no answer, but the dog licked the little girl's face furiously, tail wagging so fast it was a blur. Then she stiffened, pricked her ears and dashed off again.

'Jess!' Rachel couldn't believe it. 'Stop! Come here.'

But the bitch ignored the command and headed back through the undergrowth, the way she had come. She was barking again, loudly and continuously.

Rachel, emboldened, plunged after her. 'Jess, Jess, wait. I'm coming.'

And then, very faintly, she heard a feeble call.

She stumbled to a stop. 'Who's there?'

The faint cry came again. She could hear it just a little more clearly now. 'Help. Help me…'

'I'm coming, I'm coming.' Fighting her way through the brambles, barbs catching at her face and hands, tangled ivy and vegetation threatening to send her sprawling, Rachel ploughed on, and then suddenly burst through into a small clearing. There in front was the dreadful wreckage of the missing plane. She stopped dead, both hands going to her face. It was a horrible sight. 'Hello? Is anybody there?' Her call was meant to be loud and strong enough to carry, but it came out in a tiny squeak of fright.

'Yes, yes… I'm here.'

She crept closer, heart beating madly, looked into the cockpit and came face to face with a man. 'Oh.' The fear abruptly disappeared and her face screwed up with concern. 'Oh, you poor man. You're hurt!'

'Yes… but you've found me…' His voice was very weak.

'No, it was Jess who found you. How did she know you were here?'

He held out a shaking hand. In his palm was a dog whistle.

'You're Mr Isooba, aren't you? And… I think your wife's name is Mara?'

'Yes.'

'She's waiting for you, in our farmhouse.'

A faint smile spread across the man's face. 'My Mara…' he said, and passed out.

'Look! There's the farm.' Gregson pointed.

'Yes, that's the one. It's got all those twisty chimneys. Rawson, do a couple of circles and look for somewhere to put down. I want it really close, OK?' Smith said.

'Yes, sir.' Obediently, Rawson traced a couple of wide swings.

'Looks pretty deserted, wouldn't you say?' Gregson leaned forward in his seat, scanning the farm, the yard, the outbuildings and barns. 'Except for that Citroën. Probably means someone's home, but I don't reckon there are any men – we saw those two up on the hills, and a piffling little farm like this couldn't support any more farmhands.'

Rawson spoke up from the cockpit. 'Excuse me, sir, but the best place to land would be in that small paddock at the rear of the farm.'

Smith and Gregson looked at each other and nodded.

'Go for it,' Smith ordered.

And Rawson, dropping lower as he circled the farmhouse, obeyed.

'He obviously means the world to you; travelling all the way here from Africa.' Anne put an arm around Mara's shoulders and hugged her. They were seated at the kitchen table with steaming mugs of tea, into which Anne had poured a liberal amount of whisky.

'My Anan's the best.'

'Then you're a lucky woman.'

'The luckiest in all the world – and wherever he is, if he needs me, I'll be there.'

'And his message confirmed he's still alive. Hold on to that.'

'He said he thinks his legs are gone.'

Anne winced. 'As in bleeding?'

'No, I don't think so – he's trapped in the wreckage.'

'And Kent's gone up with Lennie to find him?'

'Yes. He said he'd inform the police.'

'Well, I'd say the police will find him. They'll probably use a heat-seeking helicopter; you can't get a normal vehicle up there.'

Mara nodded, gave a tremulous smile and took a gulp of her tea.

'And if there's that much surveillance going on up there, it's a fair bet they've found Rachel and Jess too.'

'She only went out to play... then the dog went off and the child followed her.'

Anne patted Mara's hand. 'Don't dwell on it. Rachel's got a lot of sense. I don't think she'll come to any harm. But first your husband must be found. The police will see that he gets straight to hospital.' She reached for her mug and, just as she took a drink, heard the *whump, whump* of a helicopter getting ever closer.

Mara heard it too. 'Listen – can you hear that?'

'Yes.'

'Do you think it's the police? Do you think they've found him?' Mara jumped up, slopping some of her tea.

The two women hurried to the window. They were just in time to see the helicopter circle over the yard.

'Is it the police?'

'I don't know,' Anne replied. 'That one's got a black cross painted underneath.'

FIFTY-ONE
2020

The helicopter hovered above the paddock, then, with great skill, Rawson set it down, landing strips near the tyre tracks that led from the back of the farm and across the paddock to the far gate. Away in the top corner, Victor, the aged Shire horse, lifted his head for a few moments, blew down his nose, then dismissed it and returned to the proper business of grazing.

'Don't cut the engine. We'll need it ready to take off.'

'Yes, sir.' Rawson, well used to his boss's often bizarre orders, simply stared out across the paddock at the horse. Anything else, he didn't want to see or know about. Whatever was about to kick off, it was nothing to do with him.

Smith and Gregson climbed out of the helicopter. As one, they drew their guns and, holding them down by their thighs for concealment, started to run across the paddock.

In the kitchen, as the helicopter had passed out of sight above the roof, Anne and Mara had gone to the opposite window, which gave a view of the west side of the house. They'd watched as the helicopter landed and two men, not in uniform, stepped down onto the grass. Wide-eyed in disbelief, they watched them attempt to hide their guns as they ran towards the farmhouse.

'The door – we must lock it!' Anne said, and ran from the window.

But even as she reached for the key, Smith tried the handle. He was about to barge in when the door was pressed back hard against his hand. Stepping back, he raised his boot and slammed it into the door, forcing it to spring wide. The women cowered as he and Gregson raised their guns.

'OK. Now tell me what I want to know and you'll stay in one piece. Where are they?'

'What… what are you talking about?' Anne gripped the edge of the sink with trembling fingers.

'Don't give us that, lady. Where have you hidden them?'

Anne shook her head, long black hair flying wildly. 'I… I don't know what you're looking for.'

'Oh, don't you?' With his left hand Smith grabbed at her hair, yanking her down and sideways onto her knees.

Mara screamed, hand flying to her mouth. 'Stop it! Stop it! You're hurting her.'

'Yes, well, if you don't tell me, you're both going to get hurt.' Smith jerked his head at Gregson, who pinioned Mara's arms by her sides before twisting her left arm up behind her back. She screamed in agony.

'We'll tell, we'll tell,' yelled Anne, her face wet with tears of rage and fright. 'What do you want? Money?'

'No, you stupid woman, not money. Where are the drugs?'

Leaving Lennie behind, Kent flogged the quad at a reckless speed across the grassland. Then, reaching the crest of the hill, he reduced his speed, leaned forward and cut the engine. The quad continued to roll down the steep hill, careering crazily over the tussocks, but now there was no engine noise to give away his presence. As the quad rolled to a stop just short of the yard gate, Kent leapt off and made for the kitchen window. One swift glance as he lifted his head above the sill told him all he needed to know. There were guns involved.

Dropping to his knees, he crept alongside the farmhouse wall until he was opposite the barn door. Then he sprinted for it. The men were after the drugs, he knew that, and the three bags were still where he'd hidden them: behind a stash of empty feed sacks at the back of the barn. He retrieved them, putting them down on the floor. Then from the cubbyhole in the wall, where he always left it, ready to thin out the rat population, he lifted out his twelve-bore shotgun. He didn't need to check it – he knew it was broke, ready for the insertion of cartridges. These were on the shelf above, and he quickly loaded the gun, stuffing a handful of spare cartridges into his jacket pocket. Not only was he an experienced soldier but, with the number of rats forever present on the farm providing practice, he was still an excellent shot. Snatching up the bags of cocaine with his left hand, Kent retraced his steps to the farmhouse. He could hear one of the women screaming. The kitchen door was wide open and, without hesitating, he burst in, shotgun pointing straight at Gregson's back.

'Let her go and drop your gun or I'll drill you with my twelve-bore.' It was an order, not a request. His sudden entry gave him the advantage of surprise.

With his left hand still gripping Mara's arm, Gregson wasn't about to risk turning. As the gun fell he thrust her away, and at the same time Kent brought the shotgun's stock down on the back of his neck. Gregson keeled over and joined the gun on the floor.

Swinging round, he found himself facing Smith – and the gun *he* was holding was pointing straight at Kent's heart.

'Wait.' Kent hurled the bags of cocaine onto the tiles in front of him. All three burst, white powder spraying out over the red quarries. 'Are these what you want, eh? My wife died of an overdose thanks to evil scum like you peddling drugs.'

Smith gave a howl of rage. 'Drop the gun!' His face contorted with fury. 'Drop it or she gets it first.'

Anne screamed, twisted her head sideways and buried her teeth in his hand. Kent leapt forward, swung the barrel of the shotgun and smashed Smith across the windpipe. He staggered back, let go of Anne's hair and fell to his knees, clutching his throat as he retched and gasped for breath.

Then Mara, seeing the back door opening, grabbed Gregson's gun from the tiles and screeched, 'My God, there's another.' She pulled the trigger. The bullet hit the wall, ricocheted and buried itself in the door.

'Hey, steady. Don't shoot the cavalry,' Phillip said. He stepped forward and gently removed the gun from her trembling hand.

'It's OK, Mara. He's one of us,' Kent said, before catching her as she passed out. 'Cover them, Phil.' He carried Mara through to the living room and laid her down on the settee.

Just then they heard police cars screaming up to the farm – via both the front and the back track, leaving nothing to chance. And above them, adding to the noise, was the *whump, whump, whump* of the helicopter as it took off with just Rawson aboard.

EPILOGUE
2020

'I shall *always* be so grateful,' Mara said, setting down her holdall outside the back door and putting her hand in Kent's. 'Not just for finding my Anan, but for your kindness in letting me stay here until he was out of danger. When he is fit to be transferred, they say they fly him home. But now, I am wanted there.'

'No thanks necessary.' Kent shook his head. 'You were in need, and that's enough. Anybody would have helped. I mean, apart from myself and Rachel… Anne and Lennie, there's Phillip. Oh, yes, and of course there's Petrina Milton's statement to the police. We mustn't forget her bravery in coming forward about finding the stash of cocaine at the zoo. I should think that alone will be enough to get Smith and Gregson long sentences.'

'A very bad pair of men,' Mara agreed.

'And he was a *swank*,' Rachel put in. Then added, 'But Raquel's still my friend!' She was standing beside Kent in the doorway. She rolled the intriguing word around her mouth, trying it out again. 'A *swank*.'

Kent grinned at Mara. 'I shouldn't have said that, should I?'

Rachel pouted. 'Well, you said if he hadn't been a swank, he might have got away with it. But because he painted his initial on the helicopter, you knew it couldn't have been the police heading for the farm. You *did* say that, Daddy, you *did*.'

'OK, I admit it. I did.'

Kent and Mara were both laughing openly now.

'And a good thing for all of us too.' Mara bent and kissed Rachel. 'Goodbye, little one. I shall never forget you all.'

'And Jess? She was the one who really found Mr Isooba.'

'Yes, and Jess, of course.'

Kent and Rachel went out to the gate and waved goodbye as Mara climbed into her hire car, and drove off for the airport.

As the Citroën disappeared down the track, Lennie emerged from the open doorway of the big barn and beckoned urgently to them. 'Mr Evans, Rachel, it's coming: the first one of the year.'

They raced across the yard and into the barn. In one of the lambing pens a sheep was straining to give birth. Rachel leaned over the rail. 'Come on, girl,' she cooed. 'You can do it.' With a last great effort the lamb slid from its mother's body into the straw. 'There!' Rachel said with satisfaction. 'It's precious. Every lamb is precious – you said so, Daddy.'

'I know. But my own little lamb is the most precious of all.' He wrapped his arms around her, swinging her high into the air. She squealed with delight. 'And I've got more good news for you.'

She snuggled closer. 'Tell me,' she demanded.

'How would you like to stay here at home and go to school in Redcliffe?' He held up a hand to pre-empt her squeals of joy. 'I can't look after you by myself because of work, but Lennie's mother says she would like to help. What do *you* say? Is it a deal?'

'Deal, *deal*!'

He grinned. 'Then I'll go ahead and see to it.'

'Oh, Daddy, I love you.' Rachel kissed him on the cheek.

'Wait for it; there's more.'

'More good stuff?'

'Oh, yes. I had a telephone call this morning; one I was waiting for from a farmer up in Yorkshire. His sheepdog had puppies about four weeks ago. How would you like to go up today and choose one? It'll be big enough to come and live with us in a few weeks' time.'

Rachel pressed herself away from the circle of his arms as she smiled up at him. 'I say… you're the best daddy in the world.'

Even as he accepted the compliment, Kent's mouth twitched as he recalled another call he'd received that morning, from one of the constables who had been engaged in searching the wood for Isooba.

'Thought you'd want to know, sir, we found what was left of a sheep's carcass in the wood. Obviously a fox ate it.'

Kent had hesitated, and then decided not to enlighten him.

The pilot had been helpless – easy prey – yet the panther, for whatever reason, had spared Isooba.

'You're probably right, Constable,' he said.

ACKNOWLEDGEMENT

Enormous thanks to True-2-Type Printing, run by my long-time friends, Anne and David Brown. They didn't just go the extra mile; it was more like ten! Without their help, *Feral* would not have been produced.

For writing and publishing news, or recommendations of new titles to read, sign up to the Book Guild newsletter: